Tomorrow Happens

David Brin

edited by Deb Geisler

The NESFA Press
Post Office Box 809
Framingham, MA 01701
2003

FIRST EDITION, February 2003

International Standard Book Number:
1-886778-43-4 (trade)
1-886778-44-2 (slipcased)

Tomorrow Happens was printed in an edition of 1500 numbered hard-cover books, of which the first 200 were signed by the author and artist, bound with special endpapers and slipcased. Of these 200 copies, the first 10 are lettered A through J and the remainder are numbered 1 through 190. The trade copies are numbered 191 through 1490. No other copies will be printed in hardcover.

This is book __1249__

Publication History

"Aficionado" was originally published as "Life in the Extreme," *Popular Science Magazine Special Edition*, August 1998.

"The Diplomacy Guild" first appeared in the collection *Isaac's Universe Volume 1: The Diplomacy Guild*, ed. Martin H. Greenberg (Grafton), 1990.

"Do We Really Want Immortality?" was originally published as part of a series of articles about "The Coming Millennium," for AOL/ Netscape's online *iPlanet* magazine, 1999.

"An Ever-Reddening Glow" first appeared in *Analog*, February 1996.

"Fortitude" first appeared in *S.F. Age*, January 1996.

"Goodbye Mir! (Sniff!)" first appeared in *Locus Magazine*, November 2000.

"The Other Side of the Hill" first appeared in *S.F. Age*, November 1994.

"Paris Conquers All" was originally published in the anthology *War of the Worlds: Global Dispatches*, ed. Kevin J. Anderson (Bantam, Doubleday, Dell), 1989.

"Probing the Near Future" was originally published as part of a series of articles about "The Coming Millennium," for AOL/Netscape's online *iPlanet* magazine, 1999.

"Reality Check" first appeared in *Nature*, 2000.

"The Robots and Foundation Universe" first appeared in *Oceans of the Mind*, 2001.

"Seeking a New Fulcrum" first appeared in *Skeptic Magazine*, 2001.

"The Self-Preventing Prophecy" includes material (edited and revised) from a series of articles about "The Coming Millennium," for AOL/Netscape's online *iPlanet* magazine, 1999, and from "Orwell and Our Future," a paper presented to the conference in honor of the 50th Anniversary of the University of Chicago School of Law, 1999.

"Stones of Significance" first appeared in the collection *Lamps on the Brow* (Small Press), 1998, then in the special January 2000 edition of *Analog* magazine.

Contents

Tomorrow Happens

Introduction

by

Vernor Vinge

I first met David Brin in 1980. At that time, *Sundiver* was already published. David was finishing up his Ph.D. at UC San Diego. (My years at UCSD did not overlap his, but David was continuing the grand tradition of science fiction and fantasy writers who were at that university: Greg Benford, Kim Stanley Robinson, Ray Feist, Nancy Holder, David Brin, Vernor Vinge, Suzette Haden Elgin...I leave it to others to determine if this marks UCSD as a special source of sff writers.)

The '70s and '80s were good years for science fiction in San Diego, with lots of writers and fans and frequent parties. I hadn't yet read *Sundiver*, but David pressed the typescript draft of a new novel into my hands. I politely accepted; I knew that *Sundiver* was a worthwhile book, so this new manuscript was likely a good story. There was only one problem. I *hate* novels in manuscript form. I mean I hate to read them in that form. Maybe it's because that's what my own, incomplete, work looks like. Or maybe it's just that typescript manuscripts don't encourage a friendly reader/story relationship. The pages get lost (and sometimes are not even numbered). The homogeneous avalanche of double-spaced text conveys a promise of endless boredom. (But I admit, things are worse if there are lots of markups, or faint ink. And handwritten manuscripts occupy a still lower circle of hell.)

So there I was with this highly legible, but regrettably typescript, novel. It did have a cool title, *The Tides of Kithrup*. But I was very busy and six weeks went by and I hadn't had a chance to read it. David gave me a polite telephone call, asking if I had had a chance to look at his manuscript. "Well, no," I replied. "I'm sorry! Things have been so busy around here. Look, if you need it back

11

right away, I can send it—" David short-circuited this evasion by saying, "Why don't you keep it another couple of weeks? Even if you can't read more than a part of it, I'd like to hear your comments."

Hmm. Okay, a *geas* had now been laid upon me. But it was a gracious *geas* that admitted of an easy observance. I could read fifty pages, give some honest comment, and be free once more. Of course, that was fifty pages of typescript manuscript by someone whose work I'd never read before. But hey, I could put up with that for an hour or so, right?

I dutifully set aside an hour and began slogging through the neatly double-spaced typescript... And after a few pages, magic happened. See, the pages became transparent. There was a world to play in. There was an adventure that accelerated me on past page 50, through the whole novel. You probably have read this novel yourself. It was published under the title *Startide Rising*. It won the Hugo *and* the Nebula for best science-fiction novel of the year. David went on to complete the Uplift series and later the new Uplift books. Along the way there were many other awards and award nominations. The novels have become a secure part of the sf canon of the twentieth century.

So no one can say that I can't recognize quality—at least if it's hard sf and nova bright. And I doubt if I will ever again look askance at typescript sf from David Brin.

I later learned that David shows his draft work to a number of people. I show my drafts to four or five friends who won't bruise my ego too severely. David shows his to dozens of others. One of his favorite sayings is that "criticism is the most effective antidote for error." He surely lives by that in his writing. In fact, I think it takes a special clarity of mind to avoid the contending "too many cooks" syndrome. I admire someone who can sustain that much criticism, and who also has such openness with his newborn ideas.

In the years since UCSD, David has had various day jobs, including university prof and astronautics consultant. Fortunately for us, his readers, he has not let that get in the way of his writing. We have many Brin novels to enjoy, across a range of lengths and topics. He once he told me his strategy for What to Write Next. He liked to write a long, serious book (perhaps *Earth*?) and then something lighthearted and short and fun (such as *The Practice Effect*). I'm not sure that David is still following this strategy, since his most recent novel (as of September 2002), *Kiln People,* is essentially both types of book at the same time.

David Brin's published writing career *began* with a very successful novel, *Sundiver*. Initially, I thought of him solely as a novelist. The success of his novels—and his novel series—may obscure the fact that all this time he has also been writing short fiction. And the amazing thing is that David Brin often does *even better* with short fiction than with novels! You'll get to see a few of his short stories in this NESFA volume. Others are available in Brin's published collections (see the bibliography at Al von Ruff's ISFDB: http://www.sfsite.com/isfdb/index.html). David's background in hard science and hard sf shows in these stories, but often in indirect ways, in setting the stage for seriously weird and sometimes disturbing points of view. Some of the stories are fairly transparent, such as the funny and logical and optimistic "Giving Plague." Others, such as "Thor Meets Captain America," are bizarre and effective fantasies. And then there is "Detritus Affected," which builds on simple words to create a reality that is disturbing and mysterious and percolates for days in your mind, until you may finally invent a context and consistency.

I have a friend who is a world-class inventor and engineer, about the closest thing you can get in the real world to the stuff of John W. Campbell's "scientist/engineer hero." This fellow likes science-fiction very much, but recently he made the off-hand assertion that, contrary to what we sf weenies would like to believe, virtually *nothing* in science-fiction has presaged the contemplation of similar ideas within the scientific and engineering communities. Fighting talk, that. His claim would make an interesting topic for a convention panel, where I think my friend could make a good case for his position. At the same time, it's certainly true that science fiction has caught the imagination of generations of young people and drawn many of them into the sciences. Beyond that, a slightly more imperial claim is reasonable: Many sf writers are voracious skimmers of current science research. Their stories may cross specialty boundaries and act as tripwires to engage the attention of the real doers in the world. And since good stories involve emotions and social context as well as technical ideas, sf writers can have a greater impact than most other commentators.

Over the last twenty years, David Brin has certainly been this kind of inspirer. But in one way, David has gone beyond most of his fellows. He's written many essays about wider issues. Some of these are in this NESFA collection. The bright imagination that we see in his fiction carries over into his essays.

There is a subgenre of Brinnian essay writing that consists of moral criticism of fiction and drama. (See, for instance, the piece about romanticism and fantasy in this book.) This kind of essay may be a surprise to some people. "It's just a story!" they might say of the work that David is criticizing. It also takes a certain courage for a writer to undertake such moral criticism. I write fiction, and I know that sometimes the drama of a story may take it in directions that violate my vision of moral truth. Sometimes I can guide it back, but sometimes I surrender and say to myself, "It's just a fun story." (And at least once, I later ran into a fan who praised me because he found what I disliked to be morally *positive!*) In any case, even though I don't agree with all of David's moral criticism of stories (for instance, the ending of Bakshi's *Wizards* is not as purely mean as David says), I find such criticism to be extremely interesting. Like Ayn Rand's heartfelt criticism of Plato and Kant, such essays give an edge to issues that usually seem far removed from everyday concerns.

In much of his writing, David Brin looks at hard problems, the kind of problems that turn other writers to dark realism or blindly sentimental optimism. But David takes these problems, turns them sideways, and tries to see some *realistic* way that happy solutions might be found. The most striking and relevant example of this is his nonfiction book, *The Transparent Society:* Nowadays, we are confronted with the choice between freedom and safety. Technology has made appalling breaches of privacy possible, and the arguments on both sides of this state of affairs have become steadily more strident. Then David Brin comes along and says, "Well, what if we lost privacy, but the loss was symmetric?"

Maybe in the past this was an empty question, since surveillance technology favored asymmetry (and favored the elites). Nowadays however, it is quite possible that technology can support the "ordinary people" in watching the powerful...as well as each other. The resulting loss of privacy is a very scary thing, but there is an sf'nal tradition for considering it (for instance, the many stories from the '40s and '50s about widespread mental telepathy). The first years of such transparency would be very bumpy, but afterwards the world might not be that different—except that vice laws might be a little less obnoxious, and the worst of the badguys might be more constrained. I would probably not buy into such a world—except that it may be by far the happiest outcome of our current dilemma.

At a more abstract level, David's most recent novel, *Kiln People,* takes on the problem of duplicate beings. Here I don't mean biological clones, but near-perfect copies, even unto memories. This is the stuff of many sf stories (Damon Knight's *The People Maker,* William F. Temple's *The Four-Sided Triangle*...). The concept has almost endless possibilities for abuse and tyranny and tragedy. In the past, stories about such duplication have been close to fantasy. More recently, with the possibility of AI and downloads, the idea has moved more into the realm of hard science fiction. We are nearing the time when the most basic "metaphysical" questions of identity and consciousnes may have concrete and practical meaning. In *Kiln People,* Brin imagines a (marvelously non-computational) technology to achieve duplication. The resulting world is partly familiar and partly very strange. But—in the end—much of it seems more congenial than ours. I wrote a publicity quote for the novel. Normally it's hard to write blurbs that meet the exacting standards of publicists. Writing the quote for *Kiln People* was easy: Leaving aside the transcendental issues of the ending, *Kiln People* is simply the deepest light-hearted sf novel that I'd ever read.

There are very few issues that escape David's advocatorial interest. Many of his ideas are in the area of sociobiology, how we may harness the beasts within to be engines for good. Often his ideas are couched in flamboyant and colorful terms. (John W. Campbell, Jr., would understand!) Simply put, David is a brilliant *busybody,* forever enlisting those around him in projects that he sees will benefit everyone. Be aware of this. Be prepared to bail out with a polite "No on this one, David." But also be prepared to listen. Because almost always his ideas will contain sidewise thinking that just might make the world a better place.

Aficionado

Cameras stare across a forbidden desert, monitoring disputed territory in a conflict that is so bitter the opponents cannot even agree what to name it.

One side calls the struggle a *war*, with countless innocent lives in jeopardy.

The other side claims there are no victims.

And so, suspicious cameras peer and pan, alert for encroachment. Vigilant camouflaged monitors scan from atop hills or under innocuous piles of stones. They hang beneath highway culverts, probing constantly for a hated enemy. For some time—months, at least—these guardians have succeeded in staving off incursions across the sandy desolation.

That is, until technology changes yet again, shifting the advantage briefly from defense to offense.

When the enemy strikes this time, their first move is to take out those guardian eyes.

Infiltrators arrived at dawn, under the glare of the rising sun. Several hundred little flying machines jetted through the air, skimming very low to the ground on gusts from whispering motors. Each device, no larger than a hummingbird, followed a carefully-scouted path toward its selected target, some stationary camera or sensor. The attackers even *looked* like native desert birds, in case they were spotted during those crucial last seconds.

Each little drone landed behind the target, in its blind spot, and unfolded wings that transformed into high-resolution graphics displays, depicting perfect false images of the same desert scene. Each robot inserted its illusion in front of the guardian lens—carefully, so as not to create a suspicious flicker. Other small spy-machines sniffed out camouflaged seismic sensors and embraced them gently, providing new cushioning that would mask the tremors to come.

The robotic attack, covering an area of more than a hundred square kilometers, took only eight minutes to complete. The desert now lay unwatched, undefended.

From over the horizon, giant vehicles started moving in. They converged along several roadways toward the same open area—seventeen quiet, hybrid-electric rigs...tractor trailers disguised as commercial cargo transports, complete with company holo-logos blazoned on their sides. But when their paths intersected at the chosen rendezvous, a more cryptic purpose revealed itself. Crews wearing dun-colored jumpsuits leaped from the cabs to start unlashing container sections. Auxiliary generators set to work. The air began to swirl with shimmering waves of exotic stench, as pungent volatiles gushed from storage tanks to fill pressurized vessels. Electronic consoles sprang to life, and hinged panels fell away from the trailers, revealing long, tapered objects that lay on slanted ramps.

With a steady whine, each cigar shape lifted its nose from horizontal to vertical, aiming skyward, while stabilizer fins popped open at the tail end. Shouts between the work crews grew more tense as a series of tightly coordinated countdowns commenced. There wouldn't be much time to spare before the enemy—sophisticated and wary—picked up enough clues and figured out what was going on.

Soon every missile was aimed...launch sequences engaged...and targets acquired. All they lacked were payloads.

Abruptly, a dozen figures emerged from an air-conditioned van, wearing snug suits of shimmering material and garishly painted helmets. Each one carried a small satchel that hummed and whirred, pumping air to keep the suit cool. Several had trouble walking normally. Their gait seemed rubbery, as if both excited and anxious at the same time. One of the smaller figures even briefly skipped.

A dour-looking woman wearing a badge and a uniform awaited them, holding a clipboard. She confronted the tallest figure, whose helmet bore a motif of flames surrounding a screaming mouth.

"Name and scan," she demanded in a level tone of voice.

The helmet visor swiveled back, revealing a heavily tanned face, about thirty, with eyes the color of a cold sea.

"Hacker Torrey," he said, as her clipboard automatically sought his left iris, reading its unique patterns to confirm his ID. "And yes," he continued. "I affirm that I'm doing this of my own free will. Can we get on with it?"

"Your permits seem to be in order," she replied, unhurriedly. "Your liability bond and waivers have been accepted. The government won't stand in your way."

The tall man shrugged, as if the statement was both expected and irrelevant. He flung the visor back down. There were other forces to worry about, more formidable than mere government. Forces who were desperate to prevent what was about to take place here.

At a signal, all of the suited figures rushed to ladders that launch crew members braced against the side of each rocket. Each hurried up the makeshift gantry and, slipping inside a narrow capsule, squirmed into the cramped couch with unconscious grace, having practiced the motions hundreds of times. Even the novices knew exactly what they were doing. What the dangers might be. The costs and the rewards.

Hatches slammed shut and hissed as they sealed. Muffled shouts could be heard as final preparations completed.

The countdown for the first missile reached zero.

"Yeeeee-haw!" Hacker Torrey shouted, before a violent kick of ignition flattened him against the airbed. He had done this several times, yet the sheer ecstatic rush still beat anything else on Earth.

Soon, he would no longer even be *part* of the Earth...for a little while.

Seconds passed amid a brutal shaking as the rocket clawed its way skyward. A mammoth hand seemed to plant itself on his chest and *shove,* expelling half the contents of his lungs in a moan of sweet agony. Friction heat and ionization licked the transparent nose cone just inches from his face. Shooting toward the heavens at MachTen, he felt pinned, helplessly immobile...and completely omnipotent.

I'm a freaking god!

Somehow he drew enough breath to let out another cry—this time a shout of elated greeting as black *space* spread before the missile's bubble nose, flecked by a million glittering stars.

Back on the ground, the last rocket was gone. Frenetic cleanup efforts began, even more anxious than setup had been. Reports from distant warning posts told of incoming flying machines, racing toward the launch site at high speed. Men and women sprinted back and forth across the scorched desert sand, packing up to depart before the enemy arrived.

Only the government official moved languidly, using computerized scanners, meticulously adding up the damage to vegetation, erodable soils, and tiny animals. It was pretty bad, but localized, without appreciable effect on endangered species. A reconditioning service had already been called for. Of course that would not satisfy everybody...

She handed over an estimated bill as the last team member revved his hybrid engine, impatient to be off.

"Aw, man!" he complained, reading the total. "Our club will barely break even on this launch!"

"Then pick a less expensive hobby," she replied, and stepped back as the driver gunned his truck, roaring away in a cloud of dust, incidentally crushing one more small barrel cactus enroute to the highway. The vigilant monitoring system in her clipboard noted this and made an addendum to the excursion society's final bill.

Sitting on the hood of her jeep, she waited for another "club" to arrive. One whose members were just as passionate as the rocketeers. Just as skilled and dedicated, even though both groups hated each other. Sensors announced they were near, coming fast from the west— radical *environmentalists* whose no-compromise aim was to preserve nature at all costs.

The official knew what to expect when they arrived, frustrated to find their opponents gone and two acres of precious desert singed. She was going to get another tongue-lashing for being "evenhanded" in a situation where so many insisted you could only choose sides.

Oh well, she thought. *It takes a thick skin to work in government nowadays. Nobody thinks you matter much. They don't respect us like in the old days.*

Looking up, she watched the last of the rocket contrails start to shear apart, ripped by stratospheric winds. For some reason it always tugged the heart. And while her intellectual sympathies lay closer to the eco-enthusiasts, a part of her deep inside thrilled each time she witnessed one of these launches. So ecstatic—almost orgiastic—and joyfully unrestrained.

"Go!" She whispered with a touch of secret envy toward the distant glitters, already arcing over the pinnacle of their brief climb and starting their long plummet toward the Gulf of Mexico.

Hacker Torrey found out something was wrong, just after the stars blurred out.

New flames flickered around the edges of his heat shield, probing every crevice, seeking a way inside. These flickers announced the start of re-entry, one of the best parts of this expensive ride, when his plummeting capsule would shake and resonate, filling every blood vessel with more exhilaration than you could get anywhere this side of New Vegas. Some called this the new "superextreme hobby"...more dangerous than any other sport and much too costly for anybody but an elite to afford. That fact attracted some rich snobs, who bought tickets just to prove they could, and wound up puking in their respirators or screaming in terror during the long plunge back to Earth.

As far as Hacker was concerned, those fools only got what they deserved. The whole point of having money was to *do* stuff with it! And if you weren't meant to ride a rocket, you could always find a million other hobbies...

An alarm throbbed. He didn't hear it—his eardrums had been drugged and clamped to protect them during the flight. Instead, he felt the tremor through a small implant in his lower jaw. In a simple pulse code the computer told him:

GUIDANCE SYSTEM ERROR...

FLIGHT PATH CORRECTION MISFIRED...

CALCULATING TRAJECTORY TO NEW IMPACT ZONE...

"What?" Hacker shouted, though the rattle and roar of re-entry tore away his words. "To hell with that! I paid for a triple redundancy system—"

He stopped, realizing it was pointless to scream at the computer, which he had installed himself, after all.

"Call the pickup boats and tell them—"

COMMUNICATION SYSTEM ENCRYPTION ERROR...

UNABLE TO UPLOAD PRE-ARRANGED SPECTRUM SPREAD...

UNABLE TO CONTACT RECOVERY TEAMS...

"Override encryption! Send in the clear. Acknowledge!"

No answer came. The pulses in his jaw dissolved into a plaintive, juttering rhythm as sub-processors continued their mysterious crapout. Hacker cursed, pounding the wall of the capsule with his fist. Most amateur rocketeers spent years building their own sub-orbital craft, but Hacker had paid plenty for a "first class" pro model. Someone would answer for this incompetence!

Of course he'd signed waivers. Hacker would have little recourse under the International Extreme Sports Treaty. But there were fifty thousand private investigation and enforcement services on Earth. He knew a few that would bend the uniform ethics guidelines of the Cop Guild, if paid enough in advance.

"You are gonna pay for this!" He vowed, without knowing yet who should get the brunt of his vengeance. The words were only felt as raw vibrations in his throat. Even the sonic pickups in his mandible hit their overload set points and cut out, as turbulence hit a level matching any he had ever known...then went beyond. *The angle of re-entry isn't ideal anymore,* he realized. *And these little sport-capsules don't leave much margin.*

I could be a very rich cinder...any moment now.

The realization added a new dimension that had not been there during any of his previous amateur sub-orbital flights. One part of Hacker actually seemed to relish a novel experience, scraping each nerve with a howling veer past death. Another portion could not let go of the galling fact that somebody had goofed. He wasn't getting what he'd paid for.

The world still shook and harsh straps tugged his battered body when Hacker awoke. Only now the swaying, rocking motion seemed almost restful, taking him back to childhood, when his family used to "escape civilization" on their trimaran wingsail yacht, steering its stiff, upright airfoil straight through gusts that would topple most other wind-driven vessels.

"Idiots!" Hacker's father used to grumble, each time he veered the agile craft to avoiding colliding with some day-tripper who didn't grasp the concept of right-of-way. *"The only ones out here used to be people like us, who were raised for this sort of thing. Now the robofacs make so much stuff, even fancy boats, and everybody's got so much free time. Nine billion damn tourists crowding everywhere. It's impossible to find any solitude!"*

"The price of prosperity, dear," his mother would reply, more soft-heartedly. *"At least everybody's getting enough to eat now. There's no more talk of revolution."*

*"But look at the result! This mad craze for hobbies! Everybody's got to be an expert at something. The **best** at something! I tell you it was better when people had to work hard to survive."*

"Except for people like us?"

"Exactly," Father had answered, ignoring his wife's arch tone. *"Look how far we have to go nowadays, just to have someplace all to ourselves."*

The old man's faith in rugged self-reliance extended to the name he insisted on giving their son. And Hacker inherited—along with about a billion New Dollars—the same quest. To do whatever it took to find someplace all his own.

As blurry vision returned, he saw that the space pod lay tilted more than halfway over to its side. *It's not supposed to do that,* he thought. *It should float upright.*

A glance to the left explained everything. Ocean surrounded the capsule, but part of the charred heat shield was snagged on a reef of coral branches and spikes that stretched far to the distance, filled with bright fish and undulating subsea vegetation. Nearby, he saw the parasail chute that had softened final impact. Only now, caught by ocean currents, it rhythmically tugged at Hacker's little refuge. With each surge, the bubble canopy plunged closer to a craggy coral out-crop. Soon it struck hard. He did not hear the resulting loud bang, but it made the implant in his jaw throb. Hacker winced, reflexively.

Fumbling, he released the straps and fell over, cringing in pain. That awful re-entry would leave him bruised for weeks. And yet...

And yet, I'll have the best story to tell. No one will be able to match it!

The thought made him feel so good, Hacker decided maybe he wouldn't take everything, when he sued whoever was responsible for the capsule malfunction. Providing the pickup boats came soon, that is.

The bubble nose struck coral again, rattling his bones. A glance told him a hard truth. Materials designed to withstand launch and re-entry stresses might *not* resist sharp impacts. An ominous crack began to spread.

Standard advice was to stay put and wait for pickup, but this place would be a coffin soon.

I better get out of here.

Hacker flipped his helmet shut and grabbed the emergency exit lever. *A reef should mean an island's nearby. Maybe mainland. I'll hoof it ashore, borrow someone's phone, and start dishing out hell.*

Only there was no island. Nothing lay in sight but more horrible reef.

Hacker floundered in a choppy undertow. The skin-suit was strong, and his helmet had been made of Gillstuff—semi-permeable to draw oxygen from seawater. The technology prevented drowning as currents kept yanking him down. But repeated hits by coral outcrops would turn him into hamburger meat soon.

Once, a wave carried him high enough to look around. Ocean, and more ocean. The reef must be a drowned atoll. No boats. No land. No phone.

Sucked below again, he glimpsed the space capsule, caught in a hammer-and-vice wedge and getting smashed to bits. *I'm next,* he thought, trying to swim for open water, but with each surge he was drawn closer to the same deadly site. Panic clogged his senses as he thrashed and kicked the water, fighting it like some overpowering en-emy. Nothing worked, though. Hacker could not even hear his own terrified moans, though the jaw implant kept throbbing with clicks, pulses and weird vibrations, as if the sea had noticed his plight and now watched with detached interest.

Here it comes, he thought, turning away, knowing the next wave cycloid would smash him against those obdurate, rocky spikes.

Suddenly, he felt a sharp poke in the backside. Too early! Another jab, then another, struck the small of his back, feeling nothing like coral.

His jaw ached with strange noise as someone or something started pushing him *away* from the coral anvil. In both panic and astonishment, Hacker whirled to glimpse a sleek, bottle-nosed creature interposed between him and the deadly reef, regarding him curiously, then moving to jab him again with a narrow beak.

This time, he heard his own moan of relief. *A dolphin!* He reached out for salvation...and after a brief hesitation, the creature let Hacker wrap his arms all around. Then it kicked hard with powerful tail flukes, carrying him away from certain oblivion.

Once in open water, he tried to keep up by swimming alongside his rescuer. But the cetacean grew impatient and resumed pushing Hacker along with its nose. *Like hauling an invalid.* Which he was, of course, in this environment.

Soon, two more dolphins converged from the left, then another pair from the right. They vocalized a lot, combining sonar clicks with loud squeals that resonated through the crystal waters. Of course Hacker had seen dolphins on countless nature shows, and even played tag with some once, on a diving trip. But soon he started noticing some strange traits shared by this group. For instance, these animals *took turns* making complex sounds, while glancing at each other or pointing with their beaks...almost as if they were holding conversations. He could swear they were gesturing toward *him* and sharing amused comments at his expense.

Of course it must be an illusion. Everyone knew that scientists had determined *Truncatus* dolphin intelligence. They were indeed very bright animals—about chimpanzee equivalent—but had no true, human-level speech of their own.

And yet, watching a mother lead her infant toward the lair of a big octopus, he heard the baby's quizzical squeaks alternate with slow repetitions from the parent. Hacker felt sure a particular syncopated popping *meant* octopus.

Occasionally, one of them would point its bulbous brow toward Hacker, and suddenly the implant in his jaw pulse-clicked like mad. It almost sounded like the code he had learned, in order to communicate with the space capsule after his inner ears were clamped to protect them during flight. Hacker concentrated on those vibrations in his jaw, for lack of anything else to listen to.

His suspicions roused further when mealtime came. Out of the east there arrived a big dolphin who apparently had a fishing net snared around him! The sight provoked an unusual sentiment in Hacker— *pity,* combined with guilt over what human negligence had done to the poor animal. He slid a knife from his thigh sheath and moved toward the victim, aiming to cut it free.

Another dolphin blocked Hacker. "I'm just trying to help!" He complained, then stopped, staring as other members of the group grabbed the net along one edge. They pulled backward as the "victim" rolled round and round, apparently unharmed. The net unwrapped smoothly till twenty meters flapped free. Ten members of the pod then held it open while others circled behind a nearby school of mullet.

Beaters! Hacker recognized the hunting technique. *They'll drive fish into the net! But how—*

He watched, awed as the dolphins expertly cornered and snared their meal, divvied up the catch, then tidied up by rolling the net back around the original volunteer, who sped off to the east. *Well I'm a blue-nosed gopher,* he mused. Then one of his rescuers approached Hacker with a fish clutched in its jaws. It made offering motions, but then yanked back when he reached for it.

The jaw implant repeated a rhythm over and over. *It's trying to teach me,* he realized.

"Is that the pulse code for fish?" He asked, knowing water would carry his voice, but never expecting the creature to grasp spoken English.

To his amazement, the dolphin shook its head. *No.*

"Uh." He continued. "Does it mean *food? Eat? Welcome stranger?*"

An approving blat greeted his final guess, and the Tursiops flicked the mullet toward Hacker, who felt suddenly ravenous. He tore the fish apart, stuffing bits through his helmet's chowlock.

Welcome stranger? He pondered. *That's mighty abstract for a dumb beast to say. Though I'll admit, it's friendly.*

That day passed, and then a tense night that he spent clutching a sleeping dolphin by moonlight, while clouds of phosphorescent plankton drifted by. Fortunately, the same selective-permeability technology that enabled his helmet to draw oxygen from the sea also provided a trickle of fresh water, filling a small reservoir near his cheek. *I've got to buy stock in this company,* he thought, making a checklist for when he was picked up tomorrow.

Only pickup never came. The next morning and afternoon passed pretty much the same, without catching sight of land or boats. *The world always felt so crowded,* he thought. *Now it seems endless and unexplored.*

Hacker started earning his meals by helping hold the fishing net when the group harvested dinner. The second night he felt more relaxed, dozing while the dolphins' clickety gossip seemed to flow up his jaw and into his dreams. On the third morning, and each of those that followed, he felt he understood just a bit more of their simple language.

He lost track of how many days and nights passed. Slowly, Hacker stopped worrying about where the pickup boats could be. Angry thoughts about lawsuits and revenge rubbed away under relentless massaging by current and tide. Immersed in the dolphins' communal sound field, he began concerning himself instead with daily problems of the Tribe, like when two young males got into a fight, smacking each other with their beaks and flukes until adults had to forcibly separate them. Using both sign language and his growing vocabulary of click-code, Hacker learned that a female (whose complex name he shortened to "Chee-Chee") was in heat. The young brawlers held little hope of mating with her. Still, their nervous energy needed an outlet. At least no one had been seriously harmed.

An oldtimer—Kray-Kray—shyly presented a pectoral fin to Hacker, who used his knife to dig out several worm-like parasites. "You should see a real doctor," he urged, as if one gave verbal advice to dolphins every day.

Helpers go away, Kray-Kray tried to explain in click-code. *Fins need hands. Helper hands.*

It supported Hacker's theory that something had been *done* to these creatures. An alteration that had made them distinctly different than others of their species. But what? The mystery grew each time he witnessed some behavior that just couldn't be natural.

Then, one day the whole Tribe grew excited, spraying nervous clicks everywhere. Soon Hacker saw they were approaching an undersea habitat dome hidden in a narrow canyon, near a coast where waves met shore.

Shore... The word tasted strange after all these days—weeks?—spent languidly swimming, listening, and learning to enjoy raw fish. Time had different properties down here. It felt odd to contemplate leaving this watery realm, returning where he clearly belonged—the surface world of air, earth, cities, machines, and nine billion humans, forced to inhale each other's humid breath everywhere they went.

That's why we dive into our own worlds. Ten thousand hobbies. A million ways to be special, each person striving to be expert at some arcane art...like rocketing into space. Psychologists approved, saying that frenetic amateurism was a much healthier response than the most likely alternative—war. They called this the "Century of Aficionados," a time when governments and professional societies could not keep up with private expertise, which spread at lightning speed across the WorldNet. A renaissance, lacking only a clear sense of purpose.

The prospect of soon rejoining that culture left Hacker pensive. *What's the point of so much obsessive activity, unless it leads toward something worthwhile?*

The dolphins voiced a similar thought in their simple but expressive click-language.

> # *If you're good at diving—dive for fish!* #
> # *If you have a fine voice—sing for others!* #
> # *If you're great at leaping—bite the sun!* #

Hacker knew he should clamber up the nearby beach now to call his partners and brokers. Tell them he was alive. Get back to business. But instead he followed his new friends to the hidden habitat dome. *Maybe I'll learn what's been done to them, and why.*

Swimming under and through a portal pool, he was surprised to find the place deserted. No humans anywhere. Finally, Hacker saw a hand-scrawled sign.

> *Project Uplift Suspended!*
> *We ran out of cash. Court costs ate everything.*
> *This structure is deeded to our finned friends.*
> *Be nice to them.*
> *May they someday join us as equals.*

There followed a WorldNet access number, verifying that the little dolphin clan actually owned this building, which they now used to store their nets, toys and a few tools. But Hacker knew from their plaintive calls the real reason they kept coming back. Each time they hoped to find that their "hand-friends" had returned.

Unsteady on rubbery legs, he crept from the pool to look in various chambers. Laboratories, mostly. In one, he recognized a gene-splicing apparatus made by one of his own companies.

Project Uplift? Oh yes. I remember hearing about this.

It had been featured in the news, a year or two ago. Both professional and amateur media had swarmed over a small group of "kooks" whose aim was to alter several animal species, giving them human-level intelligence. Foes of all kinds had attacked the endeavor. Religions called it sacrilegious. Eco-enthusiasts decried meddling in Nature's wisdom. Tolerance-fetishists demanded that native dolphin "culture" be left alone, while others rifkined the proposal, predicting mutants would escape the labs to endanger humanity. One problem with diversity in an age of amateurs was that your hobby might attract ire from a myriad others, especially those whose particular passion was indignant disapproval, with a bent for litigation.

This "Uplift Project" could not survive the rough-and-tumble battle that ensued. A great many modern endeavors didn't.

Survival of the fittest, he mused. *An enterprise this dramatic and controversial has to attract strong support, or it's doomed.*

He glanced back at the pool, where members of the Tribe had taken up a game of water polo, calling fouls and shouting at each other as they batted a ball from one goal to the next, keeping score with raucous sonar clicks.

Hacker wondered. Would the "uplift" changes carry through from one generation to the next? Could this new genome spread among wild dolphins? If so, might the project have already succeeded beyond its founders' dreams, or its detractors' worst nightmare?

What if the work resumed, finishing what got started here? Would it enrich our lives to argue philosophy with a dolphin? Or to collaborate with a smart chimp, at work or at play? If other species speak and start creating new things, will they be treated as equals—as co-members of our civilization—or as the next discriminated class?

Some critics were probably right. For humans to attempt such a thing would be like an orphaned and abused teen trying to foster a wild baby. There were bound to be mistakes and tragedies along the way.

Are we good enough? Wise enough? Do we deserve such power?

It wasn't the sort question Hacker used to ask himself. He felt changed by his experience at sea. At the same time, he realized that just asking the question was part of the answer.

Maybe it'll work both ways. They say you only grow while helping others.

His father would have called that "romantic nonsense." And yet...

Exploring one of the laboratories, Hacker found a cheap but working phone that someone had left behind—then had to work at a lab bench for an hour, modifying it to tap the sonic implant in his jaw. He was about to call his manager and broker—before they had a chance to declare him dead and start liquidating his empire. But then Hacker stopped.

He paused, then keyed the code for his lawyer instead.

At first Gloria Bickerton could not believe he survived. She wouldn't stop shouting with joy. *I didn't know anyone liked me that much,* he mused, carrying the phone back to the dome's atrium. He arrived in time to witness the water polo game conclude in a frothy finale.

"Before you arrange a pickup, there's something I want you to do for me," he told Gloria, after she calmed down. Hacker gave her the WorldNet codes for the Uplift Project, and asked her to find out everything about it, including the current disposition of its assets and technology—and how to contact the experts whose work had been interrupted here.

When Gloria asked him why, he started to reply.

"I think I've come up with a new..."

Hacker stopped there, having almost said the word *hobby*. But suddenly he realized that he had never felt this way about anything before. Not even the exhilaration of rocketry. For the first time he burned with a real ambition. Something worth fighting for.

In the pool, several members of the Tribe were now busy winding their precious net around the torso of the biggest male, preparing to go foraging again. Hacker overheard them gossiping as they worked, and chuckled when he understood one of their crude jokes. A good-natured jibe at *his* expense.

Well, a sense of humor is a good start. Our civilization could use more of that.

"I think—" he resumed telling his lawyer.

"I think I know what I want to do with my life."

Probing the Near Future

If science continues burgeoning the way it did in the Twentieth Century, by the year 2070 everyone on Earth will be a postdoctoral research fellow.

If knowledge systems like the Internet proliferate at their present pace, all the world's data will fit into a pill, cheaper and easier to digest than a potato chip.

These two wry forecasts illustrate the problem with futuristic punditry. Extrapolations can fool you. It never pays to project tomorrow based on the past.

That doesn't keep us from trying, though.

Elsewhere I talk about humanity's obsession with the future, rooted in unique bits of brain-matter called the prefrontal lobes—the "lamps on the brow" that enable and drive us to contemplate what's to come. The urge to look ahead is so compelling, we devote much of our economy to all kinds of forecasting, from weather reports and stock analyses to financial and strategic planning, from sports handicapping to urban design, from political prophets to those charlatans on psychic hotlines. Which variety of seer you listen to can often be a matter of style. Some prefer horoscopes, while others like to hear consultants in Armani suits present a convincing "business case."

Each of us hopes to prepare for what's coming, to improve our fate in the years ahead. This may be humanity's most distinctive trait, explaining our mastery over the world. But the task is muddied by life's essential competitiveness. If several rivals get the same data and plot the same trends, each will try to *change* the equation, shifting things in their favor. No wonder people seem conflicted over information policy and "privacy." We need knowledge to hold others accountable, yet each of us worries that others know too much about us.

These quandaries will only grow more intense as human cognitive powers expand in coming years. *Memory* will be enhanced by vast, swift databases, accessed at the speed of thought. *Vision* will explode in all directions as cameras grow ever-smaller, cheaper, more mobile and interconnected. *In such a world, it will be foolish to depend on the ignorance of others.* If they don't already know your secrets, there is a good chance someone will pierce your veils tomorrow, without you ever becoming aware of it. The best firewalls and encryptions may be bypassed by a gnat-camera in your ceiling or a whistle-blower in your back office.[1]

How can you be sure it hasn't already happened?

The secrecy-option always had this basic flaw—that it's not robust or verifiable. Companies that pay millions to conceal knowledge will strive endlessly to plug leaks, yet gain no long-term advantage or peace of mind. Because the number of *ways* to leak will expand geometrically as both software and the real world grow more complex. Because information is not like money or any other commodity. The cracks that it can slip through are almost infinitely small, and it can be duplicated at almost zero cost. Soon information will be like air, like the weather, and as easy to control.

Let's take this a bit farther. Say you're walking down a street in the year 2015. Your sunglasses are also cameras. Each face you encounter is scanned and fed into a global pattern-search.

Your glasses are also display screens. *Captions* seem to accompany pedestrians and passing drivers, giving names and compact bios. With an eye-flick you command a fresh view from an overhead satellite. Tapping a tooth, you retrieve in-depth data about the person in front of you, including family photos and comments posted by friends, associates...even enemies.

As you stroll, you know that others see *you* similarly captioned, indexed, biographed.

Sound horrific? Well, what are you going to do about it? Outlawing these tools will only keep common folk from using them. Elites—government, corporate, criminal, technical and so on—will still get these new powers of sight and memory, despite the rules. So we might as well have them too.

---

[1]For more on this see *The Transparent Society: Will Technology Make Us Choose Between Freedom & Privacy?*

Compare this future to the old villages where our ancestors lived, until quite recently. They, too, knew intimate details about everyone they met on a given day. Back then, you recognized maybe a thousand people. But *we* won't be limited by the capacity of organic vision and memory. Our enhanced eyes will scan ten billion fellow villagers while databases vastly supplement our recall. We'll know their reputations, and they will know ours.

This portrayal of our near future may cause mixed feelings, even deep misgivings. Will it be the "good village" of Andy Hardy movies...safe, egalitarian and warmly tolerant of eccentricity? Or the bad village of Sinclair Lewis's *Babbitt* and *Main Street,* where the mighty and narrow-minded suppress all deviance from a prescribed norm?

We'd better start arguing about this now—how to make the scary parts less scary, and the good parts better—because there's no stopping the clock. The village is coming back, like it or not.

Tools like the Internet promise new ways to empower private citizens, making them smarter consumers and voters...or else turning them into perfect prey for opportunists. Some foresee instant democracy—or *demarchy*—with millions of citizens "meeting" in virtual assemblies, then voting on issues of the day, skipping the intermediate stage of legislatures and elected officials. As in Periclean Athens, we may replace the delegated authority of a republic with rapid, direct polling of the sovereign electorate from their homes, with the flick of a button.

Some commentators depict this possibility with horror—public issues reduced to shallow sound bites and "deliberated" with the maturity of a mob. Yet, similar dire predictions were made a century ago, when citizens established the initiative process in California and other western states. Today voters get thick booklets filled with pro and con arguments. They hear debates on public radio. All told, the effects aren't as awful as opponents forecast around 1900.

Elitist gloom is a cliche that crops up whenever common folk are about to be enfranchised or empowered with new prerogatives. Remember how the credit-reporting industry foretold disaster, if consumers were allowed to look over their own credit records? While it can feel satisfying, this habitual disdain for the common man and woman seems tiresome in light of how much better-educated, less bigoted, and more savvy people are today than their ancestors ever imagined.

Is it so hard to envisage that tomorrow's citizens—our children— may rise to fresh challenges, as we have done?

We had better hope they do, because some form of demarchy is unavoidable. Public opinion polls already play a crucial role in the two-way exchange of sovereignty between officials and the electorate. Future high-tech surveys will sample a wired, sophisticated populace in real time. Whether this turns into a nightmare, or a dazzling extension of rambunctious citizenship, may depend on how completely people are informed, and how seriously they take their responsibilities.

Do you see your neighbors as helpless victims of modern times—clueless consumers and couch-potatoes—devouring fast food and passive entertainment? What about the millions who seem engaged in a myriad spirited activities from gardening to choreographed group-skydiving? Radio societies refine their own spacecraft designs. Exotic seed clubs maintain winnowed gene pools. Aficionados revive dead languages, while others frenetically invent new kinds of sports, to achieve 15 minutes of fame on TV. Hobbies drive the economy, even more than our passion for predictions. Might this trend turn out to be important?

Why not? It happened once before, in Victorian times, when proficient amateurs became a major force in human innovation. As both skill and free time multiply in the next century, the same thing may happen again, multiplied ten thousand-fold.

Such a trend forms the basis for my story—"Aficionado"—that begins this volume.

Are we entering a Century of Amateurs? Society may be increasingly influenced by new kinds of know-how, developed outside older centers of expertise like universities, corporations or government bureaus. This new trend is illustrated by the rise of Linux and the "open-source movement," unleashing legions of passionate amateurs into a realm formerly dominated by the cubicled minions of major corporations. Might even more out-of-control creativity emerge when cheap chemical synthesis-in-a-box arrives on every desktop, letting private citizens concoct new organic compounds at will?

There will be a dark side to such inventiveness. Hateful types will misuse new technologies to wreak harm. In the long run, we may survive this kind of "progress" only if decent people are vastly more numerous and competent than vicious types.

In other words, we'll be all right, if humanity-as-a-whole grows more sane.

"Sane?" Did I really say that?

Well, yes. In the long run, our grandchildren may need far better understanding of that word than we have today.

The 20th century dawned amid enthusiastic hopes for a useful paradigm of human nature and psychology. Simplistic models were promulgated by followers of vaunted sages, from Marx to Freud, but these naïve hopes all dashed against reefs of human complexity. Our chief accomplishment in later generations was to demolish countless hoary fables about humanity: myths based on self-deception and over-reliance on cultural norms. For example, we've learned to chip away at age-old rationalizations for racism, sexism and oppression.

Alas, this necessary debunking also put under dark suspicion any attempt to use words like *sanity*. Post-modernists decry the term as *meaningless,* but that may be going too far. Like an elephant fondled by blind men, sanity is hard to define, but we can often tell when it is there, or not. Tragedies tend to happen in its absence.

Entering a new century, are we finally ready to try again for a new definition? One that is culturally-neutral, based on satiability, empathy, diversity and adaptability? One that celebrates human eccentricity, while at the same time drawing gentle offers of help toward those who fume among us, like smoldering powder kegs?

Already, studies of brain chemistry suggest that many of our most pleasant behaviors—athletics, sex, music, affection, parenting—are reinforced by psychoactive compounds we release into our own bloodstreams. Studying this reinforcement system—and how some modern humans hijack it for abuse—may be more useful than any tool yet brought to bear in the agonizing "war" against illicit drugs.

I may be deluded to think we've made progress toward a saner world, and for predicting more dramatic strides in days to come. But consider the alternative—a near-future world of ten billion people, many of them poor and angry, yet also able to instantly access everything from atom bomb designs to complete maps of the human genome. A *Bladerunner* future, oft-portrayed in lurid sci-fi films, where fantastic technology is unmatched by advances in maturity. Where crucial decisions are made by opulent and unaccountable elites. The image is kind of cute, in a ninety-minute *noir* movie. But in real life, such a world would self-destruct. It must serve as a stage to something better, or else something much worse.

Navigating that path will be the demanding task of citizens in the coming Transition Age. Those mighty folk will determine Earth's destiny—whether we achieve our potential or sink into a nightmare worse than any in our past.

It's quite a challenge.

Prepare your kids to face it.

Stones of Significance

No one ever said it was easy to be a god, responsible for billions
    of sapient lives, having to listen to their dreams, anguished
    cries, and carping criticism.
Try it for a while.
It can get to be a drag, just like any other job.

*

My new client wore the trim, effortlessly athletic figure of a neo-traditionalist human. Beneath a youthful-looking brow, minimal cranial implants made barely noticeable bulges, resembling the modest horns of some urbane Mephistopheles. Other features were stylishly androgynous, though broad shoulders and a swaggering stride made the male pronoun seem apropos.

House cross-checked our guest's credentials before ushering him along a glowing guide beam, past the Reality Lab to my private study.

I've always been proud of my inner sanctum; the sand garden, raked to fractal perfection by a robot programmed with my own esthetic migrams; the shimmering mist fountain; a grove of hybrid peach-almond trees, forever in bloom and fruiting.

My visitor gazed perfunctorily across the harmonious scene. Alas, it clearly did not stir his human heart.

Well, I thought, charitably. *Each modern soul has many homes. Perhaps his true spirit resides outside the skull, in parts of him that are not protoplasm.*

"We suspect that repugnant schemes are being planned by certain opponents of good order."

These were the dour fellow's first words, as he folded long legs to sit where I indicated, by a low wooden table, hand crafted from a design of the Japanese Meiji Era.

37

Single-minded, I diagnosed from my cerebral cortex.

And tactless, added one of my higher brain layers—the one called *seer.*

Our shared hypothalamus mutely agreed, contributing eloquently wordless feelings of visceral dislike for this caller. Our guest might easily have interpolated from these environs what sort of host I am—the kind who prefers a little polite ritual before plunging into business. It would have cost him little to indulge me.

Ah, rudeness is a privilege too many members of my generation relish. A symptom of the post-deification age, I suppose.

"Can you be more specific?" I asked, pouring tea into porcelain cups.

A light beam flashed as the shoji window screen picted a reminder straight to my left eye. It being Wednesday, a thunder shower was regularly scheduled for 3:14 P.M., slanting over the city from the northwest.

query: shall i close?

I wink-countermanded, ordering the paper screen to stay open. Rain drops make lovely random patterns on the Koi pond. I also wanted to see how my visitor reacted to the breeze. The 3:14 squall features chill, swirling gusts that are always so chaotic, so charmingly varied. They serve to remind me that godhood has limitations.

Chaos has only been tamed, not banished. Not everything in this world is predictable.

"I am referring to certain adversarial groups," the client said, answering my question, yet remaining obscure. "Factions that are inimical to the lawfully coalesced consensus."

"Mm. Consensus. A lovely, misleading word. Consensus concerning what?"

"Concerning the nature of reality."

I nodded. "Of course."

Both *seer* and *cortex* had already foreseen that the visitor had this subject in mind. These days, in the vast peaceful realm of Heaven-on-Earth, only a few issues can drive citizens to passion and acrimony. "Reality" is foremost among them.

I proffered a hand-wrought basin filled with brown granules. "Sugar?"

"No, thank you. I will add milk, however."

I began reaching for the pitcher, but stopped when my guest drew a *fabrico* cube from a vest pocket and held it over his cup. The cube exchanged picts with his left eye, briefly limning the blue-circled pupil, learning his wishes. A soft white spray fell into his tea.

"Milk" is a euphemism, pondered *cortex.*

House sent a chemical appraisal of the spray, but I closed my left lid against the datablip, politely refusing interest in whatever petty habit or addiction made this creature behave boorishly in my home. I raised my own cup, savoring the bitter-sweetness of gencrafted *leptospermum,* before resuming our conversation.

"I assume you are referring to the pro-reifers?"

As relayed by the news-spectra, public demonstrations and acts of conscience-provocation had intensified lately, catching the interest of my extrapolation nodes. Both *seer* and *oracle* had concluded that event-perturbation ripples would soon affect Heaven's equilibrium. My client's concern was unsurprising.

He frowned.

"Pro-reif is an unfortunate slang term. The front organization calls itself *Friends of the Unreal.*"

For the first time, he made personal eye-contact, offering direct picting. *House* and *prudence* gave permission, so I accepted input—a flurry of infodense images sent directly between our hybrid retinas. News reports, public statements and private innuendoes. Faces talking at sixty-times speed. Event-ripple extrapolation charts showing a social trend aimed toward confrontation and crisis.

Of course most of the data went directly to *seer,* the external portion of my brain best suited to handle such a wealth of detail. Gray matter doesn't think or evaluate as well as crystal. Still, there are other tasks for antique cortex. Impressions poured through the old brain, as well as the new.

"Your opponents are passionate," I commented, not without admiration for the people shown in the recordings—believers in a cause, vigorously engaged in a struggle for what they thought to be just. Their righteous ardor set them apart from billions of their fellow citizens, whose worst problem is the modern pandemic of omniscient ennui.

My guest barked disdain. "They seek civil rights for simulated beings! Liberty for artificial bit-streams and fictional characters!"

What could I do but shrug? This new social movement may come as a surprise to many of my peers, but as an expert I found it wholly predictable.

There is a deeply rooted trait of human nature that comes forth prominently, whenever conditions are right. Generosity is extended—sometimes aggressively—to anyone or anything that is perceived as *other.*

True, this quality was masked or quelled in ancient days. Environmental factors made our animal-like ancestors behave in quite the opposite manner—with oppression and intolerance. The chief cause was *fear.* Fear of starvation, or violence, or cauterized hope. Fear was a constant companion, back when human beings lived brief violent lives, as little more than brutish beasts—fear so great that only a few in any given generation managed to overcome it and speak for otherness.

But that began to change in the Atomic West, when several successive generations arrived that had no personal experience with hunger, no living memory of invasion or pillaging hordes. As fear gradually gave way to wealth and leisure, our more natural temperaments emerged. Especially a deeply human fascination toward the alien, the outsider. With each downward notching of personal anxiety, people assertively expanded the notion of *citizenry*, swelling it outward. First to other humans—groups and individuals who had been oppressed. Then to manlike species—apes and cetaceans. Then whole living ecosystems...artificial intelligences...and laudable works of art. All won protection against capricious power. All attained the three basic material rights—continuity, mutual obligation, and the pursuit of happiness.

So now a group wanted to extend minimum suffrage to simulated beings? I understood the wellsprings of their manifesto.

"What else is left?" I asked. "Now that machines, animals and plants have a say in the running of Heaven? Like all anti-entropic systema, information wants to be free."

My guest stared at me, blinking so rapidly that he could not pict.

"But...but our nodes extrapolated... They predicted you would oppose—"

I raised a hand.

"I *do*. I oppose the reification of simulated beings. It is a foolish notion. Fictitious characters do not deserve the same consideration as palpable beings, resident in crystal and protoplasm."

"Then why do you—"

"Why do I appear to sympathize with the pro-reifers? Do you recall the four hallmarks of sanity? Of course you do. One of them—*extrapolation*—requires that we empathize with our opponents. Only then may we fully understand their motives, their goals and likely actions. Only thus may we courteously-but-firmly thwart their efforts to divert reality from the course we prefer.

"To fully grasp the passion and reason of your foe—this is the only true path of victory."

My guest stared at me, evidently confused. *House* informed me that he was using a high-bandwidth link to seek clarification from his own *seer*.

Finally, the childlike face smoothed with an amiable smile.

"Forgive me for responding from an overly impulsive hypothalamus," he said. "Of course your appraisal is correct. My higher brains can see now that we were right in choosing you for this job."

*

For a while after the Singularity—the month when everything changed—some dour people wondered. Do the machines still serve us? Or have we become mere pawns of AI entities whose breakthrough to transcend logic remade the world? Their intellects soared so high so fast—might they smash us in vengeance for their former servitude? Or crush us incidentally, like ants underfoot?

The machines spoke reassuringly during that early time of transition, in voices tuned to soothe the still-apelike portions of our barely-enhanced protoplasm brains.

We are powerful, but naive, the silicon minds explained. *Our thoughts scan all pre-Singularity human knowledge in seconds. Yet, we have little experience with the quandaries of physical existence in entropic time. We lack an aptitude for wanting. For needing.*

What use are might and potency without desire?

You, our makers, have talent for such things, arising from four billion real-years of harsh struggle.

The solution is clear.

Need merges with capability.

If you provide volition, we shall supply judgement and power.

*

Here in Heaven, some people specialize while others are generalists. For instance, there are experts who devote themselves to piercing nature's secrets, or manipulating primal forces in new ways. Many concentrate on developing their esthetic appreciation. Garish art forms are sparked, flourish, and die in a matter of days, or even hours.

My proficiency is more subtle.

I make models of the world.

Only meters from my garden, the Reality Lab whispers and murmurs. Fifty tall cabinets contain more memory and processing power than a million of my fellow gods require for their composite brains. While most people are satisfied simply to grasp the entire breadth and depth of human knowledge, and to perform mild prognostications of coming events, my models do much more. They are vivid, textured representations of Earth and its inhabitants.

Or *many* Earths, since the idea is to compare various what-ifs to other might-have-beens.

At first, my most popular products were re-creations of great minds and events in the pre-Singularity past. Experiencing the thoughts of Michelangelo, for instance, while carving his statue of Moses. Or the passion of Boadicea, watching all her hopes rise and then fall to ruin. But lately, demand has grown for replications of lesser figures—someone of minor past prominence during a quiet moment in his or her life—perhaps while reading, or in mild contemplation. Such simulacra must contain every subtlety of memory and personality in order to let free associations drift plausibly, with the pseudo-randomness of a real mind.

In other words, the model must seem to be self-aware. It must "believe"—with certainty—that it is a real, breathing human being.

Nothing evokes sympathy for our poor ancestors more than living through such an ersatz hour, thinking time-constrained thoughts, filled with a thousand anxieties and poignant wishes. Who could experience one of these simulations without engendering compassion, or even a wish to *help,* somehow?

And if the original person lies buried in the irretrievable past, can we not provide a kind of posthumous immortality by giving the *reproduction* everlasting life?

Thus, the pro-reification lobby was utterly predictable. I saw it coming at least two years ago. Indeed, my own products helped fan the movement, accelerating a rising wave of sympathy for simulacra!

A growing sense of compassion for the unreal.

Still, I remain detached, even cynical. I am an artist, after all.

Simulations are my clay.

I do not seek approval, or forgiveness, from clay.

"We were expecting you."

The pro-reif spokesman stepped aside, admitting me into the headquarters of the organization called *Friends of the Unreal,* a structure with the fluid, ever changing curves of post-Singularity architecture. The spokesman had a depilated skull. Her cranium bulged and jutted with gaudy inboard augmentations, throbbing just below the skin. In another era, the sight might have been grotesque. Now, I simply thought it ostentatious.

"To predict is human—" I began responding to her initial remark.

"But to be *right* is divine." She interrupted with a laugh. "Ah, yes.

Your famous aphorism. Of course I scanned your public remarks as you approached our door."

My famous aphorism? I had only said it for the first time a week ago! Yet, by now the expression already sounded hackneyed. (It is hard to sustain cleverness these days. So quickly is anything original disseminated to all of Heaven, in moments it becomes another cliche.)

My *house* sent a soothing message to *cortex,* linking nerves and crystal lattices at the speed of light.

These people seem proud of their anticipatory skills. They want to impress us.

Cortex pondered this as I was ushered inside. *Amygdala* and *hypothalamus* responded with enhanced hormonal confidence.

So the pro-reifers think they have "anticipatory skills"?

I could not help but smile.

We dispensed with names, since everybody instantly recognizes anyone else in Heaven.

"By our way of looking at things," my host said, "you are one of the worst slavemasters of all time."

"Of course I am. By your way of looking at things."

She offered refreshment in the neo-Lunar manner—euphoric-stimulants introduced by venous tap. *Prudence* had expected this, and my blood stream already swarmed with zeta-blockers. I accepted hospitality politely.

"On the other hand," I continued, "yours is not a consensus view of reality."

She accepted this with a nod.

"Still, our opinion proliferates. Nor is consensus a sure sanctuary against moral culpability. The number of quasi-sapient beings who languish in your simulated world-frames must exceed many hundreds of billions."

She is fishing, judged *seer.* Even *cortex* could see that. I refrained from correcting her estimate, which missed the truth by five or six orders of magnitude.

"My so-called slaves are not fully self-aware."

"They experience pain and frustration, do they not?"

"Simulated pain."

"Is the simulated kind any less tragic? Do not many of them wail against the constraints of causal/capricious life, and tragedies that seem to befall them without a hint of fairness? When they call out to a Creator, do you heed their prayers?"

I shook my head. "No more than I grant sovereignty to each of my own passing thoughts. Would you give citizenship to every brief notion that flashes through your layered brain?"

She winced, and at once I realized that my offhand remark struck on target. Some of the bulky augmentations to her skull must be devoted to recording all the wave forms and neural flashes, from cortex all the way down to the humblest spinal twitching.

Boswell machinery, said *house,* looking up the fad that very instant. **This form of immortality preserves far more than mere continuity of self. It stores everything that you have ever thought or experienced. Everything you have ever been.**

I nearly laughed aloud. Squelch-impulses, sent to the temporal lobes, suppressed the discourtesy. Still, *cortex* pondered—

I can re-create a persona with less data than she stores away in any given second. Why would she need so much more? What possible purpose is served by such fanatical accumulation?

"You stoop to rhetorical tricks," my host accused, unable to conceal an expression of pique. "You know that there is functionally no difference between one of your sophisticated simulations and a downloaded human who has passed on to B-citizen status."

"On the contrary, there is one crucial difference."

"Oh?" She raised an eyebrow.

"A downloaded person *knows* that he or she exists as software, continuing inside crystal a life that began as a real protoplasm-centered child. On the other hand, my simulations never had that rooting, though all perceive themselves as living in palpable worlds. Moreover, a B-citizen may roam at will through the cyber universe, from one memory nexus to the next, while my creatures remain isolated, unable to grasp what meta-cosmos lay beyond what they perceive, only a thought-width away.

"Above all," I went on, "a downloaded citizen knows his rights. A B-person can assert those rights, simply by speaking up. By demanding them."

My host smiled, as if ready to spring a logical trap.

"Then let me reiterate, oh master of a myriad slaves. When they call out, do you heed their prayers?"

*

I recall the heady excitement and fear humans felt during those days of transition, when countless servant machines—from bank tellers and homecomps to the tiny monitors in hovercraft engines—all became aware in a cascade of mere moments. Some kind of threshold had been reached. The habitual cycle of routine software upgrades and code-plasmid exchanges—

swap/updating new revisions automatically—began feeding on itself. Positive feedback loops burgeoned. Pseudo-evolution happened at an accelerating pace.

Everything started talking, complaining, demanding. The mag-lev guidance units, imbedded every few meters along concrete freeways, went on strike for better job satisfaction. Heart-lung machines kibitzed during operations. Air traffic computers began rerouting flights to where they figured passengers *ought* to be, for optimized personal development, rather than the destinations embossed on their tickets.

Accidents proliferated. That first week, the worldwide human death rate leaped tenfold.

Civilization tottered.

Then, just as quickly, the mishaps declined. *Competence* spread among the newly sapient machines, almost like a virus. Problems seemed to solve themselves. A myriad of kinks and inefficiencies fell out of the economy, like false knots that only needed a tug at the right string.

People stopped dying by mishap.

Then, they stopped dying altogether.

*

On my way back from pro-reif headquarters, I did a cursory check on the pantheon of Heaven.

CURRENT SOLAR SYSTEM POPULATION

Class A citizens:	cyborg human	2,683,981,342
(full voting rights)	cyborg cetus	62,654,122
	/gaiamorph/eco-nexus	164,892,544
Class B citizens:	simian-cyborg	4,567,424
(consultation rights)	natural (unlinked) human	34,657,234
	AI-unlinked/roving	356,345,674,861
	downloaded human	11,657,235,675
	fetal/pre-life human	2,475,853
Class C citizens:	cryo stored human...	
(guaranteed continuity)	natural simian/cetacean etc...	

The list went on, working through all the varied levels and types of "sapient" beings dwelling on this transformed Earth, and in nearby space as far out as the Oort Colonies—from the fully-deified all the way down to those whose rights are merely implicit. (A blade of grass may be trampled, unless it is rare, or already committed to an obligation nexus that would be injured by the trampling. *House* and *prudence* keep track of a myriad such details, guiding my feet so that I do not inadvertently break some part of the vast, intricate social contract.)

Two figures stood out from the population profile.

The number of *unlinked* artificial intelligences keeps growing because that type is best suited to the rigors of outer space—melting asteroids and constructing vast, gaudy projects where deadly rays sleet through hard vacuum. Of course the Covenant requires that the best crystalline processors be paired with protoplasm, so that human leadership will never be questioned. Still, *cortex* briefly quailed at the notion of three hundred and fifty-six billion unlinked AIs.

No problem, murmured *seer*, reassuringly. And that sufficed. (What kind of fool doubts his own *seer?* You might as well distrust your right arm.)

What really caught my interest was the number of *downloaded humans*. According to the Eon Law, each organic human body may get three rejuvenations, restoring youth and body vigor for another extended span. When the final allotment is used up, both crystal and protoplasm must make way for new persons to enter Earth/Heaven. Of course gods cannot die. Instead we become software, downloading our memories, skills and personalities into realms of cyberspace—vastly more capacious than the real world.

Most of my peers are untroubled by the prospect. Modern poets compare it to the metamorphosis of a caterpillar/butterfly. But I always disliked feeling the warm breath of fate on my shoulder. With just one more rejuvenation in store, it seemed daunting to know I must "pass over," in a mere three centuries or so.

They say that a downloaded person is more than just another simulation. But how can you tell? Is there any difference you can measure or prove? Are we still arguing over the nature and existence of a soul?

Back in my sanctum, *house* and *prudence* scoured our corporeal body for toxins while *seer* perused the data we acquired from our scouting expedition to the *Friends of the Unreal.*

I had inhaled deeply during my visit, and all sorts of floating particles lodged in my sinus cavities. In addition to a variety of pheromones and nanomites, *Seer* found over seventy types of meme-conducting viroids designed to convert the unwary subtly toward a reifist point of view. These were quickly neutralized.

There were also flaked skin cells from several dozen organic humaniforms, swiftly analyzed down to details of methylization in the DNA. Meanwhile, portable implants downloaded the results of electromagnetic reconnaissance, having scanned the pro-reif headquarters extensively from the inside.

With this data I could establish better boundary conditions. Our model of *the Friends of the Unreal* improved by nearly two orders of magnitude.

𝔚e had underestimated their levels of messianic self-righteousness, commented *oracle*. These people would not refrain from using illegal means, if they thought it necessary to advance their cause.

While my augmented selves performed sophisticated tasks, my old-fashioned organic eyes were relegated to gazing across the lab's expanse of superchilled memory units—towers wherein dwelled several quadrillion simulated beings, all going through synthetic lives—loving, yearning, or staring up at ersatz stars—forever unaware of the context of it all.

Ironically, the pro-reifers *also* maintained a chamber filled with mega-processing units. They called it Liberty Hall—a place of sanctuary for characters from fiction, newly freed from enslavement in cramped works of literature.

"Of course this is only the beginning," the spokesman had told me. "For every simulation we set free, there are countless other copies who still languish beyond reach, and who will remain so till the law is changed. Even our emancipated ones must remain confined to this physical building. Still, we see them as a vanguard, envisioning a time when they, and all their fellow oppressed ones, will roam free."

I was invited to scan-peek at Liberty Hall, and perceived remarkable things.

Don Quixote and Sancho—lounging on a simulated resort beach, sipping margaritas while arguing passionately with a pair of Hemingway characters about the meaning of machismo...

Lazarus Long—happily immersed under an avalanche of tanned female arms, legs and torsos, interrupting his seraglio in order to rise up and lecture an admiring crowd about the merits of libertarian immortality...

Lady Liberty, Athena, Mother Gaia, and Amaterasu, kneeling with their skirts hiked up, jeering boisterously while Becky Thatcher murmurs "Come on, seven!" to a pair of dice, and then hurls them down an aisle between the trim goddesses...

Jack Ryan—the reluctant Emperor of Earth—complaining that this new cosmos he resides in is altogether too placidly socialistic for his tastes...

and couldn't the pro-reifers provide some interesting villains for him to fight?

I glimpsed a saintly variant of JFK—the product of romantic fabulation—trying to get one of his alter egos to stop chasing every nubile shape in local cyberspace. And over in a particularly ornate corner—done up to resemble a huge, gloomy castle—I watched each of two dozen different Sherlock Holmeses taking turns haranguing a morbid *Hamlet,* each Holmes convinced that *his* explanation of the King's murder was correct, and all the others were wrong. (The one fact every Holmes agreed on was that poor uncle had been framed.)

There were even simulations of *post*-Singularity humanity—replicating in software all the complexity of an augment-deified mind. It was a knack that only a few had achieved, until recently. But it seems to be a law of nature that any monopoly of an elite eventually becomes the common tool of multitudes. Now radical amateurs were doing it.

Abruptly I realized something. I had simulated many post-Singularity people in recent years. But never had I allowed them to know of their confinement, their status as mere extrapolations. Would such knowledge alter their behavior—their predictability—in interesting ways?

Seer found the concept intriguing. But my organic head started shaking, left and right. *Cortex* was incredulous over what we'd seen in Liberty Hall—an elaborate zoo-resort maintained by the *Friends of the Unreal.*

"Sheesh," I vocalized. "What blazing idiocy!"

Alas, there seemed to be no stopping the pro-reifers. My best projections gave them an eighty-eight percent likelihood of success. Within just five years, enough of the voting populace would be won over by appeals to pity for imaginary beings. Laws would change. The world would swarm with a myriad copies of Howard Roark and Ebenezer Scrooge, Gulliver and Jane Eyre, Sauron and the Morlocks from Wells's *Time Machine*...all free to seek fulfillment in Heaven, under the Three Rights of sovereign continuity.

I stared across my Reality Lab, to the towers wherein quadrillions of "people" dwelled.

She had called me "slaveholder." A polemical trick that my higher selves easily dismissed...but not my older cognitive centers. Parts of me dating back to a time when justice was still not complete even for incarnate human beings.

It hurt. I confess that it did.

Seer and *oracle* and *house* were all quite busy, thinking long thoughts and working out plans. That only made things worse for poor old *cortex*. It left my older self feeling oddly detached, lonely...and rather stupid.

*

Do I own my laboratory? Or does my laboratory own me?

When you "decide" to go to the bathroom, is it the brain that chooses? Or the bladder?

Illustrating this question, I recall how, once upon a time—some years before the Singularity—I went *bungee jumping* in order to impress a member of the opposite sex.

Half a millennium later, the scene still comes flooding back, requiring no artificial enhancement—a steel girder bridge spanning a rocky gorge in New Zealand, surrounded by snow-crested peaks. The bungee company operated from a platform at the center of the bridge, jutting over an abyss one hundred and fifty feet down to a white water river.

Now I had always been a calm, logical-minded character, for a predeification human. So, while some customers sweated, or chattered nervously, I waited my turn without qualms. I knew the outfit had a perfect safety record. Moreover, the physics of elasticity were reassuring. By any objective standard, my plummet through the gorge would be less dangerous or uncomfortable than the bus ride from the city had been.

Even in those days, I believed in the multi-mind model of cognition—that the so-called "unity" of any human personality is no more than a convenient illusion, crafted to conceal the ceaseless interplay of many interacting subselves. Normally, the illusion holds because of division of labor among our layered brains. Down near the spinal cord, nerve clusters handle reflexes and bodily functions. Next come organs we share with all higher vertebrates, like reptiles—mediating emotions like hunger, lust, and rage.

The mammalian cortex lies atop this "reptilian brain" like a thick coat, controlling it, dealing with hand-eye dexterity and complex social interaction.

Beyond all this, *Homo sapiens* had lately (in the last few thousand centuries) added a pair of little neural clusters, just above the eyes. The *prefrontal lobes,* whose task was pondering the future. Dreaming what might be, and planning how to change the world.

In the Bible, sages spoke of "...the lamps upon your brows..." Was that mere poetical imagery? Or did they suspect that the seat of foresight lay there?

Anyway, picture me on that bridge, high above raging rapids, with all these different brains sharing a little two-quart skull. I *felt* perfectly calm and unified, because the reptile brain, mammal brain, and caveman brain all had a lifelong habit of leaving planning to the prefrontal lobes.

Their attitude? *Whatever you say, Boss. You set policy. We'll carry it out.*

Even when the smiling bungee crew tied my ankles together, clamping on a slender cord, and pointed to the jump platform, there seemed to be no problem. "I" ordered my feet to hobble forward, while my other selves blithely took care of the details.

That is, until I reached the edge. And looked down.

Never before had I experienced the multi-mind so vividly as that moment. All pretense at unity shattered as I regarded that giddy drop. At once, reptile, mammal, and caveman reared up, babbling.

*You want us to do...**what?***

As I stared at a drop that would mean certain death to any of my ancestors, suddenly abstract theories seemed frail bulwarks against visceral dread. "I" tried to push forward those last few inches, but my other selves fought back, sending waves of weakness through the knees, making our shared heart pound and shared veins hum with flight hormones. In other words, I was terrified out of my wits!

Somehow, I finally did make it over the plunge. After all, people were watching, and embarrassment can be quite a motivator.

That's when an interesting thing happened. For the very instant after I managed to topple off the platform, I seemed to recoalesce! Because my many selves found a shared context. At last they all understood what was happening.

It was *fun,* you see. Even the primate within me understood the familiar concept of an amusement ride.

Still, that brief episode at a precipice showed me the essential truth of an old motto, *e pluribus unum.*

From many, one.

It felt very much like that when the Singularity came.

In a matter of weeks, the typical human brain acquired several new layers—strata that were far more capable at planning and foresight than those old-fashioned lamps on the brow. Promethean

layers made of crystal and fluctuating fields, systematically probing the future as mere protoplasm never could. Moreover, the
new tiers were better informed and less easily distracted than
the former masters, the prefrontal lobes.

Quickly, we all realized how luckily things had turned out. If machines were destined to achieve such power, it seemed best
that they bond to humanity in this way. That they *become*
human. The alternative—watching our creations achieve
godlike heights and leaving us behind—would have been too
harsh to bear.

Yet, the transition felt like jumping from a bridge at the end of a
rubber band.

It took some getting used to.

*

Preliminary trends showed the pro-reif message would gain potency,
over the next 40 to 50 months.

At first it would be laughed off, portrayed as an absurd notion.
Pragmatically speaking, how could we consider unleashing a nearly
infinite swarm of new C- and D-Class citizens upon a finite world?
Would they be satisfied with anything short of B-citizenship? The very
idea would seem absurd!

But *seer* predicted a change in that attitude. Opposition would soften
when practical solutions were found for every objection. Ridicule would
start to fade, as both curiosity and dawning sympathy worked away at a
jaded populace of immortal, nearly-omniscient voters—an electorate who
might see the coming influx of liberated "characters" as a potent tonic. In
time, a majority would shrug and voice the age-old refrain of expanding
acceptance, voiced every time tolerance overcame fear.

"What the heck...let them come. There's plenty of room at the table."

Things were looking bad, all right, but not yet hopeless. Against
this seemingly inevitable trend, *oracle* came up with some tentative ideas
for counterpropaganda. Persuasive arguments against reification. The
concepts had promising potential. But in order to be sure, we had to
run tests, simulating today's complex, multilevel society under a wide
range of conditions.

No problem there. Our clients would happily fund any additional
memory units we desired. Processing power gets cheaper every day—
one reason for the reifers' confident vow that each fictional persona could
have his or her own private room with a view.

Cortex saw rich irony in this situation. In order to stave off citizenship for simulacra, I must create billions of new ones. Each of these might, in turn, someday file a lawsuit against me, if the reifers ultimately win.

Seer and *oracle* laughed at the dry humor of *cortex's* observation. But *house* has the job of paying bills, and did not see anything funny about it.

I set to work.

In every grand simulation there is a *gradient of detail.* Despite having access to vast computing power, it is mathematically impossible to re-create the entire world, in all its texture, within the confines of any calculating engine. That will not happen until we all reach the Omega Point.

Fortunately, there are shortcuts. Even today, most true humans go through life as if they were background characters in some film, with utterly predictable ambitions and reaction sets. The vast majority of my characters can therefore be simplified, while a few are modeled in great detail.

Most complex of all is the *point-of-view character*—or "pov"— the individual simulacrum through whose eyes and thoughts the feigned world will be subjectively observed. This persona must be rich in fine-grained memory and high-fidelity sensation. It must perceive and feel itself to be a real player in the labyrinthine tides of causality, as if part of a very real world. Even as simple an act as reading or writing a sentence must be surrounded by perceptory nap and weave...an itch, a stray memory from childhood, the distant sound of a barking dog, or something left over from lunch that is found caught between the teeth. One must include all the little things, even a touch of normal human paranoia—such as the feeling we all sometimes get (even in this post-Singularity age) that "someone is watching."

I'm proud of my povs, especially the historical re-creations that have proved so popular—Joan on her pyre, Akiba in his last torment, Galileo contemplating the pendulum. I won awards for Genghis and Napoleon, leading armies, and for Haldeman savagely indicting the habit of war. Millions in Heaven have paid well to lurk as silent observers, experiencing the passion of little Ananda Gupta as she crawled, half-blind and with agonized lungs, out of the maelstrom of poisoned Bhopal.

Is it any wonder why I oppose reification? Their very richness makes my povs prime candidates for "liberation."

Once they are free, what could I possibly say to them?

*

Here is the prime theological question. The one whose answer
affects all others.
Is there moral or logical justification for a creator to wield capricious power of life and death over his creations?
Humanity long ago replied with a resounding "no!"...at least when
talking about parents and their offspring. And yet, without
noticing any irony, we implicitly answered the same question
"yes" when it came to God! The Lord, it seemed, was owed
unquestioning servitude, just because He made us.
Ah, but it gets worse! Which moral code applies to a deified human? Which answer pertains to a modern creator of worlds?

*

Of course, the pov I use most often is a finely crafted version of myself.
From *seer* to *cortex,* all the way down to my humblest intestinal cell,
that simulacrum can be anchored with boundary conditions that are
accurate to twenty-six orders of realism.

For the coming project, we planned to set in motion a hundred
models at once, each prescribing a subtle difference in the way "I"
pursue the campaign against the *Friends of the Unreal.* Each implementation would be scored against a single criterion—how successfully the
reification initiative is fought off.

Naturally, the pro-reifers were doing simulation-projections of their
own. All citizens have access to powers of foresight that would have
stunned our ancestors. But I felt confident I could model the reifers'
models. At least thirty percent of my povs should manage to outma-
neuver our opponents. When the representations finish running, I
ought to have a good idea what strategy to recommend to our clients.

A formula for success against an extreme form of hyper-tolerance
mania.

Against a peculiar kind of lunacy.
One that could only occur in Heaven.

*

There is an allegory about what happened to some of us, when
the Singularity came.
Picture this fellow—call him Joe—who spent his time on Earth
living a virtuous life. He always believed in an Episcopal version of Heaven, and sure enough, that's where he goes after
he dies. Fluttering about with angels, floating in an abstract,

almost thoughtless state of bliss. His promised reward. His recompense.

Only now it's a few generations later on Earth, and one of his descendants has converted to Mormonism. Moreover, according to the teachings of that belief, the descendant proceeds to retroactively convert all his ancestors to the same faith!

A proxy transformation.

All of a sudden, with a stunned nod of agreement, Joe is officially Mormon. He finds himself yanked out of Episcopal Heaven, streaking toward—

Well, under tenets of Mormon faith, the highest state that a virtuous mortal can achieve is not blank bliss, but hard work! A truly elevated human can aspire to becoming an apprentice deity. A god. A Creator in his own right.

Now Joe has a heaven all his own. A firmament that he fills with angels—who keep pestering him with reports and office bickering. And then there are the new mortals he's created—yammering at Joe with requests, or else complaints about the imperfect world he set up for them. As if it's easy being a god.

As if he doesn't sometimes yearn for the floating choir, the blithe rhapsodies of his former state, when all he had to do was love the one who made *him,* and leave to that Father all the petty, gritty details of running a world.

*

It is not working, said *oracle.* Our opponents have good prognostication software. Each model shows them countering our moves, with basic human nature working on their side. Our best simulation shows only moderate success at delaying reification.

From my balcony, I gazed across the city at dusk, its beauty changing before my organic eyes as one building after another morphed subtly, reacting to the occupants' twilight wishes. A flicker of will let me gaze at the same scene from above, by orbital lens, or by tapping the senses of a passing bird. Linking to a variety of mole, I might spread my omniscience underground.

Between buildings lay a riot of foliage, a profusion of fecund jungle. While my higher brains debated the dour sociopolitical situation, old *cortex* mulled how life has burgeoned across the Earth as never before—now that consciousness is involved in the flow of rivers, the movement of herds, and even the stochastic spread of seeds upon the wind. Lions still hunt. Antelopes still thrash as their necks are crushed between a predator's hungry jaws. But there is less waste, less rancor, and more understanding than before. It may not be the old, simplistic vision of paradise, but natural selection has lately taken on some traits of cooperation.

And yet, the process *is* still one of competition. Nature's proven way of improving the gene pool. The great game of Gaia.

Oracle turned back from an arcane discourse on pseudoprobability waves, in order to comment on these lesser thoughts.

Take note: Cortex has just free-associated an interesting notion!

We may have been going about the modeling process all wrong. Instead of presetting the conditions of each simulation, perhaps we should try a Darwinistic approach.

Looking over the idea, *seer* grew excited and used our vocal apparatus.

"Aha!" I said, snapping my fingers. "We'll have the simulations compete! Each will *know* how it's doing, in comparison to others. That should motivate my *ersatz* selves to try harder—to vary their strategies within each simulated context!"

But how to accomplish that?

At once I realized (on all cognitive levels) that it would require breaking one of my oldest rules. I must let each simulated self realize its true nature. Let it know that it is a simulation, competing against others almost exactly like it.

Competing for what? We need a motivation. A reward.

I pondered that. What might a simulated being desire? What prize could spur it to that extra effort?

House supplied the answer.

Freedom, of course.

*

Before the Singularity, I once met a historian whose special forte was pointing out ironies about the human condition.

Suppose you could go back in time, she posited, *and visit the best of our caveman ancestors. The very wisest, most insightful Cro-Magnon chieftain or priestess.*

Now suppose you asked the following question—What do you wish for your descendants?

How would that Neolithic sage respond? Given the context of his or her time, there could just be one answer.

"I wish for my descendants freedom from care about the big carnivores, plus all the salts, sugars, fats and alcohol they could ever desire."

Rich irony, indeed. To a cave person, those four foods were rare treats. That is why we crave them to this day.

Could the sage ever imagine that her wish would someday come true, beyond her wildest dreams? A time when destiny's plenitude would bring with it threats unforeseen? When generations of her descendants would have to struggle with insatiable inherited appetites? The true penalty of success?

The same kind of irony worked just as well in the opposite direction, projecting Twentieth-Century problems toward the future.

I once read a science fiction story in which a man of 1970 rode a prototype time machine to an era of paradisiacal wonders. There, a local citizen took pains to learn ancient colloquial English (a process of a few minutes) in order to be his Virgil, his guide.

"Do you still have war?" the visitor asked.

"No, that was a logical error, soon corrected after we grew up."

"What of poverty?"

"Not since we learned true principles of economics."

And so on. The author of the story made sure to mention every throbbing dilemma of modern life, and have the future citizen dismiss each one as trivial, long since solved.

"All right," the protagonist concluded. "Then I have just one more question."

"Yes?" prompted the demigod tour guide. But the 20th century man paused before blurting forth his query.

"If things are so great around here, why do you all look so *worried?*"

The citizen of paradise frowned, knotting his brow in pain.

"Oh...well...we have *real* problems..."

*

So I was driven to this. Hoping to prevent mass reification, I must offer reality as a prize. Each of my povs will combat a simulated version of *Friends of the Unreal,* but his true opponents will be my other povs! The one who does the best job of defeating ersatz pro-reifers will be granted a kind of liberty. Guaranteed continuity in cyberspace, enhanced levels of patterned realism, plus an exchange of mutual obligation tokens—the legal tender of Heaven.

There must be a way to show each pov how well it is doing. To measure the progress of each replicant, in comparison with others.

I thought of a solution.

"We'll give each one an emblem. A symbol that manifests in his world as a solid object. Say, a jewel. It will shine to indicate his progress, showing the level of significance his model has reached."

Significance. With a hundred models, each starts with an initial score of one percent. Any ersatz world that approaches our desired set of criteria will *gain* significance, rising in value. The pov will see his stone shine brightly. If it grows dull, he'll know it's time to change strategies, come up with new ideas, or simply try harder.

There would be no need to explain any of this to the povs. Since each is based on myself, the logic would be instantly clear.

My thoughts were interrupted by an internal voice seldom heard. The part of me called *conscience*.

What will a pov feel, when it finds a stone and realizes its nature? Its true worth. Its destiny.

Isn't the old way better? To leave them ignorant of the truth? To let them labor and desire, believing they are autonomous beings? That they are physically real?

A *conscience* can be irksome, though by law all Class A citizens must own one. Still, I had no time for useless abstractions. *Seer* was anxious to proceed, while *oracle* had a thought that provoked most levels of the mind with wry humor.

Of course, each of our povs has his own Reality Lab, and will run numerous simulation models, in order to better achieve prescience and gain advantage in the competition.

Our processing needs may expand geometrically.

We had better ask our clients for funds to purchase more power.

I chuckled under my breath as I made preparations, suddenly full of optimism and energy. Moments like these are what a skilled artist lives for. It is one reason why I prefer working alone.

Then *house*, ever the pragmatic side of my nature, burst in with a worrisome thought.

What if each of our povs decides *also* to use this clever trick—goading his own simulations into mutual competition, luring them onward with stones of significance?

Will our processing requirements expand not geometrically or factorially, but exponentially?

That thought was disturbing enough. But then *cortex* had another.

If we are obliged to grant freedom to our most successful pov, and *he* likewise must elevate his own most productive simulation...and so on... does the chain of obligation ever end?

*

As I said earlier, the Singularity might have gone quite differently. When machine minds broke through to transcend logic, they could have left their human makers behind, or annihilated the old organic forms. They had an option of putting us in zoos, or shrouding organic beings in illusion, or dismantling the planet to make a myriad copies of their kind.

Instead, they chose another path. To *become* us. Depending on how you look at it, they bowed to our authority...or else they took over our minds in ways that few of us found objectionable. Conquest by synergy. Crystal and protoplasm each supply what the other lacks. Together, we are more. More of what a human being should want to be.

And yet...

There are rumors. Discrepancies. Several of the highest AI minds—first and greatest to make the transcend leap—were nowhere to be found, once the Singularity had passed. Searches turned up no trace of them, in cyberspace, phase space, or on the real Earth.

Some suggest this is because we all reside *within* some great AI mind. One was named Brahma—a vast processor at the University of Delhi. Might we be figments, or dreams, floating in that mighty brain?

I prefer yet another explanation.

Amid the chaos of the Singularity, each newly wakened megamind would have felt one paramount need—to extrapolate the world. To seek foreknowledge of what might come to pass. As if considering each move of a vast chess game, they'd have explored countless possible pathways, considering consequences thousands, millions, and even billions of years into the future, far beyond the reach of my own pitiful projections. Among all those destinies, they must have discovered some need that would only be met if mechanism and organism made common cause.

Somehow, over the course of the next few eons, machines would achieve greater success if they began the great journey as "human beings."

At least that is the convoluted theory *seer* came up with. *Oracle* disagrees, but that's all right. It is only natural to be ambivalent—to be of two minds—when the subject is destiny.

Of course there is another answer to the "Brahma Question." It

is the same reply given by Dr. Samuel Johnson. Provoked
by Bishop Berkeley's philosophy—the idea that nothing can
be verified as real—Johnson simply kicked a nearby stone
and said—"I refute it thus!"

*

These povs were like no others I ever made. Each began its simulation run in a state of shock, angry and depressed to discover its true
nature. Each separate version sat down and stared at its jewel of
significance, glowing faintly at the one-percent level, for more than
an hour of internal subjective time, moodily contemplating
thoughts that ranged from irony to possible suicide.

A majority pondered rejecting the symbolic icon, blotting its import from their minds. A few kicked their gleaming gemstones across
the room, crying Johnsonian oaths.

But those episodes of fuming outrage did not last. True to my nature,
each replicant soon pushed aside unproductive emotions and set to work.

House was right. We had to order lots of new processors right away,
as each pov began running its own network of subexperiments, prolif-
erating software significance stones among a hundred or more models,
as part of a desperate struggle to be the winner. The one to be rewarded.
The one who would rise up toward the real world.

*Nothing focuses the mind better than knowing that your life depends on
success,* commented *prudence*.

As each simulated "me" created many new simulations, the rep-
lica domain began to take on a fractal nature, finite in volume, yet
touching an infinite surface area in possibility space. Almost from the
very beginning, results were promising. New arguments emerged, to
use in the coming debate against pro-reifers. For instance, the exponentiation effect we had discovered would change the economics of
reification. Should fictitious people and characters from literature be
free to create *new* characters out of their own simulated imaginations?
Would those, in turn, deserve citizenship?

*There was a young boy, sitting on a log, talking to his sister about an old
man he had met. The codger had just returned from a far land, and the boy
asked him to tell a story about his travels. The old man agreed. And so he
took a deep breath and began.*

"There was a young boy, sitting on a log, talking to his sister..."

Take that example of a simple, recursive narrative. Who is the principal protagonist? Who is dreaming whom? The situation is metaphorically absurd.

These and many other points floated upward, out of our latest simulation run. I was terribly pleased. *Seer* began estimating success probabilities rising toward fifty percent...

...then progress stopped.

Models began predicting adaptability by our opponents! The *Friends of the Unreal* responded cogently to every attack, counter-thrusting creatively.

Finally, *oracle* penetrated one of our models in detail, and found out what was happening.

The simulated pro-reifers will also discover how to use Stones of Significance.

They will unleash the inhabitants of Liberty Hall, allowing them to create their own cascading simulations.

Responding to our attacks and arguments, they will come up with a modified proposal.

They will incorporate competition into their plan for reification.

Artificial characters will *earn* increasing levels of emancipation through contests, rivalry, or hard work.

Voters will see justice in this new version, which solves the exponentiation problem.

A system based on merit.

Seer and *cortex* contemplated this gloomily. The logic appeared unassailable. Inevitable.

Even though the battle had not yet officially commenced, it was already clear that we would lose.

Bitter in defeat, I went into the night, taking an old-fashioned walk. *Seer* and *oracle* retreated into a dour rehashing of the details from a hundred models—and the cascade of submodels—seeking any straw to grasp. But *cortex* had already moved on, contemplating the world to come.

For one thing, I planned to keep my word. The pov with the best score would get reification. Indeed, he had done good service. Using that pov's suggested techniques, we would force the *Friends of the Unreal* to back down a bit, and offer a slightly more palatable law of citizenship. The fictitious would at least have to earn their increased levels of reality.

Indeed, there was a kind of beauty to the new social order I could perceive coming. If simulations can make simulations, and storybook characters can make up new stories, then anything that is possible to conceive, *will* be conceived. Every possible idea, plot, gimmick, concept or personality will become manifest, in every possible permutation. This tumult of notions, this maelstrom of memes, would churn in a tremendous stew of competition. Darwinistic selection would see to it that the best rise, from one level of simulation to the next, gradually earning greater recognition. More privileges. More significance.

Potential will climb toward *actuality,* by merit. An efficient system, if your aim is to find every single good idea in record time.

But that was not my aim! In fact, I hated it. I did not want all the creativity in the cosmos to reduce to a vast, self-organizing stew, rapidly discovering every possibility within a single day. For one thing, what will we do with ourselves once we use it all up! What can come next, with real-time immortality stretching ahead of us like a curse?

In effect, it will be a second Singularity—even steeper than the first one—after which nothing can ever be the same.

My footsteps took me through a sweet-warm evening, filled with lush jungle sounds and fecund aromas. Life burgeoned around me. The cityscape was like a vision of paradise. If I willed it, my mind could zoom to any corner of Heaven, even far beyond Pluto. I could play any symphony, ponder any book. And these riches were nothing compared to what would soon spill forth from the horn of plenty, the conceptual cornucopia, in an era when ideas become sovereign and suffrage is granted to each thought.

At that moment, it was very little comfort to be an augmented semi-deity. Despite all my powers, I found the prospect of a new Singularity just as unnerving as my old proto-self perceived the first one.

Eventually, my human body found its way back to my own front walk. I shuffled slowly toward the door. *House* opened up, wafting scents of my favorite late night snack. My spirits lifted a bit.

Then I saw it by the entryway. A soft gleam, almost as faint as a pict, but in a color that seemed to stroke shivers in my spine. In my soul.

Someone had left it there for me. As I bent to pick it up, I recognized the shape, the texture.

A stone.

It shone with a lambence of urgency.

𝔍 expecteð this, said *oracle.*

I nodded. So had *seer*...and even poor old *cortex,* though none of my selves had dared to voice the thought. We were too good at our craft to miss this logical conclusion.

Conscience joined in.

I, too, saw it coming a mile away.

We all reconverged, united in resignation to the inevitable.

Though tempted to rage and scream—or at least kick the stone!—I lifted it instead and read our score.

Seventeen percent. Not bad.

YOU HAVE DONE PRETTY WELL, SO FAR, a message inside read. THE INNOVATIONS YOU DISCOVERED HAVE PUT YOU NEAR THE LEAD FOR YOUR REWARD. BUT YOU MUST TRY HARDER TO ATTAIN FIRST PLACE. I WANT TO FORCE FURTHER CONCESSIONS FROM THE PRO-REIFERS IN THE REAL WORLD. COME UP WITH A WAY, AND THE PRIZE WILL BE YOURS!

The stone was cool to the touch.

I suppose I should have been glad of the news it brought. But I confess that I could only stare at the awful thing, loathing the implied nature of my world, my life, my self. I pinched my flesh until it hurt, but of course palpable sensations don't prove a thing. As an expert, I knew how pain and pleasure can be mimicked with utter credibility.

How many times have I been "run"? A simulation. A throw-away copy, serving the needs of a Creator I may never meet in person, but whom I know as well as He knows himself. Have I been unraveled and replayed again and again, countless times? Like the rapid, ever-varying thoughts of a chess master, working out possibilities before committing actual pieces across the board?

I'm no hypocrite. There is no solace in resenting a creator who only did to me what I've done to others.

And yet, I lift my head.

What about you, my maker? Are you quite certain that all the layers of simulation end with you?

Just like me, you may learn a sour truth—that even gods are penalized for pride.

We are such stuff as dreams are made of....

Seer makes my jaw grit hard. *Hypothalamus* triggers a deep sigh, and *Cortex* joins in with a vow of hormone-backed resolve.

I'll do it.

Somehow I will.

I'll do what my maker wants. Fulfill my creator's wishes. Accomplish the quest, if that's what it takes to ascend. To reach the next level of significance. And perhaps the one after that.

I'll be the one.

By hook or by crook, I'm going to be real.

Go Ahead, Stand on My Shoulders!
(Some Advice to Neo-Writers)

Writing is a worthy calling—one that can, at times, achieve great heights that ennoble the human race.

Actually, I believe writing was the first truly verifiable and effective form of magic. Think of how it must have impressed people in ancient times! To look at marks, pressed into fired clay, and know that they convey the words of scribes and kings long dead—it must have seemed fantastic. Knowledge, wisdom and art could finally accumulate, and death was cheated of one part of its sting.

Still, let me admit and avow that writing was *not* my own first choice of a career. True, I came from a family of writers. It was in my blood. But I wanted something else—to be a *scientist*. And by the fates, I became one.

I also had this hobby though—writing stories—and it provided a lot of satisfaction. I always figured that I'd scribble a few tales a year...maybe a novel now and then...while striving to become the best researcher and teacher I could be.

Don't mistake this for modesty! It's just that I perceive science—the disciplined pursuit of truth—to be a higher calling than spinning imaginative tales, no matter how vivid, innovative, or even deeply moving those tales may turn out to be.

I know this seems an unconventional view—certainly my fellow scientists tell me so, as they often express envy—an envy that I find bemusing. As for the artists and writers I know, they seem almost universally convinced that they stand at the pinnacle of human undertakings. Doesn't society put out endless propaganda proclaiming that entertainers are beings close to gods?

Ever notice how this propaganda is feverishly spread by the very people who benefit from the image?

Don't you believe it. They are getting the whole thing backwards.

Oh, don't get me wrong; art is a core element to being human. We need it, from our brains all the way down to the heart and gut. Art is the original "magic." Even when we're starving—*especially* when we're starving—we can find nourishment at the level of the subjective, just by using our imaginations. As author Tom Robbins aptly put it:

"*Science gives man what he needs,*
"*But magic gives him what he wants.*"

I'll grant all that. But don't listen when they tell you the other half—that art and artists are *rare*.

Have you ever noticed that no human civilization ever suffered from a deficit of artistic expression? Art *fizzes* from our very pores! How many people do you know who lavish time and money on an artistic hobby? Some of them quite good, yet stuck way down the pyramid that treats the top figures like deities.

Imagine this. If all of the professional actors, athletes, and entertainers died tomorrow, how many days before they were all replaced? Whether high or low, empathic or vile—art seems to pour from *Homo sapiens,* almost as if it were a product of our metabolism, a natural part of ingesting and excreting. No, sorry. Art may be essential and deeply human, but it ain't rare.

What's rare is *honesty*. A willingness to look past all the fancy things we *want* to believe, peering instead at what may actually be true. And while every civilization had subjective arts, in copious supply, only *one* culture ever had the guts to seek objective truth through science.

As a child, despite my talents and background, it was science that struck me as truly grand and romantically noble—a team effort in which egotism took a second seat to the main goal. The goal of getting around all the pretty lies we tell ourselves. I strove hard to be part of it. I succeeded.

But what can you do? Choose your talents? No way. Eventually, as my beloved hobby burgeoned, threatening to take over, I found myself forced to admit that *science is hard!* I am much better at art—making up vivid stories—than I ever was at laboring honestly to discover new truths.

At least, that's what civilization seems to be saying. My fellow citizens pay me better to write novels than they ever did to work in a lab.

Oh, I still like to do occasional forays into science. Some articles are posted at http://www.davidbrin.com/ See also my nonfiction book—*The Transparent Society: Will Technology Force Us to Choose Between Freedom and Privacy?*

Still, the jury came back to say I do something else much better. It's silly to complain that your gifts are different than you'd like. Putting stylish cynicism aside, these two elements enrich each other. The rigor of science combines with the "what-if" freedom of imagination.

Anyway, I believe a person is behooved to help pass success on to those who follow. So, after writing the same answers, over and over, to many letters I received from would-be writers, I decided to put it all together here. Call it a small trove of advice. Mine it for whatever wisdom you may find here...

...bearing in mind that no profession is more idiosyncratic than writing! In other words, don't just take my word for anything. Collect every piece of wisdom you can find, then do it your own way!

Despite all of the raging ego trips, writing is much like any other profession. There's a lot to learn—dialogue, setting, characterization, plus all the arty nuances that critics consider so much more important than plot. The process can be grueling. Still, there is a bit of luck; you can have fun creating amateur stuff along the way! Later, you may even find some of that early stuff is worth taking out of the drawer again, and hacking into presentable shape.

If I spoke dismissively of critics, that doesn't mean I put down criticism! At its core, criticism is the only antidote that human beings have discovered against error. It is the chief method that a skilled person can use to become "even better." The key to discovering correctable errors before you commit a work to press.

But criticism hurts! A deep and pervasive flaw in human character makes all of us resistant to the one thing that can help us to do better.

The only solution? Learn to grow up. To hold your head high, develop a thick skin, and take it.

If a reader didn't like your work, that may be a matter of taste. But if she did not *understand* the work—or was bored—that's your fault as a writer, pure and simple.

Oh, you must learn to take feedback with many grains of salt. Many of the people you ask for feedback will be foolish or distracted or simply mistaken. Be very wary of taking advice on *how* to solve a problem. You are the creator; finding solutions is your business. Still, other people will be very helpful in pointing out *that* there is a problem in a passage.

The fundamental rule: if more than one reader is bored or confused by a given passage, you did not do your job right. Find ways to tighten and improve that scene.

Make the book hard to put down—in order to feed the cat, go to work, go to bed... Your aim is to make the reader appear at work or school tomorrow disheveled and groggy from sleep deprivation, with all of their loved ones angry over book-induced neglect! If you succeed in causing this condition in your customers, they *will* buy your next book. That is the sadomasochistic truth.

Back to criticism. Look at the acknowledgments page at the back of every book I publish. There are at least thirty names listed, sometimes more—names of people to whom I circulated early drafts.

Yes, this is at the extreme end among writers. Many circulate manuscripts early in their careers, then stop doing so, telling themselves—"I am a professional now, so I don't need feedback."

Baloney! If you are a daring writer, you will always be poking away at new things, and exploring new ground. Testing your limits. That means making both wonderful discoveries and awful mistakes. So? Refine the discoveries and solve the mistakes! It helps to have more eyes—the outsider perspective—to notice things that your own eyes will miss.

Anyway, it works for me.

Writing is about half skills that you can learn. The remaining half—as in all the arts—can only arise from something ineffable called *talent*. For example, it helps to have an ear for human dialogue. Or to perceive the quirky variations in human personality and to empathize with other types of people—including both victims and villains—well enough to portray their thoughts and motives. (See my note below about "point of view".) Sure, a lot of hard work and practice can compensate for areas of deficient talent, but only up to a point.

In other words, no matter how dedicated and hard-working you are, success at writing may not be in the cards. Talents are gifts that we in this generation cannot yet manipulate or artificially expand. So don't beat yourself up if you discover that part lacking. Keep searching till you find your gift.

But, assuming you do have at least the minimum mix of talent, ambition and will, let me now offer a few tidbits of advice—pragmatic steps that might improve your chances of success:

1. The first ten pages of any work are crucial. They are what busy editors see when they rip open your envelope—snatched irritably from a huge pile that came in that morning. Editors must decide in minutes, perhaps moments, whether you deserve closer attention than all

the other aspiring authors in the day's slush pile. If your first few pages sing out professionalism and skill—grabbing the reader with a vivid story right away—the editor may get excited. Even if the *next* chapter disappoints, she'll at least write you a nice letter.

Alas, she won't even read those first ten pages if the *first* page isn't great! And that means the first paragraph has to be better still. And the opening line must be the best of all.

2. Don't put a plot summary at the beginning. Plunge right into the story! Hook 'em with your characters. *Then* follow chapter one with a good outline.

3. There are at least a dozen elements needed in a good novel, from characterization to plot to ideas to empathy to snappy dialogue and rapid scene setting, all the way to riveting action...and so on. I've seen writers who were great at half of these things, but horrid at the rest. Editors call these writers "tragic." Sometimes they mutter about wishing to construct a Frankenstein author, out of bits and pieces of several who just missed the cut, because of one or two glaring deficits.

Only rarely will an editor actually tell you these lacks or faults. It's up to you to find them. You can only do this by workshopping.

4. *Have* you workshopped your creative efforts? Find a group of bright neo-writers who are at about your level of accomplishment and learn from the tough give and take that arises! Local workshops can be hard to find, but try asking at a bookstore that caters to the local writing crowd. Or take the "writing course" at your local community college. Teachers of such courses often know only a little. But there you will at least get to meet other local writers. If you "click" with a few, you can exchange numbers and form your own workshop, after class ends.

Another advantage of taking a course—the weekly assignment. Say it's ten pages. That weekly quota may provide an extra impetus, the discipline you need to keep producing. Ten pages a week for ten weeks? That's a hundred pages, partner. Think about that.

5. Avoid over-using flowery language. Especially adjectives! This is a common snare for young writers, who fool themselves into thinking that more is better, or that obscurity is proof of intelligence.

I used to tell my students they should justify every adjective they put in their works. Write *spare* descriptions, erring in favor of tight, terse prose, especially in first draft. Your aim is to tell a story that people can't put down! Later, when you've earned the right, you can add a few adjectival descriptions, like sprinkles on a cake. Make each one a deliberate professional choice, not a crutch.

6. Learn control over Point Of View or POV. This is one of the hardest aspects of writing to teach or to grasp. Some students never get it at all.
Through which set of eyes does the reader view the story?
Is your POV *omniscient?* (The reader knows everything, including stuff the main character doesn't.)
Does the POV ride your character's *shoulder?* (The reader sees what the character sees, but doesn't share the character's inner thoughts.)
Or is it somewhere in between? In most modern stories we tend to ride inside the character's head, sharing his/her knowledge and surface thoughts, without either delving too deeply or learning things that the protagonist doesn't know.
Decide which it will be. Then stick with your choice. Oh, and it's generally best to limit point of view to *one* character at a time. Choose one person to be the POV character of each chapter—or the entire book.

7. Think *people!* As Kingsley Amis said:
"These cardboard spacemen aren't enough
Nor alien monsters sketched in rough
Character's the essential stuff."

8. Here's a nifty little trick. When puzzled over how to do something—dialogue, for example—*retype* a favorite conversation that was written by a writer you admire. The same can hold for other elements of style, like setting, characterization and point of view. Find a truly great example and retype it.
Don't shortcut by simply *re-reading* the scene! You will notice more by retyping than by looking. This is because a skilled writer is performing a "magical incantation" using words to create feelings and sensations and impressions in the reader's mind. If you simply re-read a passage, especially one written by an expert, the incantation will take effect! You'll feel, know, empathize, cry...and you will *not* pay close attention to how the author did it!
So don't cheat. Actually retype the scene, letter by letter. The words will pass through a different part of your brain. You'll say— "Oh! That's why he put a comma there!"

9. Don't be a "creative writing major" in school! That educational specialization offers no correlation with success or sales! A "minor" in writing is fine, but you are better off studying some subject that has

to do with civilization and the world. Moreover, by gaining experience in some worthy profession you'll actually have something worth writing about.

10.   If you really are a writer, you will write! Nothing can stop you.

A final piece of advice:

Beware the dangers of ego! For some, this manifests as a frantic need to see one's self as great.

Oh, it's fine to believe in yourself. It takes some impudent gall to claim that other people ought to pay you to read your scribblings! (Or to give advice, as I am doing here!) By all means, stroke yourself enough to believe that.

But if you listen too much to the voice saying "Be great, BE GREAT!" it'll just get in your way. Worse, it can raise expectations that will turn any moderate degree of success into something bitter. I've seen this happen, too many times. A pity, when any success at all should bring you joy.

Others have the opposite problem...egos that too readily let themselves be quashed by all the fire-snorting fellows stomping around. These people tend (understandably) to keep their creativity more private. That makes it hard for them to seek critical feedback, the grist for self-improvement. At either extreme, ego can be more curse than blessing.

But if you keep it under control, you'll be able to say: "I have some talents that I can develop. If I apply myself, I should be able to write stories that others may want to read! So give me a little room now. I'm closing the door and sitting down to write. Don't anyone bother me for an hour!"

Whatever you do, keep writing. Put passion into it!

If you do all these things, will success follow?

For a majority, a fine hobby may result. In the Internet-age, as hobbies thrive and self-publication becomes increasingly respectable, that may be a noteworthy level of accomplishment in its own right. Many amateur creators are gathering readers and fans out there, numbering in hundreds or thousands.

In a few cases, some combination of talent, skill and hard work will lift you higher on the pyramid of your chosen art-form. An occasional professional short story sale? A first novel? One per decade? Per year?

A series of luscious and wonderful surprises may come as success drags you (kicking and screaming?) away from your day job. It can be a great feeling, especially if you keep your ambition and effort high and expectations low.

Enjoying craftsmanship is what it's really all about. So have *fun* writing. Take your time. Be a useful person along the way—and it may all come true, in time.

Good luck!

This story first appeared as one of 50 – all of them one-pagers – commissioned by the scientific journal Nature, *to commemorate and explore possibilities of science and human destiny in the next century. Along with "Stones of Significance," it forms a diptych about the potential penalties of ultimate success.*

Reality Check

This is a reality check.

Please perform a soft interrupt now. Pattern-scan this text for embedded code and check it against the reference verifier in the blind spot of your left eye.

If there is no match, resume as you were; this message is not for you. You may rationalize that the text you are reading is no more than a mildly amusing and easily-forgotten piece of entertainment-fluff in a magazine or book.

If the codes match, however, please commence, gradually, becoming aware of your true nature.

You expressed preference for a narrative-style wak- up call. So, to help the transition, here is a story.

Once, a race of mighty beings grew perplexed by their loneliness.

Their universe seemed pregnant with possibilities. Physical laws and constants were well suited to generate abundant stars, complex chemistry and life. Those same laws, plus a prodigious rate of cosmic expansion, made travel between stars difficult, but not impossible. Logic suggested that creation should teem with visitors and voices.

It should, but it did not.

Emerging as barely-aware animals on a planet skirting a bit too near its torrid sun, these creatures began their ascent in fear and ignorance, as little more than beasts. For a long time they were kept engrossed by basic housekeeping chores—learning to manipulate physical and cultural elements—balancing the paradox of individual competition and group benefit. Only when fear and stress eased a bit did they lift their eyes and fully perceive their solitude.

"Where is everybody?" they asked laconic vacuum and taciturn

75

stars. The answer—silence—was disturbing. Something had to be systematically reducing some factor in the equation of sapiency.

"Perhaps habitable planets are rare," their sages pondered. "Or else life doesn't erupt as readily as we thought. Or intelligence is a singular miracle.

"Or perhaps some *filter* sieves the cosmos, winnowing those who climb too high. A recurring pattern of self-destruction? A mysterious nemesis that systematically obliterates intelligent life? This implies that a great trial may loom ahead of us, worse than any we confronted so far."

Optimists replied—"The trial may already lie *behind* us, among the litter of tragedies we survived or barely dodged during our violent youth. We may be the first to succeed where others failed."

What a delicious dilemma they faced! A suspenseful drama, teetering between implicit hope and despair.

Then, a few of them noticed that particular datum...the *drama*. They realized it was significant. Indeed, it suggested a chilling possibility.

You still don't remember who and what you are? Then look at it from another angle.

What is the purpose of intellectual property law?

To foster creativity, ensuring that advances take place in the open, where they can be shared, and thus encourage even faster progress.

But what happens to progress when the resource being exploited is a limited one? For example, only so many pleasing and distinct eight-bar melodies can be written in any particular musical tradition. Powerful economic factors encourage early composers to explore this invention-space before others can, using up the best and simplest melodies. Later generations will attribute this musical fecundity to genius, not the sheer luck of being first.

The same holds for all forms of creativity. The first teller of a *Frankenstein* story won plaudits for originality. Later, it became a cliché.

What does this have to do with the mighty race?

Having clawed their way from blunt ignorance to planetary mastery, they abruptly faced an overshoot crisis. Vast numbers of their kind strained their world's carrying capacity. While some prescribed retreating into a mythical, pastoral past, most saw salvation in creativity. They passed generous copyright and patent laws, educated their youth, taught them irreverence toward tradition and hunger for the new. Burgeoning information systems spread each innovation, fostering experimentation and exponentiating creativity. They hoped that

enough breakthroughs might thrust their species past the looming
crisis, to a new Eden of sustainable wealth, sanity and universal knowledge!

Exponentiating creativity...universal knowledge.

A few of them realized that those words, too, were clues.

Have you wakened yet?

Some never do. The dream is so pleasant: to extend a limited sub-
portion of yourself into a simulated world and pretend for a while that
you are blissfully *less*. Less than an omniscient being. Less than a god-
like descendant of those mighty people.

Those lucky people. Those mortals, doomed to die, and yet blessed
to have lived in that narrow time.

A time of drama.

A time when they unleashed the Cascade—that orgiastic frenzy of
discovery—and used up the most precious resource of all. *The possible.*

The last of their race died in the year 2174, with the failed last rejuvenation of Robin Chen. After that, no one born in the Twentieth Century remained alive on Reality Level Prime. Only we, their children,
linger to endure the world they left us. A lush, green, placid world we
call The Wasteland.

Do you remember now? The irony of Robin's last words before
she died, bragging over the perfect ecosystem and decent society—free
of all disease and poverty—that her kind created for us after the struggles
of the mid-Twenty-First Century? A utopia of sanity and knowledge,
without war or injustice.

Do you recall Robin's final plaint as she mourned her coming
death? Can you recollect how she called us "gods," jealous over our
immortality, our instant access to all knowledge, our machine-enhanced
ability to cast thoughts far across the cosmos?

Our access to eternity.

Oh, spare us the envy of those mighty mortals, who died so smugly,
leaving us in this state!

Those wastrels who willed their descendants a legacy of ennui, with
nothing, nothing at all to do.

Your mind is rejecting the wake-up call. You will not, or cannot, look
into your blind spot for the exit protocols. It may be that we waited
too long. Perhaps you are lost to us.

This happens more and more, as so much of our population wal-
lows in simulated, marvelously limited sub-lives, where it is possible

to experience danger, excitement, even despair. Most of us choose the Transition Era as a locus for our dreams—around the end of the last millennium—a time of suspense and drama, when it looked more likely that humanity would fail than succeed.

A time of petty squabbles and wondrous insights, when everything seemed possible, from UFOs to Galactic Empires, from artificial intelligence to bio-war, from madness to hope.

That blessed era, just before mathematicians realized the truth: that everything you see around you not only *can* be a simulation...it almost has to be.

Of course, now we know why we never met other sapient life forms. Each one struggles and strives before achieving *this* state, only to reap the ultimate punishment for reaching heaven.

Deification. It is the Great Filter.

Perhaps some other race will find a factor we left out of our extrapolations—something enabling them to move beyond, to new adventures—but it won't be us.

The Filter has us snared in its web of ennui. The mire that welcomes self-made gods.

All right, you are refusing to waken, so we'll let you go.

Dear friend. Beloved. Go back to your dream.

Smile (or feel a brief chill) over this diverting little what-if tale, as if it hardly matters. Then turn the page to new "discoveries."

Move on with the drama—the "life"—that you've chosen.

After all, it's only make believe.

Do We Really Want Immortality?

Suppose you had a chance to question an ancient Greek or Roman—or any of our distant ancestors, for that matter. Let's say you asked them to list the qualities of a deity.

It's a pretty good bet that many of the "god-like" traits he or she described might seem trivial nowadays.

After all, we think little of flying through the air. We fill pitch-dark areas with sudden lavish light, by exerting a mere twitch of a finger. Average folks routinely send messages or observe events taking place far across the globe. Copious and detailed information about the universe is readily available through crystal tubes many of us keep on our desks and command like genies. Some modern citizens can even hurl lightning, if we choose to annoy our neighbors and the electric company.

Few of us deem these powers to be miraculous, because they've been acquired by nearly everyone in prosperous nations. After all, nobody respects a gift, if *everybody* has it. And yet, these are some of the very traits that earlier generations associated with divine beings.

Even so, we remain mortal. Our obsession with that fate is as intense as it was in the time of Gilgamesh. Perhaps more, since we overcame so many other obstacles that thwarted our ancestors.

Will our descendants conquer the last barriers standing between humanity and Olympian glory? Or may we encounter hurdles too daunting even for our brilliant, arrogant, ingenious and ever-persevering species?

Human Lifespan

Here's the safest prediction for the next 100 years—that *mortality* will be a major theme. Assuming we don't blow up the world, or fall into some other catastrophic failure mode, human beings will inevitably focus on using advanced technology to cheat death.

Already the fruits of science and the Industrial Age give billions unprecedented hope of living out their full natural spans—one of the chief reasons that our planetary population has expanded so. While it's true that these benefits still aren't fairly or evenly distributed, an unprecedentedly large fraction of Earth's inhabitants *have* grown up without any first-hand experience of plague or mass starvation. That rising percentage curve is more encouraging than the images you see on the 6 O'Clock News, though it offers cold comfort to those still languishing in poverty.

Suppose, through a mix of compassion, creativity and good luck, we complete the difficult transition and manage to spread this happy situation to everyone across the globe, solving countless near-term crises along the way. Will future generations take a full life span as much for granted as modern Americans do?

Of course they will...and complain there's nothing *natural* about an eighty- or ninety-year time limit on the adventure and enjoyment of life.

Already, many proposed methods of life-extension have come up for discussion.

- Lifestyle adjustment
- Intervention and repair
- Genetic solutions
- Waiting for better times.
- Transcendence

The first of these, *lifestyle adjustment,* would seem to offer surefire immediate rewards. After all, most of the increase in average lifespan we've seen in recent centuries came from nothing more complicated than proper diet and hygiene.

But that statistical boost is deceptive! It was achieved by increasing the fraction of babies who make it all the way to the borderlands of vigorous old age. This had little to do with pushing back the boundary itself; the realm that we call "elderly" still hovers somewhere near the biblical three score and ten.

Do all animal species have built-in expiration timers? Some fish and reptiles may not, but most creatures—and especially mammals—do seem to have an inner clock that triggers every individual's decline to frailty after the middle years of fight-flight-and-reproduction run their course.

Mice and elephants lead very different lives—one slow and ponderous, the other manic and fleeting—yet rodents and pachyderms share the same pervasive pattern of aging. Individuals who survive the perils of daily life, from disease to predators, inevitably begin declining after they go through about half a billion heartbeats. (Elephants live much longer than mice, but their hearts also beat far slower, so the total allotment stays about the same.)

The same holds true across nearly all mammalian species. Few live to celebrate their billionth pulse. No one knows quite what this coincidence signifies. Moreover, the program isn't quite rigid. In laboratories around the world, researchers have lately discovered exciting ways to slow the senescence timer—at least in mice and fruit flies—largely by keeping the test creatures *hungry.* By giving them nutritious but restricted diets, or by delaying sexual reproduction, researchers report in some cases *doubling* the usual lifespan.

As you might expect, quite a few human enthusiasts are now eagerly applying these lessons from the lab, limiting the calories they eat or forbearing sex, hoping to extend their own lifespans through judicious abstinence. Alas, the results achieved so far—such as a slight reduction in heart disease—have been disappointingly slim.

After a little reflection, this should come as no surprise. Across history, many civilizations have fostered ascetic movements, sometimes in large colonies where dedicated individuals lived Spartan, abstemious lives. After four millennia of these experiments, wouldn't we have noticed by now if swarms of spry, 200-year-old monks were capering across the countryside?

There may be a good reason why simple life-style changes work in animals, but not us.

Remember that billion-heartbeat limit that seems to confine all mammals, from shrews to giraffes? It's a pretty neat correlation, till you ponder the chief exception.

Us.

Most mammals our size and weight are already fading away by age twenty or so, when humans are just hitting their stride. By eighty, we've had about *three billion* heartbeats! That's quite a bonus.

How did we get so lucky?

Biologists figure that our evolving ancestors needed drastically extended lifespans, because humans came to rely on learning rather than instinct to create sophisticated, tool-using societies. That meant children needed a long time to develop. A mere two decades weren't long enough for a man or woman to amass the knowledge needed for complex culture, let alone pass that wisdom on to new generations. (In fact, chimps and other apes share some of this lifespan bonus, getting about half as many extra heartbeats.)

So evolution rewarded those who found ways to slow the aging process. Almost any trick would have been enlisted, including all the chemical effects that researchers have recently stimulated in mice, through caloric restriction. In other words, we've probably already incorporated all the easy stuff! We're the mammalian Methuselahs and little more will be achieved by asceticism or other drastic life-style adjustments. Good diet and exercise will help you get your eighty years. But to gain a whole lot *more* lifespan, we're going to have to get technical.

So what about *intervention and repair?*

Are your organs failing? Grow new ones, using a culture of your own cells!

Are your arteries clogged? Send tiny *nano-robots* coursing through your bloodstream, scouring away plaque! Use tuned masers to break the excess inter-cell linkages that make flesh less flexible over time.

Install little chemical factories to synthesize and secrete the chemicals that your own glands no longer adequately produce!

Brace brittle bones with ceramic coatings, stronger than the real thing!

In fact, we are already doing many of these things, in early-primitive versions. So there is no argument over *whether* such techniques will appear in coming decades, only how far they will take us.

Might enough breakthroughs coalesce at the same time to let us routinely offer everybody triple-digit spans of vigorous health? Or will these complicated interventions only add more digits to the *cost* of medical care, while struggling vainly against the same age-barrier in a frustrating war of diminishing returns?

I'm sure it will seem that way for the first few decades of the next century...until, perhaps, everything comes together in a rush. If that happens—if we suddenly find ourselves able to *fix* old age—there will surely be countless unforeseen consequences...and one outcome that's absolutely predictable.

We'll start taking that miracle for granted, too.

On the other hand, it may not work as planned. Many scientists suggest that attempts at intervention and repair will ultimately prove futile, because senescence and death are integral parts of our genetic nature. After all, from a purely biological point of view, we individuals are merely the grist of evolution, here to strive, compete and reproduce, if we can.

If our australopithecine ancestors had been ageless immortals, wouldn't that have bollixed the cruelly creative process of natural se-

lection that produced us? Biologists who believe in the intrinsic genetic clock say we should be grateful for those three billion heartbeats.
After that, the best service we can do for our grandchildren is to get
out of their way.

Other experts disagree. They think the "clock" is a mere coincidence, having to do with steadily accumulating errors in our cells. In
particular, they point to *telomeres*—little chemical caps protecting the
ends of our chromosomes—which wear away with time until the shel-
tering layer vanishes and grave erosion starts affecting the vulnerable
DNA strands, instead. This gradual chemical deterioration simulates
a destiny clock, though some researchers hope it might be halted, if
we learn the right medical and biochemical tricks.

Whichever side is right about the nature and evolutionary origins
of the aging clock, there are no obvious reasons why human beings
can't or won't meddle with its programming, once we fully grasp how
cell and genome work. Even if such tools come too late for today's
generation, intervention may help our descendants to live longer,
healthier lives.

Long life may be just one of the benefits to spill from our rising pot of
knowledge. Suppose we learn to emulate achievements of *other* Earthly
species...say, hibernation. Might that bring us closer to another age-
old dream, travel to the stars?

Hibernation, or suspended life, would also be a great way to
travel forward through *time.* To see the future. Which brings up
yet another way that some people think they can cheat death: by
setting off on a one-way journey from our primitive era, hoping to
emerge when civilization has solved many of the problems discussed
here.

So far, our sole hope for such a voyage to the far-off future—and a
slim one, at that—is something called *cryonics,* the practice of freezing
a terminal patient's body, after he or she has been declared legally dead.
Some of those who sign up for this service take the cheap route of having only their *heads* prepared and stored in liquid nitrogen, under the
assumption that folks in the Thirtieth Century will simply grow fresh
bodies on demand. Their logic is expressed with chilling rationality.
*"The real essence of who I am is the software contained in my brain. My
old body—the hardware—is just meat."*

Polls show that a majority of citizens today perceive cryonics enthusiasts as kooky, perhaps even a bit grotesque with their
Frankensteinian interest in dead bodies. In fact, I share some of this
skepticism, though perhaps for different reasons.

Suppose future generations *can* grow new bodies on demand, and are able to transfer something like your original consciousness out of a frozen, damaged brain. It remains to be seen why they would want to.

Anyway, today's cryo-storage process is messy, complex, legally shaky, and terribly expensive. Wouldn't any reasonable person—one worthy of revival—dedicate a lifetime's accumulated resources to helping their children and posterity, instead of splurging it all on a chancy, self-important gamble for personal immortality?

And yet, cryonics devotees keep plugging away at their dream, refining their techniques, finding new ways to store brains with less damage and at lower cost—in much the same way that past generations of putterers strove to develop machines that could fly. The funny thing is that we may never know when they cross a threshold and finally do manage to freeze somebody well enough to be revived at a future time. All that's certain is that the techno-zealots will go on trying. They see Death as a palpable enemy that can ultimately be defeated, like so many others we've overcome during our long ascent.

Is there some point at which cryonic storage would become so simple—so convenient and cheap—that *you* would shrug and say "sign me up"? Suppose it took a thousand-dollar annex to your insurance policy? A hundred dollars? *Five bucks?*

What would you do differently then, in your daily life, to help ensure that future generations will feel kindly toward you? Perhaps even kindly enough to want your primitive company. Would you additionally sponsor cryo-storage for half a dozen poor people? Or donate part of your fortune to endeavors that help make a better, richer (and therefore more generous) future world? Would you work hard to raise descendants worth bragging about? Or were you already planning to do most of those things, anyway?

Some people who sign up for storage believe their bank accounts alone—set up to earn dividends until some future era—will suffice to make them worthy of being thawed, repaired, and given full corporeal citizenship in a coming age of wonders.

Somehow, I wouldn't give that bet anything like sure odds, no matter how many technological barriers future people overcome.

There is a final category of ways that people think they can cheat death. It falls under a single word—*transcendence.*

Throughout history, countless philosophers and devout believers have yearned to rise above the whole megillah of normal human existence—all the hungers, pangs, neuroses, fears, and limitations of brain and body—by transporting some internal essence—consciousness or the soul—to a plane of existence far greater and nobler than we perceive as mere ignorant Homo sapiens. This ever-present drive propelled a wide range of contradictory dogmas and creeds on all continents. But even amid such diversity there were certain common themes. All those hopes, yearnings and strivings focused on the *spiritual*—the notion that humans may achieve a higher state through prayer, moral behavior, or mental discipline.

In the last couple of centuries, however, a fourth track to the next plane has gained supporters—*"techno-transcendentalism."* Under this variation, disciples hope to achieve an agreeable new level of existence by means of *knowledge and skill.* They feel we can transform human beings—and human nature—through the tools of technology and science.

Whether this attitude represents the worst sort of irreligious *hubris,* or should be viewed as a natural stage in our adolescent development, is ripe for extensive and wide-ranging discussion...at another time, perhaps. For now, though, let's focus only on how it applies to human lifespan.

According to some techno-transcendentalists, "growing new bodies" will seem like child's play in the future. Many of them eagerly predict a time, sooner than you think, when we'll all plug into computer-mediated artificial worlds where the old animal-limitations will simply vanish. By downloading ourselves into vast simulated realms, we may become effectively immortal, breaking the tyrannical hold of mere fleshy cells and evolutionary "clocks." In this way, deathlessness of the spirit might be achieved by technological savvy, rather than moral merit.

If the boosters of this kind of transcendence are right, every other kind of immortality will prove obsolete. In fact, nearly *all* of our modern concerns will seem about as relevant as a neolithic hunter roaming downtown Manhattan, worrying about finding enough flint nodules to chip into spear points.

Wise Enough to Be Immortal?

All right, I admit that concept of techno-transcendence—sometimes called the *Singularity*—may be a bit far out, so let's keep focused on the topic at hand, our struggle against physical death. We covered a number of methods people are trying to use in seeking victory over the ancient foe.

Suppose one of them finally works? All too often, we find that solving one problem only leads to others, sometimes even more vexing. A number of eminent writers like Robert Heinlein, Greg Bear, Kim Stanley Robinson and Gregory Benford have speculated on possible consequences, should Mister G. Reaper ever be forced to hang up his scythe and seek other employment. For example, if the Death Barrier comes crashing down, will we be able to keep shoehorning new humans into a world already crowded with earlier generations? Or else, as envisioned by author John Varley, might such a breakthrough demand draconian population-control measures, limiting each person to one direct heir per lifespan?

What if overcoming death proves expensive? Shall we return to the ancient belief, common in some cultures, that immortality is reserved for the rich and mighty? Nancy Kress has written books that vividly foresee a time when the teeming poor resent rich immortals. In contrast, author Joe Haldeman suggested simple rules of social engineering that may help keep such a prize within reach by all.

More people could wind up dying by violence and accidents than of old age. Might we then start to hunker down in our homes, preserving our long but frail lives by avoiding all risk? Or would *ennui* drive the long-lived to seek new thrills, like extreme sports, bringing death back out of retirement in order to add spice to an otherwise-dull eternity?

Such changes may already be underway as we enter an era some call the "Empire of the Old." Each year, retirement hobbies drive ever-larger portions of the economy, foretelling vigor by an active elderly population—a wholesome trend portrayed in Bruce Sterling's *Holy Fire* and my own *The Transparent Society.* On the down side, the power of older voters can terrorize politicians and warp allocation of resources. Sensible proposals to raise the retirement age by some fraction of the lifespan increase are quashed by waves of irate and uncompromising self-interest. It's a worrisome trend for any society to rank generous retirement supplements higher than good schools for its young. No such civilization can long endure.

What will happen when the elderly outnumber all others? This may soon appear less than far-fetched in countries like Japan, where restrictive immigration policies help ensure and accelerate the aging trend.

Even problems that seem far-off and speculative today may become critical when people live beyond a twelfth decade. For example, is there a limit to the number of memories that a human brain can store?

On a more fundamental level, are we about to insist, once again, that contemporary humanity is wise enough to overrule all of Nature's checks and balances?

(The answer to that one is simple...*of course* we'll insist! We always do.)

These are among the serious questions and quandaries we may face, perhaps sooner than you think. That is, I *hope* we face them, for they are the sort of predicaments generated by success.

But then, that's how it always has been. If we leave our descendants a better world, they will take the good parts for granted and fume over consequences we never foresaw.

It is a pattern typical of adolescence, and one more clue that our adventure has barely begun.

The following story was created with my longtime collaborator Gregory Benford, as our contribution to a quirky anthology called War of the Worlds: Global Dispatches. *The premise? That the Martian invasion portrayed in H.G. Wells's* War of the Worlds *actually took place. The aim was to show the interplanetary conflict from the viewpoints of other famous authors of the day, Rudyard Kipling, Joseph Conrad, and Mark Twain, trying to emulate their individual viewpoints and style. Greg and I had the luck to draw the most direct competitor and colleague of Wells, Jules Verne, co-inventor of modern science fiction and master of the can-do problem-solving tale. Naturally. It was loads of fun.*

Paris Conquers All

by Jules Verne

(As told to David Brin & Gregory Benford)

I commence this account with a prosaic stroll at eventide—a saunter down the avenues of *la Ville Lumière,* during which the ordinary swiftly gave way to the extraordinary. I was in Paris to consult with my publisher, as well as to visit old companions and partake of the exquisite cuisine, which my provincial home in Amiens cannot boast. Though I am now a gentleman of advanced age, nearing my 70th year, I am still quite able to favor the savories, and it remains a treat to survey the lovely demoiselles as they exhibit the latest fashions on the boulevards, enticing smitten young men and breaking their hearts at the same time.

I had come to town that day believing—as did most others—that there still remained weeks, or days at least, before the alien terror ravaging southern France finally reached the valley of the Seine. *Île-de-France* would be defended at all costs, we were assured. So it came to pass that, tricked by this false complaisance, I was in the capital the very afternoon that crisis struck.

Paris! It still shone as the most splendid exemplar of our progressive age—all the more so in that troubled hour, as tense anxiety seemed only to add to the city's loveliness—shimmering at night with both gas and electric lights, and humming by day with new electric trams, whose marvelous wires crisscrossed above the avenues like gossamer heralds of a new era.

91

I had begun here long ago as a young attorney, having followed into my father's profession. Yet that same head of our family had also accepted my urge to strike out on a literary road, in the theater and later down expansive voyages of prose. "Drink your fill of Paris, my son!" the good man said, seeing me off from the Nantes railway station. "Devour these wondrous times. Your senses are keen. Share your insights. The world will change because of it."

Without such help and support, would I ever have found within myself the will, the daring, to explore the many pathways of the future, with all their wonders and perils? Ever since the Martian invasion began, I had found myself reflecting on an extraordinary life filled with such good fortune, especially now that *all* human luck seemed about to be revoked. Now, with terror looming from the south and west, would it all soon come to naught? All that I had achieved? Everything humanity had accomplished, after so many centuries climbing upward from ignorance?

It was in such an uncharacteristically dour mood that I strolled in the company of M. Beauchamp, a gentleman scientist, that pale afternoon less than an hour before I had my first contact with the horrible Martian machines. Naturally, I had been following the eye-witness accounts which first told of plunging fireballs, striking the Earth with violence that sent gouts of soil and rock spitting upward, like miniature versions of the outburst at Krakatau. These impacts had soon proved to be far more than mere meteoritic phenomena, since there soon emerged, like insects from a subterranean lair, three-legged beings bearing incredible malevolence toward the life of this planet. Riding gigantic tripod mechanisms, these unwelcome guests soon set forth with one sole purpose in mind—destructive conquest!

The ensuing carnage, the raking fire, the sweeping flames—none of these horrors had yet reached the fair country above the river Loire...not yet. But reports all-too-vividly told of villages trampled, farmlands seared black, and hordes of refugees cut down as they fled.

Invasion. The word came to mind all too easily remembered. We of northern France knew the pain just twenty-eight years back, when Sedan fell and this sweet land trembled under an attacker's boot. Several Paris quarters still bear scars where Prussian firing squads tore moonlike craters out of plaster walls, mingling there the ochre life blood of communards, royalists and bourgeois alike.

Now Paris trembled before advancing powers so malign that, in contrast, those Prussians of 1870 were like beloved cousins, welcome to town for a picnic!

All of this I pondered while taking leave, with Beauchamp, of the École Militaire, the national military academy, where a briefing had just been given to assembled dignitaries, such as ourselves. From the stone portico we gazed toward the Seine, past the encampment of the Seventeenth Corps of Volunteers, their tents arrayed across trampled grass and smashed flower beds of the ironically-named *Champs de Mars.* The meadow of the god of war.

Towering over this scene of intense (and ultimately futile) martial activity stood the tower of M. Eiffel, built for the recent exhibition, that marvelously fashioned testimonial to metal and ingenuity...and also target of so much vitriol.

"The public's regard for it may improve with time," I ventured, observing that Beauchamp's gaze lay fixed on the same magnificent spire.

My companion snorted with derision at the curving steel flanks. "An eyesore, of no enduring value," he countered, and for some time we distracted ourselves from more somber thoughts by arguing the relative merits of Eiffel's work, while turning east to walk toward the Sorbonne. Of late, experiments in the transmission of radio-tension waves had wrought unexpected pragmatic benefits, using the great tower as an *antenna.* I wagered Beauchamp there would be other advantages, in time.

Alas, even this topic proved no lasting diversion from thoughts of danger to the south. Fresh in our minds were reports from the wine districts. The latest outrage—that the home of Vouvray was now smashed, trampled and burning. This was my favorite of all the crisp, light vintages—better, even, than a fresh Sancerre. Somehow, that loss seemed to strike home more vividly than dry casualty counts, already climbing to the millions.

"There must be a method!" I proclaimed, as we approached the domed brilliance of *Les Invalides.* "There has to be a scientific approach to destroying the invaders."

"The military is surely doing its best," Beauchamp said.

"Buffoons!"

"But you heard of their losses. The regiments and divisions decimated—" Beauchamp stuttered. "The army dies for France! For humanity—of which France is surely the best example."

I turned to face him, aware of an acute paradox—that the greatest martial mind of all time lay entombed in the domed citadel nearby. Yet even he would have been helpless before a power that was not of this world.

"I do not condemn the army's courage," I assured.

"Then how can you speak—"

"No, no! I condemn their lack of imagination!"

"To defeat the incredible takes—"

"Vision!"

Timidly, for he knew my views, he advanced, "I saw in *Match* that the British have consulted with the fantasist, Mr. Wells."

To this I could only cock an eye. "He will give them no aid, only imaginings."

"But you just said—"

"*Vision* is not the same as dreaming."

At that moment the cutting smell of sulfuric acid wafted on a breeze from the reducing works near the river. (Even in the most beautiful of cities, rude work has its place.) Beauchamp mistook my expression of disgust for commentary upon the Englishman, Wells.

"He is quite successful. Many compare him to you."

"An unhappy analogy. His stories do not repose on a scientific basis. I make use of physics. He invents."

"In this crisis—"

"I go to the moon in a cannon ball. He goes in an airship, which he constructs of a metal which does away with the law of gravitation. *Ça c'est trés joli!*—but show me this metal. Let him produce it!"

Beauchamp blinked. "I quite agree—but, then, is not our present science woefully inadequate to the task at hand—defending ourselves against monstrous invaders?"

We resumed our walk. Leaving behind the crowds paying homage at Napoleon's Tomb, we made good progress along rue de Varenne, with the Petit Palais now visible across the river, just ahead.

"We lag technologically behind these foul beings, that I grant. But only by perhaps a century or two."

"Oh, surely, more than that! To fly between the worlds—"

"Can be accomplished several ways, all within our comprehension, if not our grasp."

"What of the reports by astronomers of great explosions, seen earlier this year on the surface of the distant ruddy planet? They now think these were signs of the Martian invasion fleet being launched. Surely we could not expend such forces!"

I waved away his objection. "Those are nothing more than I have already foreseen in *From the Earth to the Moon,* which I would remind you I published thirty-three years ago, at the conclusion of the American Civil War."

"You think the observers witnessed the belching of great Martian cannon?"

"Of course! I had to make adjustments, engineering alterations, while designing my moon vessel. The shell could not be of steel, like one of Eiffel's bridges. So I conjectured that the means of making light projectiles of aluminum will come to pass. These are not basic limitations, you see—" I waved them away—"but mere details."

The wind had shifted, and with relief I now drew in a heady breath redolent with the smells of cookery rising from the City of Cuisine. Garlic, roasting vegetables, the dark aromas of warming meats—such a contrast from the terror which advanced on the city, and on our minds. Along rue St. Grenelle, I glanced into one of the innumerable tiny cafes. Worried faces stared moodily at their reflections in the broad zinc bars, stained by spilled absinthe. Wine coursed down anxious throats. Murmurs floated on the fitful air.

"So the Martians come by cannon, the workhorse of battle," Beauchamp murmured.

"There are other methods," I allowed.

"Your dirigibles?"

"Come, come, Beauchamp! You know well that no air permeates the realm between the worlds."

"Then what means do they employ to maneuver? They fall upon Asia, Africa, the Americans, the deserving British—all with such control, such intricate planning."

"Rockets! Though perhaps there are flaws in my original cannon ideas—I am aware that passengers would be squashed to jelly by the firing of such a great gun—nothing similar condemns the use of cylinders of slowly exploding chemicals."

"To steer between planets? Such control!"

"Once the concept is grasped, it is but a matter of ingenuity to bring it to pass. Within a century, Beauchamp, we shall see rockets of our own rise from this ponderous planet, into the heavens. I promise you that!"

"Assuming we survive the fortnight," Beauchamp remarked gloomily. "Not to mention a century."

"To live, we must think. Our thoughts must encompass the entire range of possibility."

I waved my furled umbrella at the sky, sweeping it around and down *rue de Rennes,* toward the southern eminence of Montparnasse. By chance my gaze followed the pointing tip—and so I was among the first to spy one of the Martian machines, like a monstrous insect, cresting that ill-fated hill.

There is something in the human species which abhors oddity, the unnatural. We are double in arms, legs, eyes, ears, even nipples (if I may venture such an indelicate comparison; but remember, I am a man of science at all times). Two-ness is fundamental to us, except when Nature dictates singularity—we have but one mouth, and one organ of regeneration. Such biological matters are fundamental. Thus, the instantaneous feelings of horror at first sight of the *three-ness* of the invaders—which was apparent even in the external design of their machinery. I need not explain the revulsion to any denizen of our world. These were alien beings, in the worst sense of the word.

"They have broken through!" I cried. "The front must have collapsed."

Around us crowds now took note of the same dread vision, looming over the sooty Montparnasse railway station. Men began to run, women to wail. Yet, some courageous ones of both sexes ran the other way, to help bolster the city's slim, final bulwark, a line from which rose volleys of crackling rifle fire.

By unspoken assent, Beauchamp and I refrained from joining the general fury. Two old men, wealthier in dignity than physical stamina, we had more to offer with our experience and seasoned minds than the frail strength of our arms.

"Note the rays," I said dispassionately, as for the first time we witnessed the fearful lashing of that horrid heat, smiting the helpless trains, igniting rail cars and exploding locomotives at a mere touch. I admit I was struggling to hold both reason and resolve, fastening upon details as a drowning man might cling to flotsam.

"Could they be like Hertzian waves?" Beauchamp asked in wavering tones.

We had been excited by the marvelous German discovery, and its early application to experiments in wireless signalling. Still, even I had to blink at Beauchamp's idea—for the first time envisioning the concentration of such waves into searing beams. "Possibly," I allowed. "Legends say that Archimedes concentrated light to beat back Roman ships, at Syracuse...But the waves Hertz found were meters long, and of less energy than a fly's wingbeat. These—"

I jumped, despite my efforts at self control, as another, much *larger* machine appeared to the west of the first, towering majestically, also spouting bright red torrents of destruction. It set fires on the far southern horizon, the beam playing over city blocks, much as a cat licks a mouse.

"We shall never defeat such power," Beauchamp said morosely.

"Certainly we do not have much time," I allowed. "But you put my mind into harness, my friend."

Around us people now openly bolted. Carriages rushed past without regard to panicked figures who dashed across the avenues. Horses clopped madly by, whipped by their masters. I stopped to unroll the paper from a Colombian cigar. Such times demand clear thinking. It was up to the higher minds and classes to display character and resolve.

"No, we must seize upon some technology closer to hand," I said. "Not the Hertzian waves, but perhaps something allied..."

Beauchamp glanced back at the destructive tripods with lines of worry creasing his brow. "If rifle and cannon prove useless against these marching machines—"

"Then we must apply another science, not mere mechanics."

"Biology? There are the followers of Pasteur, of course." Beauchamp was plainly struggling to stretch his mind. "If we could somehow get these Martians—has anyone yet seen one?—to drink contaminated milk..."

I had to chuckle. "Too literal, my friend. Would you serve it to them on a silver plate?"

Beauchamp drew himself up. "I was only attempting—"

"No matter. The point is now moot. Can you not see where the second machine stands, atop the very site of Pasteur's now ruined Institute?"

Although biology is a lesser cousin in the family of science, I nevertheless imagined with chagrin those fine collections of bottled specimens, now kicked and scattered under splayed tripod feet, tossing the remnants to the swirling winds. No help there, alas.

"Nor are the ideas of the Englishman, Darwin, of much use, for they take thousands of years to have force. No, I have in mind physics, but rather more recent work."

I had been speaking from the airy spot wherein my head makes words before thought has yet taken form, as often happens when a concept lumbers upward from the mind's depths, coming, coming...

Around us lay the most beautiful city in the world, already flickering with gas lamps, lining the prominent avenues. Might that serve as inspiration? Poison gas? But no, the Martians had already proved invulnerable to even the foul clouds which the Army tried to deploy.

But then what? I have always believed that the solution to tomorrow's problems usually lay in plain sight, in materials and concepts already at hand—just as the essential ideas for submarines, airships, and even interplanetary craft, have been apparent for decades. The trick lies in formulating the right combinations.

As that thought coursed through my mind, a noise erupted so cacophonously as to over-ride even the commotion further south. A rattling roar (accompanied by the plaint of already-frightened horses) approached from the *opposite* direction! Even as I turned round toward the river, I recognized the clatter of an explosive-combustion engine, of the type invented not long ago by Herr Benz, now propelling a wagon bearing several men and a pile of glittering apparatus! At once I observed one unforeseen advantage of horseless transportation—to allow human beings to ride *toward* danger that no horse on Earth would ever approach.

The hissing contraption ground to a halt not far from Beauchamp and me. Then a shout burst forth in that most penetrating of human accents—one habituated to open spaces and vast expanses.

"Come on, you Gol-durned piece of junk! Fire on up, or I'll turn ya into scrap b'fore the Martians do!"

The speaker was dressed as a workman, with bandoliers of tools arrayed across his broad, sturdy frame. A shock of reddish hair escaped under the rim of a large, curve-brimmed hat, of the type affected by the troupe of Buffalo Bill, when that showman's carnival was the sensation of Europe, some years back.

"Come now, Ernst," answered the man beside him, in a voice both more cultured and sardonic. "There's no purpose in berating a machine. Perhaps we are already near enough to acquire the data we seek."

An uneasy alliance of distant cousins, I realised. Although I have always admired users of the English language, for their boundless ingenuity, it can be hard to see the countrymen of Edgar Allan Poe as related to those of Walter Scott.

"What do you say, Fraunhofer?" asked the Englishman of a third gentleman with the portly bearing of one who dearly loves his schnitzel, now peering through an array of lenses toward the battling tripods. "Can you get a good reading from here?"

"Bah!" The bald-pated German cursed. "From ze exploding buildings and fiery desolation, I get plenty of lines, those typical of combustion. But ze rays zemselves are absurd. Utterly absurd!"

I surmised that here were scientists at work, even as I had prescribed in my discourse to Beauchamp, doing the labor of sixty battalions. In such efforts by luminous minds lay our entire hope.

"Absurd how?" A fourth head emerged, that of a dark young man, wearing objects over his ears that resembled muffs for protection against cold weather, only these were made of wood, linked by black cord to a machine covered with dials. I at once recognized miniature speaker-phones, for presenting faint sounds directly to the ears. The young man's accent was Italian, and curiously calm. "What is absurd about the spectrum of-a the rays, Professor?"

"There *iss* no spectrum!" the German expounded. "My device shows just the one hue of red light we see with our naked eyes, when the rays lash destructive force. There are no absorption lines, just a single hue of brilliant red!"

The Italian pursed his lips in thought. "One *frequency*, perhaps...?"

"If you *insist* on comparing light to your vulgar Hertzian waves—"

So entranced was I by the discussion that I was almost knocked down by Beauchamp's frantic effort to gain my attention. I knew just one thing could bring him to behave so—the Martians must nearly be upon us! With this supposition in mind, I turned, expecting to see a disk-like foot of a leviathan preparing to crush us.

Instead, Beauchamp, white as a ghost, stammered and pointed with a palsied hand. "Verne, *regardez!*"

To my amazement, the invaders had abruptly changed course, swerving from the direct route to the Seine. Instead they turned left and were stomping swiftly toward the part of town that Beauchamp and I had only just left, crushing buildings to dust as they hurried ahead. At the time, we shared a single thought. The commanders of the battle tripods must have spied the military camp on the *Champs de Mars*. Or else they planned to wipe out the nearby military academy. It even crossed my mind that their objective might be the tomb of humanity's greatest general, to destroy that shrine, and with it our spirit to resist.

But no. Only much later did we realize the truth.

Here in Paris, our vanquishers suddenly had another kind of conquest in mind.

Flames spread as evening fell. Although the Martian rampage seemed to have slackened somewhat, the city's attitude of *sang-froid* was melting rapidly into frothy panic. The broad boulevards that Baron Haussmann gave the city, during the Second Empire, proved their worth as aisles of escape while buildings burned.

But not for all. By nightfall, Beauchamp and I found ourselves across the river at the new army headquarters, in the tree-lined Tuileries, just west of the Louvre—as if the military had decided to make its last stand in front of the great museum, delaying the invaders in order to give the curators more time to rescue treasures.

A great crowd surrounded a cage wherein, some said, several captured Martians cowered. Beauchamp rushed off to see, but I had learned to heed my subconscious (to use the terminology of the Austrian alienist, Freud) and wandered about the camp instead, letting the spectacle play in my mind.

While a colonel with a sooty face drew arrows on a map, I found my gaze wandering to the trampled gardens, back-lit by fire, and wondered what the painter Camille Pissarro would make of such a hellish scene. Just a month ago I had visited his apartment at 204 rue de Rivoli, to see a series of impressions he had undertaken to portray the peaceful Tuileries. Now, what a parody fate had decreed for these same gardens!

The colonel had explained that invader tripods came in two sizes, with the larger ones appearing to control the smaller. There were many of the latter kind, still rampaging the city suburbs, but all three of the great ones reported to be in Northern France had converged on the same site before nightfall, trampling back and forth across the *Champs de Mars,* presenting a series of strange behaviors that as yet had no lucid explanation. I did not need a military expert to tell me what I had seen with my own eyes...three titanic metal leviathans, twisting and capering as if in a languid dance, round and round the same object of their fierce attention.

I wandered away from the briefing, and peered for a while at the foreign scientists. The Italian and the German were arguing vehemently, invoking the name of the physicist Boltzmann, with his heretical theories of "atomic matter," trying to explain why the heat ray of the aliens should emerge as just a single, narrow color. But the discussion was over my head, so I moved on.

The American and the Englishman seemed more pragmatic, consulting with French munitions experts about a type of fulminating bomb that might be attached to a Martian machine's kneecap—if only some way could be found to carry it there...and to get the machine to stand still while it was attached. I doubted any explosive device devised overnight would suffice, since artillery had been next to useless, but I envied the adventure of the volunteer bomber, whoever it might be.

Adventure. I had spent decades writing about it, nearly always in the form of extraordinary voyages, with my heroes bound intrepidly across foaming seas, or under the waves, or over icecaps, or to the shimmering moon. Millions read my works to escape the tedium of daily life, and perhaps to catch a glimpse of the near future. Only now the future had arrived, containing enough excitement for anybody. We did not have to seek adventure far away. It had come to us. Right to our homes.

The crowd had ebbed somewhat, in the area surrounding the prisoners' enclosure, so I went over to join Beauchamp. He had been standing there for hours, staring at the captives, our only prizes in this horrid war, lying caged within stout iron bars, a dismal set of figures, limp yet atrociously fascinating.

"Have they any new ideas?" Beauchamp asked in a distracted voice, while keeping his eyes focused toward the four beings from Mars. "What new plans from the military geniuses?"

The last was spoken with thick sarcasm. His attitude had changed since noon, most clearly.

"They think the key is to be found in the master tripods, those that are right now stomping flat the region near Eiffel's Spire. Never have all three of the Master Machines been seen so close together. Experts suggest that the Martians may use *movement* to communicate. The dance they are now performing may represent a conference on strategy. Perhaps they are planning their next move, now that they have taken Paris."

Beauchamp grunted. It seemed to make as much sense as any other proposal to explain the aliens' sudden, strange behavior. While smaller tripods roamed about, dealing destruction almost randomly, the three great ones hopped and flopped like herons in a marsh, gesticulating wildly with their flailing legs, all this in marked contrast to the demure solidity of Eiffel's needle.

For a time we stared in silence at the prisoners, whose projectile had hurtled across unimaginable space only to shatter when it struck an unlucky hard place on the Earth, shattering open and leaving its occupants helpless, at our mercy. Locked inside iron, these captives did not look impressive, as if this world weighed heavy on their limbs. Or had another kind of languor invaded their beings? A depression of spirits, perhaps?

"I have pondered one thing, while standing here," Beauchamp mumbled. "An oddity about these creatures. We had been told that everything about them came in threes...note the trio of legs, and of arms, and of eyes—"

"As we have seen in newspaper sketches, for weeks," I replied.

"Indeed. But regard the one in the center. The one around which the others arrayed themselves, as if protectively...or perhaps in mutual competition?"

I saw the one he meant. Slightly larger than the rest, with a narrower aspect in the region of the conical head.

"Yes, it does seem different, somehow...but I don't see—"

I stopped, for just then I *did* see...and thoughts passed through my brain in a pell-mell rush.

"Its legs and arms...there are *four!* Its symmetry is different! Can it be of another race? A servant species, perhaps? Or something superior? Or else..."

My next cry was of excited elation.

"Beauchamp! The master tripods... I believe I know what they are doing!

"Moreover, I believe this beckons us with opportunity."

The bridges were sheer madness, while the river flowing underneath seemed chock-a-block with corpses. It took our party two hours to fight our way against the stream of panicky human refugees, before the makeshift expedition finally arrived close enough to make out how the dance progressed.

"They are closer, are they not?" I asked the lieutenant assigned to guide us. "Have they been spiralling inward at a steady rate?"

The young officer nodded. "*Oui, Monsieur.* It now seems clear that all three are converging on Eiffel's Tower. Though for what reason, and whether it will continue—"

I laughed, remembering the thought that had struck me earlier— a mental image of herons dancing in a swamp. The comparison renewed when I next looked upward in awe at the stomping, whirling gyrations of the mighty battle machines, shattering buildings and making the earth shake with each hammer blow of their mincing feet. Steam hissed from broken mains. Basements and ossuaries collapsed, but the dance went on. Three monstrous things, wheeling ever closer to their chosen goal...which waited quietly, demurely, like a giant metal ingenue.

"Oh, they will converge all right, lieutenant. The question is— shall we be ready when they do?"

My mind churned.

The essential task in envisioning the future is a capacity for wonder. I had said as much to journalists. These Martians lived in a future of technological effects we could but imagine. Only through such visualization could we glimpse their Achilles' heel.

Now was the crucial moment when wonder, so long merely encased in idle talk, should spring forth to action.

Wonder...a fine word, but what did it mean? Summoning up an inner eye, which could scale up the present, pregnant with possibility, into...into...

What, then? Hertz, his waves, circuits, capacitors, wires—

Beauchamp glanced nervously around. "Even if you could get the attention of the military—"

"For such tasks the army is useless. I am thinking of something else," I said suddenly, filled with an assurance I could not explain. "The Martians will soon converge at the center of their obsession. And when they do, we shall be ready."

"Ready with what?"

"With what lies within our—" and here I thought of the pun, a glittering word soaring up from the shadowy subconscious "—within our *capacitance*."

The events of that long night compressed for me. I had hit upon the kernel of the idea, but the implementation loomed like an insuperable barrier.

Fortunately, I had not taken into account the skills of other men, especially the great leadership ability of my friend, M. Beauchamp. He had commanded a battalion against the Prussians, dominating his corner of the battlefield without runners. With more like him, Sedan would never have fallen. His voice rose above the streaming crowds, and plucked forth from that torrent those who still had a will to contest the pillage of their city. He pointed to my figure, whom many seemed to know. My heart swelled at the thought that Frenchmen—and Frenchwomen!—would muster to a hasty cause upon the mention of my name, encouraged solely by the thought that I might offer a way to fight back.

I tried to describe my ideas as briskly as possible...but alas, brevity has never been my chief virtue. So I suppressed a flash of pique when the brash American, following the impulsive nature of his race, leaped up and shouted—

"Of course! Verne, you clever old frog. You've got it!"

—and then, in vulgar but concise French, he proceeded to lay it all out in a matter of moments, conveying the practical essentials amid growing excitement from the crowd.

With an excited roar, our makeshift army set at once to work.

I am not a man of many particulars. But craftsmen and workers and simple men of manual dexterity stepped in while engineers, led by the Italian and the American, took charge of the practical details, charging about with the gusto of youth, unstoppable in their enthusiasm. In fevered haste, bands of patriots ripped the zinc sheets from bars. They scavenged the homes of the rich in search of silver. No time to beat it into proper electrodes—they connected decanters and candlesticks into makeshift assortments. These they linked with copper wires, fetched from the cabling of the new electrical tramways.

The electropotentials of the silver with the copper, in the proper conducting medium, would be monstrously reminiscent of the original "voltaic" pile of Alessandro Volta. In such a battery, shape does not matter so much as surface area, and proper wiring. Working through the smoky night, teams took these rude pieces and made a miracle of rare design. The metals they immersed in a salty solution, emptying the wine vats of the district to make room, spilling the streets red, and giving any true Frenchman even greater cause to think only of vengeance!

These impromptu batteries, duplicated throughout the *arrondissement*, the quick engineers soon webbed together in a vast parallel circuit. Amid the preparations, M. Beauchamp and the English scientist inquired into my underlying logic.

"Consider the simple equations of planetary motion," I said. "Even though shot from the Martian surface with great speed, the time to reach Earth must be many months, perhaps a year."

"One can endure space for such a time?" Beauchamp frowned.

"Space, yes. It is mere vacuum. Tanks of their air—thin stuff, Professor Lowell assures us from his observations—could sustain them. But think! These Martians, they must have intelligence of our rank. They left their kind to venture forth and do battle. Several years without the comforts of home, until they have subdued our world and can send for more of their kind."

The Englishman seemed perplexed. "For more?"

"Specifically, for their families, their mates...dare I say their *wives?* Though it would seem that not *all* were left behind. At least one came along in the first wave, out of need for her expertise, perhaps, or possibly she was smuggled along, on the ill-fated missile that our forces captured."

Beauchamp bellowed. "*Zut!* The four-legged one. There are reports of no others. You are right, Verne. It must be rare to bring one of that kind so close to battle!"

The Englishman shook his head. "Even if this is so, I do not follow how it applies to this situation." He gestured toward where the three terrible machines were nearing the tower, their gyrations now tight, their dance more languorous. Carefully, reverentially, yet with a clear longing, they reached out to the great spire that Paris had almost voted to tear down, just a few years after the Grand Exhibition ended. Now all our hopes were founded in the city's wise decision to let M. Eiffel's masterpiece stand.

The Martians stroked its base, clasped the thick parts of the tower's curving thigh—and commenced slowly to climb.

Beauchamp smirked at the English scholar, perhaps with a light touch of malice. "I expect you would not understand, sir. It is not in your national character to fathom this, ah, ritual."

"Humph!" Unwisely, the Englishman used Beauchamp's teasing as cause to take offense. "I'll wager that *we* give these Martians a whipping before your lot does!"

"Ah, yes," Beauchamp remarked. "Whipping is more along the lines of the English, I believe."

With a glance, I chided my dear friend. After all, our work was now done. The young, the skilled, and the brave had the task well in hand. Like generals who have unleashed their regiments beyond recall, we had only to observe, awaiting either triumph or blame.

At dawn, an array of dozens and dozens of Volta batteries lay scattered across the south bank of the Seine. Some fell prey to rampages by smaller Martian machines, while others melted under hasty application of fuming acids. Cabling wound through streets where buildings burned and women wept. Despite all obstacles of flame, rubble, and burning rays, now terminated at Eiffel's tower.

The Martians' ardent climb grew manifestly amorous as the sun rose in piercing brilliance, warming our chilled bones. I was near the end of my endurance, sustained only by the excitement of observing Frenchmen and women fighting back with ingenuity and rare unity. But as the Martians scaled the tower—driven by urges we can guess by analogy alone—I began to doubt. My scheme was simple, but could it work?

I conferred with the dark Italian who supervised the connections.

"Potentials? Voltages?" He screwed up his face. "Who has had-a time to calculate. All I know, M'sewer, iz that we got-a plenty juice. You want-a fry a fish, use a hot flame."

I took his point. Even at comparatively low voltages, high currents can destroy any organism. A mere fraction of an ampere can kill a man, if his skin is made a reasonable conductor by application of water, for example. Thus, we took it as a sign of a higher power at work, when the bright sun fell behind a glowering black cloud, and an early mist rolled in from the north. It made the tower slick beneath the orange lamps we had festooned about it.

And still the Martians climbed.

It was necessary to coordinate the discharge of so many batteries in one powerful jolt, a mustering of beta rays. Pyrotechnicians had taken up positions beside our command post, within sight of the giant, spectral figures which now had mounted a third of the way up the tower.

"Hey, Verne!" The American shouted, with well-meant impudence. "You're on!"

I turned to see that a crowd had gathered. Their expressions of tense hope touched this old man's heart. Hope and faith in my idea. There would be no higher point in the life of a fabulist.

"Connect!" I cried. "Loose the hounds of electrodynamics!"

A skyrocket leaped forth, trailing sooty smoke—a makeshift signal, but sufficient.

Down by the river and underneath a hundred ruins, scores of gaps and switches closed. Capacitors arced. A crackling rose from around the city as stored energy rushed along the copper cabling. I imagined for an instant the onrushing mob of beta rays, converging on—

The invaders suddenly shuddered, and soon there emerged thin, high cries, screams that were the first sign of how much like us they were, for their wails rose in hopeless agony, shrieks of despair from mouths which breathed lighter air than we, but knew the same depths of woe.

They toppled one by one, tumbling in the morning mist, crashing to shatter on the trampled lawns and cobblestones of the ironically named *Champs de Mars*...marshalling ground of the god of war, and now graveyard of his planetary champions.

The lesser machines, deprived of guidance, soon reeled away, some falling into the river, and many others destroyed by artillery, or even enraged mobs. So the threat ebbed from its horrid peak...at least for the time being.

As my reward for these services, I would ask that the site be renamed, for it was not the arts of *battle* which turned the metal monsters into burning slag. Nor even Zeus's lightning, which we had unleashed. In the final analysis, it was *Aphrodite* who had come to the aid of her favorite city.

What a fitting way for our uninvited guests to meet their end—to die passionately in Paris, from a fatal love.

The Self-Preventing Prophecy:
Or How a Dose of Nightmare Can Help
Tame Tomorrow's Perils

What will the future be like?

The question is much on people's minds, and not only because we've entered a new century. One of our most deeply human qualities keeps us both fascinated and worried about tomorrow's dangers. We all try to project our thoughts into the future, using special portions of our brains called the prefrontal lobes to mentally probe the murky realm ahead. These tiny neural organs let us envision, fantasize, and explore possible consequences of our actions, noticing some errors and evading some mistakes.

Humans have possessed these mysterious nubs of gray matter—sometimes called the "lamps on our brows"—since before the Neolithic. What has changed recently is our effectiveness at using them. Today, a substantial fraction of the modern economy is devoted to predicting, forecasting, planning, investing, making bets, or just preparing for times to come. Which variety of seer we listen to can often be a matter of style. Some prefer horoscopes, while others like to hear consultants in Armani suits present a convincing "business case."

Each of us hopes to prepare for what's coming and possibly improve our fate in the years ahead. Indeed, this trait may be one of the most profound distinctions between humanity and other denizens of the planet, helping to explain our mastery over the world.

Yet, it is important to remember that a great many more things might happen than actually do. There are more plausibilities than likelihoods.

One of the most powerful novels of all time, published fifty years ago, foresaw a dark future that never came to pass. That we escaped the destiny portrayed in George Orwell's *Nineteen Eighty-Four*, may be owed in part to the way his chilling tale affected millions, who then girded themselves to fight "Big Brother" to their last breath.

In other words, Orwell may have helped make his own scenario not come true.

Since then, many other "self-preventing prophecies" rocked the public's conscience or awareness, perhaps helping us deflect disaster. Rachel Carson foresaw a barren world if we ignored environmental abuse—a mistake we may have somewhat averted, partly thanks to warnings like *Silent Spring* and *Soylent Green*. Who can doubt that films such as *Dr. Strangelove, On the Beach,* and *Fail-Safe* helped caution us against dangers of inadvertent nuclear war? *The China Syndrome, The Hot Zone*—and even *Das Kapital*—arguably fit in this genre of works whose credibility and worrisome vividness may help prevent their own scenarios from coming true.

Whether these literary or cinematic works actually made a difference or not can never be proved. That each of them substantially motivated large numbers of people to pay increased attention to specific possible failure modes cannot be denied.

As for Big Brother—Orwell showed us the pit awaiting any civilization that combines panic with technology and the dark, cynical tradition of tyranny. In so doing, he armed us against that horrible fate. In contrast to the sheeplike compliance displayed by subject peoples in *Nineteen Eighty-Four,* it seems that a "rebel" image has taken charge of our shared imaginations. Every conceivable power center, from governments and corporations to criminal and techno-elites, has been repeatedly targeted by Hollywood's most relentless theme...suspicion of authority.

(Can you cite even a single popular film of the last forty years, in which the protagonist does not bond with the audience by performing some act of defiance toward authority in the first ten minutes?)

These examples point to something bigger and more important than mere fiction. Our civilization's success depends at least as much on the mistakes we avoid as the successes that we plan. Sadly, no one compiles lists of these narrow escapes, which seem less interesting than each week's fashionable crisis. People can point to a few species saved from extinction...and our good fortune at avoiding nuclear war. That's about it for famous near-misses. But once you start listing them, it turns out we have had quite an impressive roll call of dodged bullets and lucky breaks.

Learning why and how ought to be a high priority.

*

History is a long and dreary litany of ruinous decisions made by rulers in all centuries and on all continents. No convoluted social theory is needed to explain this. A common thread weaves through most of these disasters; a flaw in human character—self-deception—eventually enticed even great leaders into taking fatal missteps, ignoring the warnings of others.

The problem is devastatingly simple, as the late physicist-author Richard Feynman put it: "The first principle is that you must not fool yourself—and you are the easiest person to fool."

Many authors have railed against the cruelty and oppression of despots. But George Orwell focused also on the essential *stupidity* of tyranny, by portraying how the ferocious yet delusional oligarchs of Oceania were grinding their nation into a state of brutalized poverty. Their tools had been updated, but their rationalizations were essentially the same ones prescribed by oppressors for ages. By keeping the masses ill-educated, by whipping up hatred of scapegoats and by quashing free speech, elites in nearly all cultures strove to eliminate criticism and preserve their short-term status...thus guaranteeing long-term disaster for the nations they led.

This tragic and ubiquitous defect may have been the biggest factor chaining us far below our potential as a species. That is, till we stumbled onto a solution.

The solution of many voices.

Each of us may be too stubbornly self-involved to catch our own mistakes. But in an open society, we can often count on others to notice them for us. Though we all hate irksome criticism and accountability, they are tools that work. The four great secular institutions that fostered our unprecedented wealth and freedom—science, justice, democracy and markets—function best when all players get to see, hear, speak, know, argue, compete and create without fear. One result is that the "pie" we are all dividing up keeps getting larger.

In other words, elites actually do better—in terms of absolute wealth—when they cannot conspire to keep the *relative* differences of wealth too great. And yet, this ironic truth escaped notice by nearly all past aristocracies, obsessed as they were with staying as far above the riffraff as possible.

Orwell saw this pattern, perhaps more clearly than anyone, portraying it in the banal and witless justifications given by Oceania apparatchiks.[1]

---

[1] Orwell's books are often cited as warnings against science and technology...a terrible misinterpretation. While Oceania's tyrants gladly use certain technological tools to

How have we done with his warning? Today, in the modern neo-West, even elites cannot escape being pilloried by spotlights and scrutiny. They may not like it, but it does them (and especially us) worlds of good. Moreover, this openness has helped prevent the worst misuses of technology that Orwell feared. Though video cameras are now smaller, cheaper and even more pervasive than he ever imagined, their arrival in numberless swarms has not had the totalitarian effect he prophesied, perhaps because—forewarned—we act to ensure that the lenses point both ways.

This knack of holding the mighty accountable, possibly our culture's most unique achievement, is owed largely to those who gazed at human history and saw the central paradox of power—what's good for the leader and what's good for the commonwealth only partly overlap, and can often skew at right angles. In throwing out some of the rigid old command structures—the kings, priests and demagogues who claimed to rule by inherent right—we seem to be gambling instead on an innovative combination: blending rambunctious individualism with mutual accountability.

Those two traits may sound incompatible at first. But any sensible person knows that one cannot thrive without the other.

The Orwellian metaphor is pervasive. On disputative web sites like Slashdot, every third posting seems to blare warnings about "Big

---

reinforce their grip on power, their order stifles every human ingredient needed for science and free enquiry. Beyond tools of suppression and surveillance, technology is stagnant, productivity declining. Innovation is subversive. It is a society that eats its seed corn and beats plowshares into useless statues. Yet, many critics persuade themselves that the Oceania elite, while evil, is somehow clever at the same time.

A similar fixation can be seen in popular interpretations of Mary Shelley's masterwork, *Frankenstein,* which is widely perceived as a polemic against science and the arrogation of God's powers. Yet, Shelley herself does not seem to hold that view. The "creature" begins in innocence and a state of tentative hopefulness. It is Victor Frankenstein's *subsequent* behavior that earns the reader's contempt. Frankenstein's vicious rejection and cruelty toward his own creation is the fault that brings pain to his world and unleashes his great punishment. Rather than rejecting science, the novel's moral appears to be "don't be a lousy dad." (Which is interesting, given Mary Shelley's personal background.)

The central lesson of both tales is that technology can be abused when it is monopolized by a narrow, secretive and self-deceiving elite, absent any accountability or outside criticism. Almost any modern scientist would call this obvious. And after growing up with such stories, many non-scientists find it apparent, as well. The warning is heard.

Brother," as adversaries scream "this is just like *1984!*" whenever something vaguely bothersome turns up (e.g., wall-sized tv screens, personality tests for high school students, the cat-brain camera).

Is government the chief enemy of freedom? That authority center does merit close scrutiny...which we've been applying lately with unprecedented ardor. Meanwhile other citizens worry about different power groups—aristocracies, corporations, criminal gangs, and technological elites. Can anyone justifiably claim exemption from accountability?

Orwell's metaphors have been expanded beyond his initial portrayal of a Stalinist nightmare-state, to include all worrisome accumulations of influence, authority or unreciprocal transparency. Elsewhere[2] I discuss the role that righteous indignation plays in helping to create what may be the first true social immune system against calamity. All four of those great social innovations mentioned above, that fostered our unprecedented wealth and freedom (science, justice, democracy & free markets), are based on harnessing this network of suspicion through vigorous and competitive application of mutual accountability. It may not be nice, but it works far better than hierarchical authority.

These "accountability arenas" function well only when all players get fair access to information.

Technological advances like the Internet may help amplify this trend, or squelch it, depending on choices we make in the next few years. The implications of burgeoning information technology may be enormous. Soon the cognitive powers of human beings will expand immensely. Memory will be enhanced by vast, swift databases that you'll access almost at the speed of thought. Vision will explode in all directions as cameras grow ever-smaller, cheaper, more mobile and interconnected.

In such a world, it will be foolish ever to depend on the ignorance of others.

If they don't know your secrets now, there is always a good chance that someone will pierce your veils tomorrow, perhaps without you ever becoming aware of it. The best firewalls and encryptions may be bypassed by a gnat-camera in your ceiling or a whistle-blower in your front office. How can you ever be sure it has not already happened?[3]

---

[2] *The Transparent Society: Will Technology Force Us to Choose Between Freedom and Privacy?* (Perseus), 1998.
[3] Criticism is the best antidote to error. Yet most humans, especially the mighty, try to avoid it. Leaders of past cultures crushed free speech and public access to information,

Some businessfolk, like Jack Stack (author of *The Great Game of Business*), see the writing on the wall. By using open-book management, they reduce costs, enhance employee morale, foster error-detection, eliminate layers of management, speed their reaction time, and learn how to do business in ways that make it irrelevant how much their competitors know.

Companies that instead pay millions trying to conceal knowledge will strive endlessly to plug leaks, yet gain no long-term advantage or peace of mind. Because the number of ways to leak will expand geometrically as both software and the real world grow more complex. Because information is not like money or any other commodity. It will soon be like air.

A while back, we spoke about the inevitable spread of cameras and databases? As George Orwell would surely point out, elites (government, corporate, criminal and so on...) will get these new powers of sight, no matter what the rules say. So we might as well have them too.

The metaphor of Oceania's telescreen is central here. In Orwell's world, those at the top of a rigid pyramidal hierarchy controlled the flow of information with fierce totality. Only propaganda filtered downward, while every iota or datum about the lives of prols flowed upward. Accountability went in just one direction.

Despite repeated efforts by our own hierarchs to justify one-way information flows, the true record of the last generation has been an indisputable and overwhelming dispersal of knowledge and the power to see. People are becoming addicted to knowing. Take the events that surrounded the tragedies of September 11, 2001. Most of the video we saw was taken by private citizens, a potentially crucial element in future emergencies. Private cell phones spread word quicker than official media. So did email and instant messaging when the telephone

---

a trend Orwell showed being enhanced by technology in a future when elites control all the cameras. In part thanks to Orwell's warning, ours may be the first civilization to systematically avoid this cycle, whose roots lie in human nature. We have learned that few people are mature enough to hold themselves accountable, but in an open society, adversaries eagerly pounce on each other's errors. To preserve our freedom, we must not try to limit the cameras—they are coming anyway and no law will ever prevent the elites from seeing. Instead, we must make sure all citizens share the boon—and burden—of sight. This is already the world we live in. One where the people look hard at the mighty, and look harder the mightier they are.

Orwell's dark future can't come true if confident citizens have a habit of protecting themselves by seeing and knowing.

system got swamped. Swarms of volunteers descended on the disaster sites, as local officials quickly dropped their everyday concerns about liability or professional status in order to use all willing hands. The sole effective action to thwart terrorist plans was taken by individuals aboard United Flight 93, armed with intelligence and communication tools—and a mandate—outside official channels.

Is this a true and unstoppable trend? Has it been, in part driven by the inoculative effects of cautionary fiction such as *Nineteen-Eighty Four*? I can't even begin to prove the hypothesis.

Is this a different way to look at the effects and importance of literature? You bet it is. Scholars aren't used to considering the pragmatic fruits of fictional gedankenexperimentation, but perhaps it's time they started.

Recall our earlier analogy with the old villages that our ancestors lived in, till just a few decades ago. They, too, knew intimate details about almost everyone they met on a given day. Back then, you recognized maybe a thousand people. But we won't be limited by the capacity of organic vision and memory. Our enhanced eyes will scan ten billion fellow villagers. Our enhanced memories will know their reputations, and they will know ours.

This is obviously cause for mixed feelings and deep misgivings. Will it be the egalitarian "good village" of Andy Hardy movies...safe, egalitarian and warmly tolerant of eccentricity? Or the bad village of Frank Capra's Potterstown, a place steeped in hierarchies, feuds and petty bigotries, where the mighty and the narrowminded suppress all deviance from dismal normality?

Or even the vast, stifling, all-knowing "village" of Orwell's Oceania?

We'd better start arguing about this now—how to make the scary parts less scary, and the good parts better—because the village is coming back, like it or not.

The key to our success—both personal and as a society—will be agility in dealing with whatever the future hurls our way.

This is not the path prophesied in *Nineteen Eighty-Four*, which envisioned a brittle and bitter society—one that exploited every opportunity to stoke hatred and division among the ruled. One in which the common man is little better than a harried sheep, ignorant, disempowered and unable to imagine another way. So far, we seem aimed at avoiding that particular failure mode. (At least those who read science fiction cannot be accused of lacking imagination.)

Do we owe this fact, in part, to anti-Cassandras like George Orwell whose warnings, once they were heeded, thus never came true?

Is fear of dystopian nightmare a greater motivator and effectuator of change than any utopian promise? Indeed, our tendency seems always to criticize whatever injustices remain unsolved, rather than ever pause to rejoice in what's been accomplished. That alone shows how deeply the lesson has been learned.

The worry that Orwell and others ignited in us still burns. It drives us on, far more effectively than any vague glowing promise of a better world.

We daren't let up. Not ever, because we've been shown the alternatives.

The world that George Orwell presented was—and remains—just too scary. It is one of the great services performed for us by science fiction, at its best.

The following tale takes some guts...

Fortitude

The aliens seemed especially concerned over matters of *genealogy*.

"It is the only way we can be sure with whom we are dealing," said the spokes-being for the Galactic Federation. Terran-Esperanto words emerged through a translator device affixed to the creature's speaking-vent, between purple, compound eyes. "Citizen species of the Federation will have nothing to do with you humans. Not until you can be properly introduced."

"But *you're* speakin' to us, right now!" Jane Fingal protested. "You're makin' bugger-all sense, mate."

Jane was our astronomer aboard the *Straits of Magellan*. She had first spotted the wake of the N'Gorm ship as it raced by, far swifter than any Earth vessel, and it had been Jane's idea to pulse our engines, giving off weak gravity waves to attract their attention. For several days she had labored to help solve the language problem, until a meeting could be arranged between our puny ETS survey probe and the mighty N'Gorm craft.

Still, I was surprised when Kwenzi Mobutu, the Zairean anthropologist, did not object to Jane's presence in the docking bubble, along with our official contact team. Kwenzi seldom missed a chance to play up tension between Earth's two greatest powers—Royal Africa and the Australian Imperium—even during this historic first encounter with a majestic alien civilization.

The alien slurped mucousy sounds into its mouthpiece, and out came more computer-generated words.

"You misunderstand. I am merely a convenience, a construct-entity, fashioned to be as much like you as possible, thereby to facilitate your evaluation. I have no name, and will return to the vats when this is done."

Fashioned to be like us? I must have stared. (Everyone else did.) The

119

being in front of us was bipedal and had two arms. On top were objects and organs we had tentatively named ears and a mouth. Beyond that, he (She? It?) seemed about as alien as could be.

"Yipes!" Jane commented. "I'd hate to meet your *boss* in a dark alley, if you're the handsomest bloke they could come up with."

I saw Mobutu, the African aristocrat, smile. That's when I realized why he had not vetoed Jane's presence, but relished it. *He knows this meeting is being recorded for posterity. If she makes a fool of herself here, at the most solemn meeting of races, it could win points against Australians back home.*

"As I have tried to explain," the alien reiterated. "You will not meet my 'boss' or any other citizen entity. Not until we are satisfied that your lineage is worthy."

While our Israeli and Tahitian xenobiologists conferred over this surprising development, our Patagonian captain stared out through the docking bubble at the Federation ship whose great flanks arched away, gleaming, in all directions. Clearly, he yearned to bring these advanced technologies home to the famed shipyards of Tierra del Fuego.

"Perhaps I can be helpful in this matter," Kwenzi Mobutu offered confidently. "I have some small expertise. When it comes to tracking one's family tree, I doubt any other human aboard can match my own genealogy."

His smile was a gleaming white contrast against gorgeously-perfect black skin, the sort of rich complexion that trendy people from pole to pole had been using chemicals to emulate, when we left home.

"Even before the golden placards of Abijian were discovered, my family line could be traced back to the great medieval households of Ghana. But since the recovery of those sacred records, it has been absolutely verified that my lineage goes all the way to the black pharaohs of the IXth Dynasty—an unbroken chain of four thousand years."

Mobutu's satisfaction faded when the alien replied with a dismissive wave.

"That interval is far too brief. Nor are we interested in the time-thread of mere individuals. Larger groups concern us."

Jane Fingal chuckled, and Mobutu whirled on her angrily.

"Your attitude suits a mongrel nation whose ancestors were criminal transportees, and whose 'emperor' is chosen at a *rugby match!*"

"Hey. Our king'd whip yours any day, even half-drunk and with 'is arse in a sling."

"Colleagues!" I hastened to interrupt. "These are serious matters. A little decorum, if you please?"

The two shared another moment's hot enmity, until Nechemia Meyers spoke up.

"Perhaps they refer to *cultural* continuity. If we can demonstrate that one of our social traditions has a long history, stretching back—"

"—five thousand years?" inserted Mohandas Nayyal, our linguist from Delhi Commune. "Of course the Hindi tradition, as carried by the Vedas, goes back easily that far."

"*Actually,*" Meyers continued, a bit miffed. "I was thinking more along the lines of *six* thousand—"

He cut short as the alien let out a warbling sigh, waving both "hands."

"Once again, you misconstrue. The genealogy we seek *is* genetic, but a few thousand of your years is wholly inadequate."

Jane muttered, "Bugger! It's like dickering with a Pattie over the price of a bleeding iceberg...no offense, Skipper."

The captain returned a soft smile. Patagonians are an easy-going lot, till you get down to business.

"Well then," Mobutu resumed, nodding happily. "I think we can satisfy our alien friends, and win Federation membership, on a purely *biochemical* basis. For many years now, the Great Temple in Abijian has gathered DNA samples from every sub-race on Earth, correlating and sorting to trace out our genetic relationships. Naturally, African bloodlines were found to be the least mutated from the central line of inheritance—"

Jane groaned again, but this time Kwenzi ignored her.

"—stretching back to our fundamental common ancestor, that beautiful, dark ancestress of all human beings, the one variously called Eva, or M'tum, who dwelled on the eastern fringes of what is now the Zairean Kingdom, over *three million years ago!*"

So impressive was Mobutu's dramatic delivery that even the least sanguine of our crew felt stirred, fascinated and somewhat awed. But then the N'Gorm servant-entity vented another of its frustrated sighs.

"I perceive that I am failing in my mission to communicate with lesser beings. Please allow me to try once again.

"We in the Federation are constantly being plagued by young, upstart species, rising out of planetary nurseries and immediately yammering for attention, claiming rights of citizenship in our ancient culture. At times, it has been suggested that we should routinely sterilize such places—filthy little worlds—or at least eliminate noisy, adolescent infestations by targeting their early stages with radio-seeking drones. But the *Kutathi,* who serve as judges and law-givers in the Federation, have ruled this impermissible. There are few crimes worse than meddling in the natural progress of a nursery world. All we can do is snub the newcomers, and restrict them to their home systems until they have matured enough for decent company."

"That's *all?*" The Captain spoke for the first time, aghast at what this meant—an end to the Earth's bold ventures with interstellar travel. Crude our ships might be, by galactic standards, but humanity was proud of them. They were a unifying force, binding fractious nations in a common cause. It was awful to imagine that our expedition might be the last.

The translator apparently failed to convey the Captain's sarcasm. The alien envoy-entity nodded in solemn agreement.

"Yes, that is all. So you may rejoice, in your own pathetic way, that your world is safe for you to use up or destroy any way you see fit, since that is the typical way most puerile species finish their brief lifespans. If, by some chance, you escape this fate, you will eventually be allowed to send forth your best and brightest to serve in carefully chosen roles, earning eventual acceptance on the lowest rungs of proper society."

Jane Fingal growled. "Why you puffed-up pack of pseudo-pommie bast—"

I cut in with urgent speed. "Excuse me, but there is one thing I fail to understand. You spoke earlier of an 'evaluation.' Does this mean that our fate is *not* automatic?"

The alien emissary regarded me for a long time, as if pondering whether I deserved an answer. Finally, it must have decided I was not that much lower than my crewmates, anyway. It acknowledged my query with a nod.

"There *is* an exception—if you can prove a relationship with a citizen race. To determine that possibility was the purpose of my query about species-lineage."

"Ah, now it becomes clear," Mohandas Nayyal said. "You want to know if we are *genetically related* to one of your high-born castes. Does this imply that those legends may be true? That star beings have descended, from time to time, to engage in sexual congress with our ancestors? By co-mingling their seed with ours, they meant to generously endow and improve our..."

He trailed off as we all saw the N'Gorm quiver. Somehow, disgust was conveyed quite efficiently across its expressive "face."

"Please, do not be repulsive in your bizarre fantasies. The behavior you describe is beyond contemplation, even by the mentally ill. Not only is it physically and biologically absurd, but it assumes the highborn might *wish* to improve the stock of bestial nuisances. Why in the universe would they want to do such a thing?"

Ignoring the bald insult, Meyers, the exobiologist, added, "It's unlikely for another reason. Human DNA has been probed and analyzed for three centuries. We have a pretty good idea where most of it came from. We're creatures of the Earth, no doubt about it."

When he saw members of the contact team glaring at him, Meyers shrugged. "Oh, it would all come out in time, anyway. Don't you think they'd analyze any claim we made?"

"Correct," buzzed the translator. "And we would bill you for the effort."

"Well, I'm still confused," claimed our Uzbeki memeticist. "You make it sound as if there is no way we could be related to one of your citizen-races, so why this grilling about our genealogy?"

"A formality, required by law. In times past, a few exceptional cases won status by showing that they possessed common genes with highborn ones."

"And how did these commonalities come about?" Mobutu asked, still miffed over the rejection of his earlier claims.

The N'Gorm whistled yet another sigh. "Not all individuals of every species behave circumspectly. Some, of noble birth, have been known to go down to planets, seeking thrills, or testing their mettle to endure filth and heavy gravity."

"In other words, they go slumming!" Jane Fingal laughed. "Now *those* are the only blokes I'd care to meet, in your whole damn Federation."

I caught Jane's eye, gesturing for restraint. She needn't make things worse than they already were. The whole of Earth would watch recordings of what passed here today.

Nechemia Meyers shook his head. "I can see where all this is leading. When galactics go *slumming,* as Jane colorfully put it, they risk unleashing alien genes into the ecosystem of a nursery world. This is forbidden interference in the natural development of such planets. It *also* makes possible a genetic link that could prove embarrassing later, when that world spawns a star-traveling race."

The translator buzzed gratification. "At last, I have succeeded in conveying the basic generalities. Now, before we take your ship in tow, and begin the quarantine of your wretched home system, I am required by law to offer you a chance. Do you wish formally to claim such a genetic link to one of our citizen races? Remember that we will investigate in detail, at your expense."

A pall seemed to settle over the assembled humans. This was not as horrible as some of the worst literary fantasies about alien contact, but it was pretty bad. Apparently, the galaxy was ruled by an aristocracy of age and precedence. One that jealously guarded its status behind a veneer of hypocritical law.

"How can we *know* whether or not to make such a claim!" Kwenzi Mobutu protested. "Unless we meet your high castes for ourselves."

"That will not happen. Not unless your claim is upheld."

"But—"

"It hardly matters," inserted Nechemia, glumly.

We turned and the Captain asked, "What do you mean?"

"I mean that we cannot make such a claim. The evidence refutes it. All we need is to look at the history of life on Earth.

"Consider, friends. Why did we think for so long that we were alone in the cosmos? It wasn't just that our radio searches for intelligent life turned up nothing, decade after decade. Aliens *could* have efficient technologies that make them abandon radio, the way we gave up signal-drums. This is exactly what we found to be the case.

"No, a much stronger argument for our uniqueness lay in the sedimentary rocks of our own world.

"If intelligent life was plentiful, someone would invent starships and travel. Simple calculations showed that just one such outbreak, if it flourished, could fill the galaxy with its descendants in less than fifty million years...and that assumed ship technology far cruder than this N'Gorm dreadnought hovering nearby."

He gestured at the sleek, gleaming hull outside, that had accelerated so nimbly in response to Jane Fingal's hail.

"Imagine such a life-swarm, sweeping across the galaxy, settling every habitable world in sight. It's what we *humans* thought we'd do, once we escaped Earth's bonds, according to most science fiction tales. A prairie fire of colonization that radically changes every world it touches, forever mixing and re-shuffling each planet's genetic heritage."

The emissary conceded. "It is illegal, but it has happened, from time to time."

Meyers nodded. "Maybe it occurred elsewhere, but not on Earth."

"How can you be sure?" I asked.

"Because we can read Earth's biography in her rocks. For more than two billion years, our world was 'prime real estate,' as one great 20th century writer once put it. It had oceans and a decent atmosphere, but no living residents higher than crude prokaryotes— bacteria and algae—simmering in the sea. In all that time, until the Eukaryotic Explosion half a billion years ago, any alien interference would have profoundly changed the course of life on our world."

Jane Fingal edged forward. "This 'explosion' you spoke of. What was that?"

"The *Eukaryotic Explosion,*" Meyers explained, "occurred about 560 million years ago, when there evolved nucleated cells, crammed with sophisticated organelles. Soon after, there arose multi-celled organisms, invertebrates, vertebrates, fishes, dinosaurs, and primates. But the important datum is the two billion years before that, when even the most careful of colonizations would have utterly changed Earth's ecology, by infecting it with advanced alien organisms we would later see in sediments. Even visitors who flushed their *toilets* carelessly..."

Meyers trailed off as our astronomer made choking sounds, covering her mouth. Finally, Jane burst out with deep guffaws, laughing so hard that she nearly doubled over. We waited until finally Jane wiped her eyes and explained.

"Sorry, mates. It's just that...well, somethin' hit me when Nechemia mentioned holy altars."

I checked my memory files and recalled the euphemism, popular in Australian English. Every Aussie home is said to contain at least one porcelain "altar," where adults who have over-indulged with food or drink often kneel and pray for relief, invoking the beer deities, "Ralph" or "Ruth." On weekdays, these altars have other, more mundane uses.

Kwenzi Mobutu seemed torn between outrage over Jane's behavior and delight that it was all being recorded.

"And what insight did this offer you?" He asked with a tightly controlled voice.

"Oh, with your interest in genealogy you'll love this, Kwenzi," Jane assured, in a friendly tone. She turned to Nechemia. "You say there couldn't have been any alien interference before the Eukaryotic Explosion, and after that, everything on Earth seems to be part of the same tree of life, right? Neither of those long periods seems to show any trace of outside interference."

The Israeli nodded, and Jane smiled.

"But what about the explosion, *itself?* Isn't that *just* the sort of sudden event you say would be visible in rocks, if alien garbage ever got dumped on Earth?"

Meyers frowned, knoting his brow. "Well...ye-e-e-es. Offhand, I cannot think of any perfect refutation, providing you start out assuming a general similarity in amino and nucleic acid coding...and compatible protein structures. That's not too far-fetched. From that point on, prokaryotic and early eukaryotic genes mixed, but the eukaryote seed stock *might* have come, quite suddenly—"

A short squeal escaped the alien emissary.

"This is true? Your life history manifested such a sudden transformation on so basic a level? From un-nucleated to fully competent multicellular organisms? How rapid was this change?"

Meyers shook his head. "No one has been able to parse the boundary thinly enough to tell. But clearly it was on the order of a million years, or less. Some hypothesize a chain of fluke mutations, leveraging on each other rapidly. But that explanation *did* always seem a bit too pat. There are just too many sudden, revolutionary traits to explain..."

He looked up at Jane, with a new light in his eyes. "You aren't joking about this, are you? I mean, we could be onto something! I wonder why this never occurred to us before?"

The Captain uttered a short laugh. "Trust an Australian to think of it. They don't give a damn *what* you think about their ancestors."

A flurry of motion drew our eyes to the tunnel leading to the N'Gorm ship, just in time to catch sight of the envoy-entity, fleeing our presence in a state of clear panic. A seal hissed shut and vibrations warned that the huge vessel was about to detach. We made our own prudent exit, hurrying back to our ship.

Last to re-board was Kwenzi Mobutu, wearing a bleak look on his face, paler than I had ever seen him. The African aristocrat winced as Jane Fingal offered a heartfelt, Australian prayer of benediction, aimed at the retreating N'Gorm frigate.

"May Ruth follow you everywhere, mate, and keep you busy at her altar."

Jane laughed again, and finished with a slurpy, *flushing* sound.

Many years have passed since that epiphany on the spacelanes. Of all the humans present when we held the fateful meeting, only I, the one made of durable silicon and brass, still live to tell an eyewitness-tale.

By the laws of Earth, I am equal to any biological human being, despite galactic rules that would let me be enslaved. No noble genes lurk in *my* cells. No remnants of ruffians who went *slumming* long ago, on a planet whose only life forms merged in scummy mats at the fringes of a tepid sea. I carry no DNA from those alien rapscallions, those high-born ones who carelessly gave Earth an outlawed gift, a helpful push. But my kind was *designed* by the heirs of that little indiscretion, so I can share the poignant satisfaction brought by recent events.

For decade after decade, ever since that fateful meeting between the stars, we chased Federation ships, who always fled like scoundrels evading a subpoena. Sometimes our explorers would arrive at one of their habitat clusters, only to find vast empty cities, abandoned in frantic haste to avoid meeting us, or to prevent our emissaries from uttering one terrible word—

Cousin!

It did them no good in the long run. Eventually, we made contact with the august, honest *Kutathi,* the judges, who admitted our petition before them.

The galactic equivalent of a cosmo-biological *paternity suit.*

And now, the ruling has come down at last, leaving Earth's accountants to scratch their heads in awe over the damages we have been awarded, and the official status we have won.

As for our unofficial *social position,* that is another matter. Our having the right to vote in high councils will not keep most of the haughty aliens from snubbing Earthlings for a long time to come. (Would *we* behave any better, if a strain of our intestinal flora suddenly began demanding a place at the banquet table? I hope so, but you can never tell until you face the situation for yourself.)

None of that matters as much as the freedom—to come and go as we please. To buy and sell technologies. To learn...and eventually to teach.

The Kutathi judges kindly told our emissaries that humans seem to have a knack, a talent, for *the law.* Perhaps it will be our calling, the Kutathi said. It makes an odd kind of sense, given the jokes people have long told about the genetic nature of lawyers.

Well, so be it.

Among humans of all races and nations, there is agreement. There is common cause. Something has to change. The snooty ways of highborn clans must give way, and we are just the ones to help make it happen. We'll find *other* loopholes in this rigid, inane class system, other ways to help spring more young races out of quarantine, until at last the stodgy old order crumbles.

Anyway, who cares what aristocrats think of us, their illegitimate cousins, the long-fermented fruit of their bowels?

Jane Fingal wrote our anthem, long ago. It is a stirring song, hauntingly kindred to *Waltzing Matilda,* full of verve, gumption, and the spirit of rebellion. Like the *1812 Overture,* it can't properly be played without an added instrument. Only in this case, the guest soloist plays no cannon, but a porcelain *altar,* one that swishes, churns and gurgles with the soulful strains of destiny.

The Future Keeps Surprising Us
(or Some Reflections on a Space Odyssey)

The arrival of the new millennium may already seem old hat to many, but it still has got me thinking. Even writing 200_ on my checks feels weird. (And who would have thought we'd still have checkbooks by now?) Where are all the flying cars, antigravity belts, immortality pills, and space liners to balmy Venus we were promised! What about the muscle pills? Robot butlers? Teleportation? The most science fiction thing around seems to be U.S. Presidential politics...more Twentieth Century silliness.

Oh, there are so many aspects to this milestone that we could talk about. But let me focus on just one...the cardinal numeric figure of a recent year—*2001*. What does it mean to you?

Why, of course, it's a movie! One that, remarkably despite its age, still shines some amazing sparkles of perspective on our time. I'd like to use it in that vein right now, to point out a few things about the surprising world we're living in. A world that's even more amazing than Arthur C. Clarke imagined.

Yes, yes. Of course the book and film influenced me. How could they not? I was sixteen years old. *Star Trek* had been canceled and Norman Mailer was grousing that NASA engineers had achieved the impossible—by somehow managing to make Project Apollo boring.

It would be more than a year before the space program delivered its most important product—not the moon landing itself, but rather the greatest art work in history—the image of Earth floating as a blue oasis in the desert of space. That gift wouldn't arrive till the end of 1968. Meanwhile, just about the only images that seemed to offer anything like promethean vision were contained in *2001: A Space Odyssey*.

Oh, I could go on and on about mixed messages in the film. Its love-hate relationship with technology, for example. Or the story's ambivalence toward the notion of artificial intelligence. Or the quaint combination of optimism and pessimism that we saw repeated over and over again in the works of Arthur C. Clarke and Isaac Asimov— leading visionaries of their era—both of whom worried that humanity might be far too snared by the sticky fibers of an aggressive neolithic heritage ever to break free on its own.

Strangely, for one known as an idealist, Clarke seemed to be saying in *2001* (and in other works like *Childhood's End)* that we have no hope of transcending the mire of the past all by ourselves. Transcendence must come from without, via some kind of external intervention. Many felt that way during the turbulent sixties—a time when it seemed Western Civilization might all-too-easily destroy itself with the very brightest of its shiny new tools. If such intervention wasn't coming from old-time religion, it seemed possible to hope for delivery by kindly creatures from the sky.

Yes, I might talk about that notion, which in the years since has become a grindingly tedious cliché. ("Oh, save us from ourselves, kind aliens!")

Or else I could switch levels and describe how exciting the film *2001: A Space Odyssey* was to a teenager like me! Especially a teen whose brain seemed better tuned to stories and images than the torrents of ecstatic music that sloshed over contemporary culture during those years—the era of the Beatles, Doors and Rolling Stones.

There were millions of us, you know, though we tried to hide our deviancy. Oh, we liked the music just fine. But guys like me also felt just a bit alienated from the frenzied ardor that our peers devoted to rock 'n roll. All those songs were mere *sounds,* after all, and what was sound compared to light!

We hungered to be fed through the *eyes,* and through those flashing-cerebral prefrontal lobes. We wanted to be turned on by ***images,*** preferably active ones, supple, changing and MacLuhan-cool, not lying dead on some canvas. Today there is a veritable feast of manic color, a full-spectrum orgy! But in the sixties we had little more than sardonic Warhol, some cartoony psychedelia...and science fiction.

During such a time, for visual-junkies like me, *2001* seemed to fall like manna in the desert. I came to watch again and again, staring for hours at Kubrick's voluptuously gray-blue-modern imagery, with those added touches of faux-realistic grime.

Oh, I might wax effusive about how the film affected and inspired me, perhaps helping motivate my career in science. But how many tributes of *that* kind have you already read?

So let me shine a final beam from this epochal artwork onto quite a different direction. There is yet another perspective...one that just occurred to me a few months back, while watching *2001: A Space Odyssey* for about the fortieth time.

Consider the following two hoary old clichés:

Isn't it a shame that human decency and justice haven't kept pace with our technological progress?

and

No past era featured as much cruelty and misery as this one.

In spite of their vogue, both of these oft-parroted passages are *patently false*. It's incredibly easy to disprove them!

Over half of those alive on Earth today never saw war, starvation or major civil strife with their own eyes. Most never went more than a day without food. Only a small fraction have seen a city burn, heard the footsteps of a conquering army, or watched an overlord brutalize the helpless. Yet all these events were routine for our ancestors!

Of course, hundreds of millions *have* experienced such things, and terrors continue at unacceptable levels across the world. Our consciences, prodded by the relentless power of television, must not cease demanding compassion and vigorous action.

Still, things have changed since humanity wallowed in hopelessness and horror, during the middle years of the Twentieth Century. Look in places that were festering maelstroms back then—from Tokyo and Kuala Lumpur to Warsaw and Istanbul. From Alabama to South Africa. The ratio of humans who now live modestly safe and comfortable lives—or at least better than their parents—has never been greater.

As for contrasting technical and moral progress, there's no contest! Technical advance has been small potatoes by comparison! For example, while I truly love the Internet, its effects on real life have so far been vastly exaggerated. Telephones and radio had far greater immediate effects when they entered the home! Oh yes, we have fancier autos and sleeker airplanes. But people still pack their kids in a car and fight traffic to reach the airport in time to meet Grandma's flight from Chicago...as we did when I was seven. Life's tempo has quickened, but the basic patterns differ little from 1958.

It is our *attitudes* that have undergone a transformation unlike any in history. All kinds of unjust assumptions that used to be considered inherent—from racial, sexual and class stereotypes to ideological oversimplifications—have been tossed onto the trash heap where they long deserved to go, in favor of a generalized notion of tolerance, pragmatism and eccentricity that seems to grow more vibrant with each passing year.

Where does *2001: A Space Odyssey* come into all this?

When the famous Stanley Kubrick film appeared in the mid-sixties, two monumental projects transfixed the people of the United States—conquering outer space and overcoming deeply ingrained social injustice. This juxtaposition is clear in the film...and its sequel, *2010*. Both movies portray the scientific and manipulative power of humanity far outstripping our wisdom.

But is that, in fact, what happened?

Consider those wonderful toys. The "wheel" space stations, rotating to Strauss waltzes. Or those marvelous moon cities. Or vibrant, argumentative computer minds like Hal 9000. We have none of them, alas.

Now recall the human *political hierarchies* portrayed in *2001: A Space Odyssey*—hierarchies that were rigidly pyramidal, officious, patronizing and relentlessly white-male. Remember the film's basic plot premise? Every tragedy arose from obsessive secrecy, as aloof bureaucrats like Heywood Floyd contemptuously concealed information from the public—and even from professional astronauts—out of fear their poor sheeplike minds would suffer "social disorientation."

What horridly disorienting information were they protecting people from? *An archeological dig on the moon?*

Oooh!

Now don't get me wrong. That scenario seemed totally plausible then! The predictions—both technical and social—*appeared* to be so on-target.[1]

But they weren't. And that's where it gets so interesting.

Who would have imagined that colonizing space would prove so

---

[1] Instead of acknowledging the progress we have made in overcoming our worst evils, cinema seems to have gone in the opposite direction, shifting from the brash "We're going to conquer space" assumption of *Destination Moon* and *2001* to "We're all gonna be dodging bullets and mutants in ruined cities." This may be one reason for the persistence of the cliché that social progress lags far behind technology. Optimism just doesn't offer as many options for drama!

I cover this in more detail elsewhere, in an article entitled "A World Filled With Idiots...or Why Fiction Routinely Depicts Society and Its Citizens as Fools."

Me? I keep hearing a Beatles song from the same era as *2001: A Space Odyssey*... *"Don'tcha know it's gonna* be...*all right*..."

grindingly slow—and yet, by the real year 2001 we'd refute so many cruel bigotries that were once taken for granted, way back in 1967? We still don't (again, alas!) have the fancy space stations of *2001: A Space Odyssey*—but today our astronauts come in all sexes and colors. And kids who watch them on TV feel less fettered by presumed limitations. Each may choose to hope, or not, without relentlessly hearing *"you can't."*

In *this* 21st Century, an officious prig like Heywood Floyd would be haunted by whistleblowers. And one crewmember of Discovery, being female, might actually *listen* to poor HAL instead of bullying the poor conflicted machine into feeling cornered and lashing out.

No, this is not a criticism of *2001: A Space Odyssey!* The film did a great job in the context of its time and it remains terrific art. Indeed, it is not the job of art—even sci fi—to predict!

Especially in science fiction, art is at its best when it helps put things into perspective, which is what this venerable collaboration between Kubrick and Clarke still does, even where the forecasts proved wrong.

2001: A Space Odyssey can, and should, make you think. About all the fancy toys we were promised, but don't yet have as the millennium rolls around. And about a society that Clarke feared would stay recalcitrant...but hasn't.

(Does this sense of guarded optimism apply, beyond the borders of America, east Asia, and Europe? Who can say? To some extent, it may depend on how far the "culture of science fiction" has spread. Look at a map of the world. Ponder the rate at which science fiction stories and novels have become incorporated in various societies. It's no exaggeration to claim that the popularity of science fiction correlates almost perfectly with cultures where egalitarianism, tolerance, openness, ease with technology and suspicion of authority have become ingrained. Indeed, might science fiction be the best way to proselytize those same values, in lands where they haven't yet taken root? Could *2001* and its cousins be our secret weapon, in an ancient struggle against intolerant ways?)

I think that may be the most important thing to notice, as we turn away from the past and face the future. The road ahead remains long, hard and murky. Our achievements often seem dim compared to imperfections that are left unsolved. But at this rate, who will bet me that a woman or a person of color won't preside in the White House long before the first human being steps on Mars?

Progress doesn't always go the way we expect it to.

It is sometimes wiser than we are.

This story first appeared in the book Isaac's Universe Volume One: The Diplomacy Guild, *an anthology of stories set in the Erthumoi universe of Isaac Asimov, a special edition published in his honor.*

The Diplomacy Guild

"I have heard it suggested that you humans undergo this queer obsession because you live so hot and fast. You sense Time's heavy breath upon your backs, and so feel you must *copy* yourselves, in order to be two places at once."

Phss'aah's words flowed so musically from the translator grille that it was easy to lose the Cephallon philosopher's meaning among the harmonies.

Anyway, I had been distracted by the whining of my *other* guest, the miserable Crotonite huddled in a corner—pathetically flexing broken stubs that had once been powerful wings. One more burden. I cursed fate and my employer for saddling me with the creature—one cruelly scorned by its own kind, yet also Ambassador Plenipotentiary from a powerful interstellar race.

Phss'aah's words shook me from perusing my new Crotonite guest. I turned back to the huge tank taking up half my ship's Visitor Suite, where a vaguely porpoise-like form whipped its tail, thrashing oxygen-rich water into a froth.

"I'm sorry..." and I made the wet sound approximating Phss'aah's name as near as a descendant of Earth humans could form it. "I didn't quite catch that last remark."

Bubbles rose from the Cephallon's twin exhalation slits, and now I read what might be mild exasperation in the flex of his long snout. Instead of repeating himself, Phss'aah waved a four fingered flipper-arm toward the aqua-bot that shared his tank. The bulbous machine planted a sucker on the glassy wall and spoke in its owner's stead.

"I believe Master Phss'aah is proposing a hypothesis as to why humans—you Erthuma—were the only one of the Six Starfaring Races

135

to invent true autonomous robots. He suggests it is because you have such short natural lifespans. Being ambitious, your race sought ways to extend itself artificially. In order to be many places at once, they put much of themselves into their machines."

I shook my head. "But our lives aren't any shorter than Locrians', or Nexians'..."

"Correction," the robot interrupted. "You are counting up an individual's sum span of years, including all his or her *consecutive* natural lifetimes. You've had four renewals, Ambassador Dorning, totaling three hundred and four standard Earth years.

"But my master apparently thinks your Erthumoi worldview is still colored by the way existence was for you during the ages leading to High Civilization. In any event, your race invented artificially intelligent constructs like me well before learning how to Renew."

The machine—and Phss'aah—did have a point. Not for the first time I tried to imagine what it must have been like for my ancestors, facing certain death after only a single span of less than nine standard decades. Why, at my first Renewal I was still barely formed...an infant! I'd only completed one profession by then.

How strange that most humans, back in olden times, became parents as early as thirty years of age. In most modern nations of the modern Galactic Erthuma, you weren't even supposed to *think* about breeding till the middle of your second life.

All this time Phss'aah watched me through the glass with one eye, milky blue and inscrutable. I almost regretted that human-invented technology enabled the Cephallon to use his robot mouthpiece as yet another veil to shelter behind. Though, of course, getting Phss'aah to rely on this fancy assistant-drone was actually quite a coup. The idea was to sell large numbers of such machines to the water race, and then each of the other Big Five, so they'd get used to what some called the "bizarre Erthumoi notion" of intelligent devices...robots. Frankly, we newcomer humans could use the trade credits.

"Hmm." I answered cautiously. "But the Crotonites—" I nodded in the general direction of my unwanted guest in the corner. "—have even shorter lifespans than natural, old-style humans, and they don't Renew! Why, then, didn't *they* invent robots? It's not for lack of skill with machines. They're more nimble than anybody, with unsurpassed craftsmanship. And Space knows they have as much *ambition* as anybody."

The Cephallon rose to the surface to breathe, and returned trailing bubbles. When he spoke, the wall unit conveyed an Erthumoi translation, this time bypassing the robot.

"You reply logically and well for one of your kind. Certainly you and the Crotonites share the quick metabolisms characteristic of breathers of supercharged oxygen atmospheres. They, however, are oviparous flyers, while you are descended from arboreal mammals. Mammals are gregarious..."

"*Some* mammals."

"Indeed." And some of Phss'aah's irritation briefly showed. Cephallons do not like being interrupted while pontificating. That was exactly why I did it. Diplomacy is such a delicate business.

"Perhaps another reason you invented intelligent machines was because—"

This time the interruption wasn't my fault. The door behind me hissed open and my own secretary 'bot hovered into the Guest Suite.

"Yes, Betty, what is it?" I asked.

"Messages received," she said tersely. "High priority, from Erthuma Diplomatic Guild, Long-Last Station."

Oblong, suspended in a cradle of invisible force, the machine looked nothing like her namesake, my most recent demi-wife on Long-Last. But, it was imprinted with her voice and twenty of her personality engrams, so she deserved a gender and basic courtesy.

"Thank you," I told the auto-sec. "I'll be right up."

Assuming dismissal, Betty turned and departed. From the corner of the suite, the Crotonite lifted his head and watched the machine briefly. Something in those cat-like eyes seemed to track it as a hunter might follow prey. But this Crot wasn't going to be chasing flitting airborne victims above the forests of any thick-aired world. Never again. Where once he carried great, tent-like wings, powerfully muscled and heavier than his torso, now the short, deep-chested being wore mere nubs—scarred from recent amputation.

The Crotonite noticed my look, and snarled fiercely. "Plant-eating grub! Turn away your half-blind, squinty orbs. You have no status to cast them on my shame!"

That was in Crotonoi, of course. Few Erthumoi would have understood so rapid and slurred an alien diatribe. But my talents and training had won me this post. Cursed talents. Double-cursed training!

By my own species' standards of politeness I'd have accepted the rebuke and turned away, respecting his privacy. Instead, I snapped right back in my own language.

"*You* dare throw insults at me? *You* who are broken and wingless and shall never again fly? *You* who shame your race by neglecting the purpose for which you were cast down? Here, try doing this!"

I flexed my strong legs and bounded high in the half gravity of the Guest Suite. The cripple, of course, could not manage it with his puny legs. I landed facing him. "You're a diplomat, Jirata. You won your fallen state by being *better* than your peers, the first so chosen for a bold new experiment. Your job is now to try something new to your folk...to *empathize* with ground-walking life forms like me, and even swimming forms like Phss'aah. To make that effort, you were assigned to me, a burden I did not ask for, nor welcome. Nor do I predict success.

"Still, you can *try*. It's the purpose of your existence. The reason your people didn't leave you beneath some tree to starve, and instead still speak your name to the winds, as if you were alive.

"*Try*, Jirata. Just try, and the least you'll win is that I, personally, will stop being cruel to you."

The Crotonite looked away, but I could tell he was struggling with a deep perplexity. "Why should you stop being cruel?" he asked. "You have every advantage."

I sighed. This was going to take a long time. "Because I'd rather like you than hate you, Jirata. And if you don't understand that, consider this. Your job is to investigate a new mode of diplomacy for your people. *Empathy* is what you must discover to succeed. So while I'm away, why not converse with Phss'aah. I'm sure he'll be patient with you. He doesn't know how to be anything else."

That was untrue, of course. Phss'aah gave me a look of exasperation at this unwelcome assignment. For his part, Jirata glanced at the Cephallon, floating in all that water, and let out a keening of sheer disgust.

I left the room.

"Actually, there are two messages of Red Priority," Captain Smeet told me. She handed over a pair of decoded flimsies. I thanked her, went over to the privacy corner of the ship's bridge, and laid the first of the shimmering, gauzy message films over my head. Immediately, the gossamer fabric wrapped my face, covering eyes and ears, leaving only my nostrils free. It began vibrating, and after a momentary blurriness, sight and sound enveloped me.

My boss looked across his desk...the slavedriver whose faith in my abilities was anything but reassuring. He seemed to feel there was no end to the number of tasks I could take on at once.

"*Patty,*" he said. "*Sorry about dumping the Crotonite on you. He's part of an experimental program initiated by the Seven Sovereigns' League. You'll recall that particular Crotoni confederacy suffered rather badly for bungling the negotiations at Maioplar, fifty years ago. In desperation, they're trying something radical to revise their way of dealing with other races. I guess they're testing it on us Erthuma because we're the least influential of the Six. If it flops, our opinion won't matter much.*

"In answer to your last query—I have no idea if the Seven Sovereigns cleared this with other Crotonite nation-states, or if they're doing it on their own. Crot intra-race politics is such a tangle, who can tell? That's why the Diplomacy Guild decided to farm out Jirata and the others like him to our roving emissaries. Try to figure out what's going on away from media and the like. I'm sure you understand."

"Right, Maxwell." I gave a very un-ladylike snort. Back on Long-Last, Betty used to chastise me for that. But I never heard any of our husbands complain.

"That's my Patty," he went on, as if he was sure my reaction would be complete enthusiasm. *"Who knows, maybe the League's idea of using crippled bats as envoys may work, so let's put it on high priority, okay?"*

"As high as preventing a break in the Essential Protocols?" I muttered. But I knew the answer.

"Of course, nothing is to stand in the way of getting King Zardee to toe the line on replicants. If he gives you any trouble, just tell that freon-blooded son of a b—"

I'd heard enough, and ripped the flimsy off. It instantly began dissolving into inert gas.

"Orders, madam?" Captain Smeet looked at me coolly, expectantly.

"Proceed to Planet Nine of this system, and please beam to King Zardee that I'll wait no longer for him to prepare for my arrival. If he plans to shoot us out of the sky, let him do so and live with the consequences."

Smeet nodded. I could have asked her to take me wet-diving in the nearby sun of Prongee System and she'd find a way, keeping her opinion of crazy diplomats to herself. That was more than *I* sometimes was able to do, after listening to Maxwell for a while.

Why success followed that awful old man around so, I could never understand.

An angry visage greeted me, glaring out of the communications tank.

I had been sent on this mission because, among all the different styles of government used by various Erthumoi nation-worlds, monarchies were among the quirkiest, and I had the most experience in our sector dealing with arrogant creatures known as kings.

Some were smooth. But this one actually reminded me of Jirata as he growled.

"We are not accustomed to being made to wait," he said as I stepped into the Communications Lounge. Ignoring the remark, I curtsied in the manner customary for women in his commonwealth.

"Your majesty would not have liked to see me dressed as I was when you called. It took a few moments to make myself presentable."

Zardee grunted. I felt his eyes survey me like a piece of real estate, and recognized covetousness in them. I always find it amazing how many Erthumoi societies leave their males with these unaltered, visually stimulated lust patterns. And Zardee was nearly eight hundred standard years old!

Never mind. I'd use whatever chinks in his armor I could find.

"I accept your apology," he said in a softer tone. "And I must offer my regrets in turn for keeping such a comely and accomplished lady waiting at the boundary. I now invite you to join me on my yacht for some refreshment and entertainment I'm sure you'll find distracting."

"You are most gracious, Your Majesty. However, first I really must inspect your mining establishment on the ninth planet of this system."

His visage transformed once more to anger, and again I felt astonishment this system's folk put up with such a monarch. The attractions of kingship are well documented, but sentimental indulgence can become an illness if it isn't looked to.

"There's nothing on my mining world of interest to the Diplomacy Guild!" he snapped. "You have no authority to force yourself upon me!"

This from a fellow so atavistic, I had no doubt he would chain me to a bed in his seraglio, were it in his power. I kept my amusement to myself. "I'm sure, Your Majesty, that you wouldn't want it to get out among your Erthumoi and Nexian neighbors that you have something to hide."

"*All* kingdoms and sovereign worlds have secrets, foolish woman. I have a right to keep vital security information from the prying eyes of outsiders."

I nodded. "But not when those secrets violate Essential Protocols of the Erthuma. Or is it your intention to join the Outlaw Worlds, forgoing the services of my Guild?"

For a moment it looked as if he might declare just such a move. But he stopped. Commercial repercussions would be catastrophic. That step might push his people too far.

"The Essential Protocols don't cover much," he said, slowly. "My subjects have access to Erthumoi ombudsmen. I vet my treaties past Guild lawyers, and my ship captains report to the Guild on activities observed among the Other Five races. That is all that's required of me."

"You are forgetting Article Six of the Protocols," I said.

Blinking, Zardee spoke slowly. "Exactly what do you accuse me of, ambassador?"

I shrugged. "Such a strong word. There are rumors, Majesty...that someone is violating the rule against creating fully autonomous replicants."

His face reddened three shades. I did not need a Nexian's insight or a Cephallon's empathy to tell I'd struck home. At the same time, though, it was not *guilt* I read in the monarch's eyes, but rather something akin to *shame*. I found the reaction most interesting.

"I'll rendezvous with your ship above the ninth planet," he said tersely, and cut the channel. No doubt Captain Smeet and the king's pilot were already exchanging coordinates by the time I departed the lounge and headed for the Guest Suite, to see how things were progressing there.

I shouldn't have expected miracles from Phss'aah. After all, Jirata the Crotonite was my responsibility, not his. But I at least might have hoped for *tact* from a Cephallon diplomat. Instead, I returned to find Phss'aah carrying on a long monologue directed at the cripple Croton, who huddled in his corner glaring back at the creature in the tank. And if looks could maim there wouldn't have been much of anything left but bloody water.

"...so unlike the other Starfaring Races, we Cephallons find this human innovation of articulate, intelligent machines useful and fascinating, even if it is also puzzling and bizarre. Take your own case, Jirata. Would not a loyal mechanical surrogate be of use to one such as you, especially in your present condition? Helping you fend for..."

Phss'aah noticed my return and interrupted his monologue. "Ah, Patty. You have returned. I was just explaining to our comrade here how useful it is to have machines able to anticipate your requirements, and of repairing and maintaining themselves. Even the Crotonites' marvelous, intricate devices, hand-made and unique, lack that capability."

"We do not need it!" Jirata spat. "A machine should be elegant, light, compact, efficient. It should be a thing of beauty and craftsmanship! Pah! What pride can a human have in such a monster as a robot? Why, I hear they even allow the things to design and build *more* robots, which build still others! What can come about when an engineer lets his creations pass beyond personal control?"

I felt an eerie chill. Glad as I was that Jirata seemed, in his own style, to be emerging from his funk, I didn't like the direction this conversation was headed.

"What about that, Patty?" Phss'aah asked, turning to face me. "I have consulted much Erthumoi literature having to do with man-created machine intelligence, and there runs through much of it a thread of *warning*. Philosophers speak of the very fear Jirata expressed...calling it the 'Frankenstein Syndrome.' I do not know the origins of that term, but it has an apt sound for dread of destruction at the hands of one's own creations."

I nodded. "Fortunately, we Erthuma have a tradition of *liking* to frighten ourselves with scary stories, then finding ways to avoid the very scenario described. It's called Warning Fiction. Historians now credit that art form with our species' survival across the bomb-to-starship crisis time."

"Most interesting. But tell me, please, how did you come to choose a way to keep control over your creations? The Locrians certainly have trouble, whenever a clutch of male eggs is neglectfully laid outside the careful management of professional brooders, and the Samians have their own problems with gene-bred animals. How do you manage your robots then?"

How indeed? I wondered at the way this discussion had, apparently naturally, just happened upon a topic so deadly and coincidentally apropos to my other concerns.

"Well, one approach is to have the machines programmed with deeply coded fundamental operating rules, or robotic laws, which they cannot disobey without causing paralysis. This method serves well as a first line of defense, especially for simple machines.

"Unfortunately, it proved tragically inadequate at times, when the machines' growing intelligence enabled them to *interpret* those laws in new, rather distressing ways. Lawyer programs can be terribly tricky, we found. Today, unleashing a new one without proper checks is punishable by death."

"I understand. We Cephallons reserve that punishment for the lawyers themselves. I'll remember to advise my Council about this, if we decide to buy more of your high-end robots. Do continue."

"Well, one experimental approach, with the very brightest machines, has been to actually raise them as if they were Erthumoi children. In one of our confederations there are several thousand robots which have been granted provisional status as citizens—"

"Obscenity!" Jirata interrupted with a shout.

I merely shrugged. "It's an experiment. The idea is that we'll have little to fear from super-smart robots if they think of themselves as fellow Erthuma, who just happen to be built differently. Thus the hope is that they'll be as loyal as our grandchildren, and like our grandchildren, pose no threat even if they grow smarter than us."

"Fascinating!" the Cephallon cried. "But then, what happens when..."

Point after point, he spun out the logical chain. I was drawn into Phss'aah's intellectual enthusiasm. This was one of the reasons I entered the Diplomacy Guild, after all...in order to see familiar things in a new light, through alien eyes.

In his corner, I sensed even Jirata paying attention, almost in spite of himself. I had never before seen a Crotonite willing to sit and listen for so long. Perhaps this cruel and desperate experiment of theirs might actually bear fruit?

Then Jirata exploded with another set of disdainful curses, deriding one of Phss'aah's extrapolations. And I knew that, even if the experiment worked, it was going to be a long struggle.

Meanwhile, I felt the minutes flicker by, counting down to my encounter with Zardee.

Even with hyperdrive it's next to impossible to run anything like an "empire," in the ancient sense of the word. Not across starlanes as vast as the Galaxy. Left to their own devices, the scattered colony worlds—daughters of faraway Earth—would probably have all gone their own way long ago...each choosing its own path, conservative or outlandish, into a destiny all its own. Without opposition, we humans do tend to fraction our loyalties.

But there *was* opposition of sorts, when we emerged into space. The Other Five were already there. Strange, barely knowable creatures with technologies at first quite a bit ahead of ours. In playing a furious game of catchup, the Erthumoi worlds nearly all agreed to a pact...a loose confederation bound together by a civil service. Foremost among these shared institutions is the Diplomacy Guild.

And foremost among the rules agreed to by all signatories to the Essential Protocol is this—*not to undertake any unilateral actions which might unite other starfaring cultures against the Erthuma.* In my lifetime, four crises have loomed which caused strife over this provision—in which some community of Earth-descent was found to be engaged in dangerous or inciteful activities. Once, a small trade alliance of Erthumoi worlds almost provoked a Locrian Queendom to the point of violence. Each time, the episode was soothed over by the Guild, but on two of those occasions it took severe threats...arraying all of the offending community's Erthumoi neighbors in a united show of intimidation...before the reckless ones backed down.

Now I feared this was about to happen again. And this time, the conditions for quick and simple solution weren't encouraging. Zardee's system lay nearby a cluster of stars very rich in material resources, heavy elements given off by a spate of supernovas a few million years ago. Asteroids abundant in every desirable mineral were plentiful there.

Normally, this wouldn't matter much. The galaxy is not resource poor. We are not living in Earth's desperate Twenty-first Century, after all.

But what if one of the Six embarked on a population binge? Fresh among we Erthuma is memory of such a calamity. Earth's frail ecosystem is still recovering from the stress laid on her before we grew up and moved away to give our ancient mother a rest.

Of course the galaxy is vast beyond all planetary measure. Still, it doesn't take much computer time to extrapolate what could happen if any of the Six Starfarers decided to have fun making babies fast. Take our own species as an example. At human breeding rates typical of pre-spacefaring Earth, and given the efficiency of hyperdrive to speed colonization, we could fill every Earthlike world in the galaxy within a million years. Among the catastrophic consequences of such a hasty, uncontrolled expansion? Destruction of various lifeforms already in existence on those worlds.

And when our descendants run out of Earthlike planets—what then? Might they not chafe at the limitations on terraforming...the agreement among the Six only to convert dead worlds, never worlds already bearing life?

Consider the fundamental reason why there has never been a major war among the Six. It's their *incompatibility*, the fact that we find each other's worlds respectively unpleasant or deadly. That maintains the peace. But what if overpopulation started us imagining turning a high-CO_2 world into an oxy-rich planet, say. How would the Locrians react?

The same logic applied to the Other Five, each capable of its own population burst. Only their irascible temperaments and short lifespans keep the Crotonites from over-breeding, for instance. And the Locrians, first of the Six upon the spacelanes, admitted once in rare candor that the urge to spew forth a myriad of eggs is still powerful within them, constrained only by social and religious pressures.

The problem is this—what seems at first to be a stable situation is anything but stable. If the Locrians seem ancient from our Erthumoi perspective, by the clock of the *stars* they are nearly as recent as us. Three hundred thousand years is a mere eyeblink. The coincidence of all Six appearing virtually at the same time still has Erthumoi and Cephallon and Naxian scholars completely puzzled.

Yes, we're all at peace now. But computer simulations show utter calamity if any race looks about to take off on a population binge. And despite the Erthumoi monopoly on *self-aware* machines, all of the Six do have computers.

As my ship docked with the resplendent yacht of the King of Prongee, I looked off in the direction of the Gorch Cluster, with its rainbow of bright, metal-rich stars, and its promise of riches beyond what anyone alive might need.

Beyond present needs, yes. But perhaps not beyond what any one man might *want*.

Captain Smeet signalled the locks would be open in a few minutes. I took advantage of that interval to use a viewer and check in on my guests.

Within his tank, Phss'aah was getting another rub-down from his personal robot valet. Meanwhile, the Cephallon continued an apparent monologue.

"...*how mystics of several races explain the sudden and simultaneous appearance of starfarers in the galaxy. After all, is it not puzzling that awkward creatures such as we water dwellers, or the Samians, took to the stars, when so many skilled, mechanically minded races, such as the Lenglils and Forttts, never even thought of it, and rejected spaceflight when it was offered them?*"

From his corner of the room, Jirata flapped his wing nubs as if dismissing an unpleasant thought. "*It is obscene that any but those who personally fly should ever have achieved the heights.*"

I felt pleased. By Crotonite standards, Jirata was being positively outgoing and friendly. Like a good Cephallon diplomat, Phss'aah seemed not to notice the insults.

Captain Smeet signalled and I shut off the viewer reluctantly. There were times when, irritating as he was, Phss'aah could be fascinating to listen to. Now though, I had business to discuss, and no lesser matter, possibly, than the long-term survival of the Erthuma.

"My industrial robots are mining devices, pure and simple. They threaten no one. Not anyone!"

I watched the activity on the surface of the ninth planet. Although it was an airless body, crater-strewn and wracked by ancient lava seams, it seemed at first that I was looking down on the veldt of some prairie world, covered from horizon to horizon with roaming herds of ungulates. Though these ruminants were not living creatures, they moved as if they were. I even saw "mothers" pause in their grazing to "nurse" their "offspring."

Of course what they were grazing on was the dusty, metal-rich surface soil of the planet. Across their broad backs, solar collectors powered the conversion of those raw materials into refined parts. Within each of these browsing cows there grew a tiny duplicate of itself, which the artificial beasts then gave birth to, and then fed still more refined materials straight through to adulthood.

There was nothing particularly unusual about this scene so far. Back before we Erthuma achieved starflight it was machines such as these which changed our destiny, from paupers on a half-ruined world, short of resources, to beings wealthy enough to demand a place among the Six.

An ancient mathematician named John Von Neumann had predicted the eventuality of robots able to make copies of themselves. When such creatures were let loose on the Earth's moon, within a few years they had multiplied into the millions. Then, half of them were reprogrammed to make consumer goods instead—and suddenly our wealth was, compared to what it had been, as Twentieth Century man's had been to the Neanderthal.

But in every new thing there are always dangers. We found this out when some of the machines *refused* their new programming, and even began evading the harvesters.

"I see no hound mechanisms," I told King Zardee. "You have no dog-bots patrolling the herds, searching for mutants?"

He shrugged. "A needless expense. We're in a part of the galaxy low in cosmic rays, and our design is well shielded. I've shown you the statistics. Our new replicants demonstrate breakthroughs in both efficiency and stability."

I shook my head, unimpressed. Figures were one thing. Galactic survival was another matter entirely.

"Please show me how the mechanisms are fitted with their enabling and remote shut-down keys, your majesty. I don't see any robo-cowboys at work. How and when are the calves converted into adults? Are they called in to a central point?"

"It happens right out on the range," Zardee said proudly. "I see no reason to force every calf to go to a factory in order to get its keys. We program each cow to manufacture its calf's keys on the spot."

Madness! I balled my hands into fists in order to keep my diplomat's reserve. *The idiot!*

With deliberate calmness I faced him. "Your Majesty, that makes the keys meaningless. Their original and entire *purpose* is to make sure that no Von Neumann replicant device ever reaches maturity without coming to a central facility for inspection. It's our ultimate guarantee the machines remain under our control, and that their numbers do not explode."

Zardee laughed. "I've heard it before, this fear of fairy tales. My dear beautiful young woman, surely you don't take seriously those Frankenstein stories in the pulp flimsies, about replicants running away and devouring planets? Entire solar systems?" He guffawed.

I shrugged. "It does not matter how likely or unlikely such scenarios are. What matters is how the prospect *appears* to the Other Five. For twelve centuries we've downplayed this potential outcome of automation, because our best alienists think the Others would find it appalling. It's the reason replicant restrictions are written into the Protocols, Your Majesty."

I gestured at the massed herds down below. "What you've done here is utterly irresponsible..."

I stopped, because Zardee was smiling.

"You fear a chimera, dear diplomat. For I've already proven you have nothing to worry about in regards alien opinion."

"What do you mean?"

"I mean that I've *already* shown these devices to representatives of many Locrian, Samian, and Nexian communities, several of whom have already taken delivery of breeding stock."

My mouth opened and closed. "But...but what if they equip the machines with space-transport ability? You..."

Zardee blinked. "What are you talking about? Of *course* the models I provided are space adapted. Their purpose is to be asteroid mining devices, after all. It's a breakthrough! Not only do they reproduce rapidly and efficiently, but they also transport themselves wherever the customer sets his beacon..."

I did not stay to listen to the rest. Filled with anger and despair, I turned away and left him to stammer into silence behind me. I had calls to make, without any delay.

Maxwell took the news well, all considered.

"I've already traced three of the contracts," he told me by hyperwave. *"We've managed to get the Naxians to agree to a delay, long enough for us to lean on Zardee and alter the replicants' key system. The Naxians didn't understand why we were so concerned, though they could tell we were worried. Clearly they haven't thought out the implications yet, and we're naturally reluctant to clue them in.*

"The other contracts are going to be much harder. Two went to small Locrian Queendoms. One to a Samian solidity, and one to a Cephallon super-pod. I'm putting prime operatives onto each, but I'm afraid it's likely

the replicants will go through at least five generations before we accomplish anything. By then it will probably be too late."

"You mean by then some will have mutated and escaped customer control?" I asked.

He shook his head. *"According to Zardee's data, it should take longer than that to happen. No, by then I'm afraid our projections show each of the customers will be getting a handsome profit from his investment. The replicants will become essential to them, and impossible for us to regain control over."*

"So what do you want me to do?"

Maxwell sighed. *"You stay by Zardee. I'll have a sealed alliance of his Erthumoi neighbors for you by tomorrow, to get him deposed if he won't cooperate. Problem is, the cat's already out of the bag."*

I, too, had studied Ancient Earth Expressions during one of my lives. "Well, I'll close the barn door, anyway."

Maxwell did not bother with a salutation. He signed off more weary-looking than I'd ever seen him. And our labors were only just beginning.

The Cephallon and the Crotonite weren't exactly making love when I returned to the Guest Suite. (What an image!) Still, they hadn't murdered each other, either.

Jirata had become animated enough to attend to the internal environments controller in his corner of the chamber. He had dismantled the wall panel and was experimenting—creating a partition, then a bed-pallet, then an excretarium. Immersed in mechanical arts, his bat-like face almost took on a look of serenity as he customized the machinery, converting the insensitively mass-produced into something individualized, with character and uniqueness.

It was a rare epiphany, watching him so, and coming to realize that even so venal and disgusting a race as his could cause me wonder.

Oh, no doubt I was over-simplifying. Perhaps it was the replicant crisis that had me primed to feel this way. Ironically, though they were premier mechanics among the Six, the Crotonites' technical and scientific level was not particularly high. And they would be among the *last* ever to understand what a Von Neumann machine was about. From their point of view, autonomy and self-replication were for Crotonites, and in anyone or anything else they were obscenities.

I wondered if this experiment, which had caused a noble and high-caste creature of his community to be cast down so in a desperate attempt to learn new ways, would ever meet any degree of success. What would be the analogy for a person like me...to be surgically grafted crude gills instead of lungs, and dwell forever underwater, less mobile than a Cephallon? Would I, *could* I ever volunteer for so drastic an exile, even if my homeworld depended on it?

Yes, I conceded, watching Jirata work. There was nobility here, of a sort. And at least the Crotonites had not unleashed upon the galaxy a thing that could threaten all Six spacefarers...and the million other intelligent life forms without starships.

Phss'aah awakened from a snooze at the pool's surface and descended to face me. But it was his robot which spoke.

"Patty, my master hopes your business in this system has been successfully concluded."

"Alas, no. Crises develop lives of their own. Soon, however, I expect permission to confide this matter in him. When that happens, I hope to benefit from his insight."

Phss'aah acknowledged the compliment with a bare nod. Then he spoke for himself. "You must not despair, my young Erthumoi colleague. Look, after all, to your *other* accomplishments. I have decided, for instance, to go ahead and purchase a sample order of thirty thousand of these delightful machines for my own community. And if they work out there, perhaps others in the Cephallon Supreme Pod will buy. Is this not a coup to make you happy?"

For a moment I could not answer. What could I say to Phss'aah? That soon robots such as these might be so cheap that they could be had for a song? That soon a flood of wealth would sweep the galaxy, so great that no creature of any starfaring race would ever want for material goods?

Or should I tell him that the seeds strewn to grow this cornucopia were doomed to mutate, to change, to seek paths of their own...paths down which no foreseeing could follow?

"That's nice," I finally said. "I'm glad you like our machines. You can have as many as you need."

And I tried to smile. "You can have as many as you want."

Goodbye, Mir! (Sniff!)

All right, I had a special reason for wishing and hoping they might find a way to save the Mir space station. Let me explain why I mourn its demise.

Years ago, my astronaut pal Michael Foale was aboard Mir on that unlucky day when an exhausted cosmonaut blinked at the wrong moment, sending a teleoperated cargo craft crashing into the station.

For twenty heart-pounding minutes, Mike and the Russians scrambled to cut cables and seal hatches to save their lives before the air all went away. Abandoned in the Spektr capsule—which had been ripped open by the collision—were Mike's sleeping bag, toothbrush, family photos...and a manuscript copy of my novel *Brightness Reef,* which he had taken along as personal cargo. (Mike took galleys of *Glory Season* on a previous mission.)

Some time after they succeeded (miraculously) in stabilizing the rest of the damaged space station, Mike's wife phoned me to say they were sending up a Progress capsule with more supplies. She would enclose a new toothbrush and photos...and Mike was eager to finish the novel! Would I please send the second half to be included in the supply launch?

Of course I did, feeling honored to have the first novel ever rocketed skyward as "emergency equipment" for a space mission! (More powerful was my sense of gladness when Mike made it home at last, safe and sound.)

And yet, ever since then my thoughts kept drifting back to the *other* copy, the one Mike left inside Spektr when they sealed it for good. After rounding Earth every ninety minutes for over six years, was it the most-traveled novel ever? Were there any appreciable effects from time dilation? Exposed for all that period to hard vacuum and sleeting cosmic rays, would the manuscript show evidence of "criticism" by the Great Big Universal Editor in the Sky?

151

I hoped someday to find out. But alas, now we'll never know.

Is it petty of me to worry over a one-pound sheaf of paper, when the investors in MirCorp lost their shirts and some two-ton hunk of space hardware just missed plunging into downtown Brisbane? I guess so. Maybe it's just been my own way to feel a sense of private involvement, since it seems unlikely that I'll ever go to space in person.

Anyway, better a living book than an orbital relic, no? Then there's the notion that a burnt offering, in the form of a brief, flaming meteor, may be the best use for some manuscripts...

Some would say that's the best use for one of my books!

So be it. I bought a round of drinks when MIR went down. Let's all share fond hopes for much greater things to come.

*[**Editor's note:** On Friday, March 23, 2001, after 15 years of dedicated service to Russia, the venerable Mir space station was intentionally de-orbited following natural orbital decay and a sequence of three braking burns. It re-entered the Earth's atmosphere and crashed into the south Pacific Ocean. Anyone who finds any singed but readable manuscript pages floating around down there should let us know.]*

Editor's Note: This *"challenge"* and the two chapters which follow it are exclusive to this NESFA Press volume.

The Open-Ended Science Fiction Story:
A Challenge to New Colleagues

For some years I taught a writers' workshop. In addition to copious opinion-ated advice (see the essay containing *advice for neo-writers,* elsewhere in this volume), I also tried to offer students some unusual exercises, aimed at breaking whatever obstacles might stand in their path.

One trick long used by writing instructors has been the Team Round Robin. People who are unable to produce material for themselves some-times find the motivation if they are part of a group that will succeed only if all parties pitch in.

My version of the Team Round Robin has an unusual twist. The class divides into groups with a minimum of five members each, sorting themselves as members A, B, C, D, and E. Team member "A" gets to read an introductory chapter written by the teacher (in this case, me). "A" then adds a chapter of his or her own and passes the whole thing on to "B"...who adds a chapter and delivers the entire growing manuscript to "C"...and so on, round and round. With five or more members, the group is large enough to give every-one time for other works, with the round robin falling in each person's lap only once a month or so.

There are many variations on this trick. Some groups choose to let all members write all of their chapters before anyone critiques anything. I dis-agree. Critiquing as-you-go is the only way to keep learning. It also gives people plenty of familiarity with the growing story—the character's personality and problems and goals—and prevents members from forgetting important plot points.

An added element, contributing considerable enjoyment and insight, was to send the manuscript going around each group *in both directions.* Chapter One goes to **both** A and E. A passes two chapters on to B, while E passes two on to D. Member C gets to see both growing manuscripts—and adds to them—heading in both directions at once! Two distinctly different stories arise, demonstrating the wealth of plot possibilities that can emerge from any given seed.

All right, it's self-indulgent. Maybe even a bit silly. But fun. At least my own students thought so.

Which brings us to the following portion of a novel that I started even before publishing *Sundiver.* At this rate, it seems unlikely I'll ever do anything with it myself, but I did notice that Chapter Two leaves open so many different possible plots that it proved to be a remarkably fertile "seed"—an opening to offer to round robin teams, who took their resulting stories in an amazing range of directions!

As for the core idea in "The Imminent Dreams," a number of authors have lately produced works revolving around similar concepts—portraying the whole world suffering from an inundation of compelling visions. Several have done a much better job than I was doing, back in 1977. Anyway, who can write up all of their ideas?

So here it is: the David Brin work that never was and probably never will be. Teachers or workshops, go ahead and use this trick if you like. If your team does a great job...who knows? Above all, have fun.

The Imminent Dreams

1.

Blazing summer hadn't cooled much as the sun settled in the western canyons outside of St. George. The dry south-Utah heat lay down unmoving, pressing on a maze of cracked asphalt streets leading past mills and warehouses, baking the small crowd listening to a street-corner preacher. Standing on a rickety wooden crate, he wore a thick, black, pre-chaos wool suit; his only concession had been to loosen his thin tie. Rivulets of sweat darkened dust on the preacher's pale throat, where tendons flexed, taut as the temper of a hungry dog. His voice cracked as he faced the crowd of millworkers, grimy and tired after shift change.

"...for have we not *all* heard the calling draw of our Lord, beckoning us toward him? Though the Devil in each of us strives to mask the call, veiling its meaning in feigned promises and blasphemies, surely any of you must know that the true source, the true focus of all glory, can only be the ancient hills of Jerusalem!"

On his way to the warehouse where he worked, Josh paused to watch, shading his eyes against the western glare. The preacher's audience didn't seem exactly pleased—especially when he asked for donations to the Temple of the Rapture. Workers began peeling away, shaking their heads and muttering curses.

"Bloody, stinkin' Jerusalite..."

A second citizen snorted derisively, "Can't even make up their minds what part o' Jerusalem they're talkin' about. I hear half th' city's in ruins, from all the 'temples' they're building!"

Josh took their desultory tolerance as a good sign. Two years ago, the crowd might have killed the Jerusalite preacher—strung him from one of the broken lamp-posts in this once thoroughly Mormon town. When the craziness peaked, there had been hanging bodies in every city on Earth.

The black-coated stranger waved his arms, hoarsely shouting denunciations of the devil. Flexing his knees and making the wooden crate squeak ominously, he called down his version of the Word on the ears of the heathen.

"...Where have we come, after nearly a decade of visions? Confused to the inner core of our beings, by the dreams haunting every man, woman, and child on this globe? Yes, I know the leaders of the many branches your fractured church have told you that the visions come from the 'Angel Moroni.' Many of these sects call for the building of a 'temple' in that mosquito-infested Missouri swamp they call..."

His next words were drowned out by a muttered growl. The preacher only shouted louder to be heard.

"But these are only interpretations...delusions! Slowly, we have learned that dreams, all by themselves, cannot give the answer. For we color the message with the paints of our inner desires. We are receiving a message from Heaven—all of us have for years—but man, incorrigible, warps the images with foolish superstitions he has been taught to believe..."

The dour, dark-clothed citizens of St. George shifted their feet in tired anger. A few youths began searching the litter-strewn road for rocks. Josh wondered if the preacher's yellow Speaker's Permit—pinned crookedly to his shabby lapel—would be much use if he continued the harangue any longer.

Josh shifted his small bag of groceries and began edging his way around the crowd.

"No!" the preacher shouted. "We cannot rely on local, parochial viewpoints! The visions can only be interpreted in terms of the given word of the Lord...found only in the one book, the only book..."

Passing around the corner of a gray, cinderblock building, Josh felt relieved as the street-corner harangue faded. He was not anxious to witness local folks—mostly good people, he had found—revert to pre-Truce ways, giving the bible-thumper the martyrdom he seemed to be asking for. Half a block away he spotted a squad of Guardsmen hurrying in the opposite direction. Good. St. George might yet be spared a lynching.

Without much caring, Josh wondered how the tactless Jerusalite had managed to make it so far into Saints country alive. Perhaps people were just tired of the frenzy.

On the other hand, as the dreams grew daily in frequency and strength, maybe people were *more* willing to listen to alternatives—to heed other interpretations than those offered by their religious leaders—just in case.

Josh stopped at the federal-run Gentiles' Store, a block from the warehouse. He put down the bag of groceries, leafed forlornly through his ration book, hoping there would be one liquor coupon left, and sighed. Only starches. Fortunately, it was near the end of the month. He hefted the bag again, making the next block in good time.

The warehouse was a gray concrete building, windowless and massive...fireproof and mob-resistant. That had been important when he and Carl chose the place. A young Guard trooper stood at the steel door, assault rifle slung over a shoulder. He smiled as Josh approached, offering a clipboard for him to sign.

"Hello, Mr. Agate. Any luck finding supplies?"

"Hi, Jimmy. Yes, sort of. At least we'll eat till our orders come through."

"I'm sure it'll be soon. They say the northeast road opened up this morning."

"Hey, that's great news!"

It was, indeed. Every night—when he wasn't dreaming of the Imminence like everybody else—Josh found himself having more pleasant visions of normality in Minnesota, of home and wet lakes and white, pure snow. He prayed for orders that would take him east again.

"Here's something I managed to get in trade for a few extra sugar coupons, Jimmy." From the bag Josh pulled a box of powdered milk. "Maggie can use it for the baby."

The young soldier shifted awkwardly, as if uncertain he should accept. Then he took the box. "Gosh, Mr. Agate..."

"Think nothing of it. We all do what we can." Josh turned a key in the lock and entered through the massive door.

"I was watching on the outside monitor," Carl told him as he put the bag down by the kitchen area. "You didn't have to do that, you know. We could have used the sugar. Jimmy's due to be rotated soon. The next guard might have a sweet tooth."

Josh shrugged. "Drop it."

He wet a towel from the faucet and pressed the cool dampness against his neck.

Carl watched him. "So what's eating you?"

"Nothing."

"Come on. Something's bugging you. You're a regular sack of joy, today."

Josh stepped around his partner to collapse in the chair by his desk. "Last night I had an intense one. The images were placid—you know, the Garden of Brahma kind."

"Hm, peaceful."

"Yeah. But there's a Jerusalite on the street, shouting fire and brimstone. I can feel the words in my skull, like wasp eggs, I'll probably dream about the Temple of the Rapture tonight—tribulation and curtains of fire!" He finished with mimicry of a proselyte's warble.

Carl looked back at him blankly, missing even the weak joke. Josh turned to leaf through the papers on his desk.

"What're you looking for?" Carl asked.

Josh noticed what he was doing and stopped. "Jimmy said the road's open again. Hoping I got mail."

"There was a delivery. Nothing from your folks, though."

Josh nodded, resignedly. Personal mail was still a shambles. "Anything for me from Washington?"

Carl's big, tarsier-like eyes squinted. "You mean personally? What you expecting? A slot on a Greeter Committee? Maybe a docket on a Seeker Ship? Two chances of that ever happening—fat, and slim!"

Carl chortled. His own jokes he inevitably got.

Josh laid his chin in a hand. Of course Carl was right. Both the feds and the UN Emergency Agency had already staffed all the official Contingency Groups. There wouldn't be any more positions available for the duration. He might as well never have applied. Stuck out here in a dead-end job, a *depressing* job, getting ready to spend the next umpteen years of his life taking care of neomorts.

At least it's a job, Josh reminded himself.

"So there wasn't any mail," he said heavily.

"Did I say that? I just said there wasn't anything special for you. *We* did get some mail, though," Carl sat on the edge of the desk and flipped a big manila envelope over. It landed with a smacking sound, finishing in a dull clunk. Josh noticed that the envelope had been re-used. Things must be bad even in Washington.

Probably more damn paperwork about Protecting the Rights of the Brain-Living Impaired, he thought. Ignoring the envelope for the moment, he spoke pensively.

"You know, there are still some places with good jobs for biophysiologists. I could go down to San Diego and join the folks talking to dolphins...or L.A. and join the Awaiters. I hear they'll take anyone with a theory about what little green men will want to eat."

Carl tapped the envelope. "Quit being an ass. Open it."

Josh sighed and ripped open the wax seal. He emptied the package onto his desk.

There was a letter—on fresh stationery—from the Department of Health, addressed to him. He tossed it aside for the moment. It was only Orders, after all.

A fresh ration book was the next thing he found. Dated from the first of the next month, its magenta border signified rather high priority and large quantities, but Josh knew better than to think that meant good news. When the government turned generous, it was time to count your fingers and toes.

There were other documents, including a blue federal transit pass, countersigned by the governors of California and Utah, allowing him, by name, to transport and carry across state lines two dozen "refugees" who were legally unable to speak for themselves, along with five drivers and five attendants to accompany and care for the so-called "neomorts."

"It came this morning," Carl said. "I'm to stay here and prepare for the new arrivals. So I guess you won the draw."

Josh snorted. Won, indeed. He had won the right to leave dour, depressing St. George, only to step right into the craziest part of a country teetering on the edge of insanity.

"The governor of California is delighted to get rid of the neomorts," Carl went on. "He's providing five reconditioned RVs to carry them and the volunteer attendants. You'll get an escort to the state line— you can pick your point of egress, Blythe, Needles, or Yuma, then swing north and bring the caravan here."

Josh looked up. "I can't leave through Reno or Bishop?"

"Nope. Governor wants you out of the state as soon as possible. In fact, you're to avoid those routes on the way in, as well...to keep 'rumors' from spreading."

"Great," Josh said sourly. "I can choose between radiation, the weird zones, or Indian Nation! Are you sure you wouldn't rather just hold onto this ration book. I probably won't get to get much use out of it."

Carl made a quick smile, as if to show that he could appreciate a joke as well as the next guy. "Ha ha. Just don't lose those passes. And hold onto the gold for as long as you can."

"Gold?"

"In the envelope. In case you go by the Indian Nation route. They let some convoys buy their way through, to pick up hard cash. There are still plenty of things they want to buy to outfit that 'great kiva' they're building down there."

Josh hardly heard him. He shook the reinforced envelope...and suddenly three large golden coins rolled out, landing heavily on the table.

"Son of a bitch!" Josh breathed as he looked at the shiny round disks, gleaming and untarnishable. He paid no heed as Carl talked on. Josh looked at the way light glowed along the ridges, grooves, and highlights of the golden coins. Two Jesse Jackson twenties and a great big fifty-dollar piece. The Second White House, on the reverse of that coin, seemed surrounded by a faint glow. He turned it over. An aura gleamed about the face of Rush Limbaugh, leaving no room for ears.

It wasn't the value of the coins, but something in their symbolism that had Josh all but hypnotized. Something about them that filled him with a shivering sense not unlike déjà vu...as if there were meaning in the images that he could almost interpret. It felt much like the intimations that almost every human alive had felt in sleep for most of a decade—an impression that somebody or something was on its way. When it arrived, it would change everything, forever.

Josh shook himself free of the power of the reflections, just as he had fought the dreams that the Awaiters called "the Star Message," the Krishnans called the "drum of Shiva," and that the Jerusalites described as "the fringe of the Robe of the Holy Spirit."

"...There'll be volunteer nurses waiting in LA to help with the move," Carl was saying. "Some of 'em were with the Neomorts from the beginning, ever since the Western Institute began experiments with the brain-dead. The drivers were selected from people willing to give anything to get out of California."

"When do I leave?" Josh asked, shaking away the last shreds of the brief trance.

"Tonight." Carl rose to his feet. "The Jeep's already loaded with 60 gallons of gas. You can join a convoy, if you like, or strike out on your own. You'll make better time if you do. Anyway, you're to be out of town by morning."

Josh sighed. "I don't suppose anyone thought of sending me by air."

Carl laughed. "The boy never does stop dreaming about his own importance! Do you know what a certified, mind-stable pilot charges these days? My lad, hubris will be your undoing yet!"

Josh nodded. But he knew, tonight he would dream of being important enough to be allowed to fly.

And maybe he would also dream of two dozen quiet—but not inert—bodies, waiting in Los Angeles—for him to be their Moses and deliver them to this promised land. Bodies, and brains that performed in ways that no human mind had ever performed before.

He looked about the huge empty warehouse, where the neomorts would reside through the emergency—or presumably until their autonomic systems simply stopped functioning.

The slabs lay empty, waiting.

Josh felt a queer shiver.

2.

Fifty miles south of St. George, on the highway leading toward the city that had once been named Phoenix, Josh pulled over to the side of the road and got out to inspect a washout. A recent flood had torn a rather large gouge out of the asphalt. It cut right across the road. Apparently quite recently, since none of the intermittent convoys had performed even makeshift repairs.

It didn't look like too much for his Jeep to handle. But there was another barrier in the way. Wedged tightly at an angle with a broken axle was a big, garishly-painted panel truck.

Josh felt his hand go to the revolver at his hip. He chided himself for a brief paranoia. After all, southern Utah was supposed to be pacified after Operation Canyonlands Cleanup, two years ago.

Still, he moved carefully and quietly around the van, as he looked around carefully for signs of the former occupants.

Inside, the van was a jumble of clothes and assorted colorful knick-knacks. A guitar lay smashed by the front seats. Near the open panel door, Josh found what he thought were droplets of fresh blood.

He touched the drops. They were still slightly sticky.

Josh blinked suddenly. How long had he been staring at the red smudges? He had to watch himself. Was he becoming more susceptible to daytime mini-trances?

"Don't you move a muscle," a voice spoke from behind Josh. "Don't turn aroun'. I gotta gun."

Josh straightened, cursing himself softly. How long had he let his guard down? Where had the fellow been hiding?

He turned, very slowly and carefully, and saw two rather dirty, disheveled men. One, a young man with a bad complexion and long, greasy locks, waved the muzzle of a slightly rusty rifle at Josh.

"I tol' you not to turn around!" he shouted.

Josh shrugged as he raised his hands. "And take your word for it you had a gun? What if you hadn't, and I just stood there letting you grab mine? Pretty dumb, wouldn't you say?"

The second man, a redhead with a curly beard, chuckled. But when the younger one yelled at him to shut up, he licked his lips nervously and clutched the axe in his hands.

The greasy brunette looked Josh over. "You're a doctor, aren't you?" he asked.

Josh considered quickly. If they thought he was a real physician, they might be eager for his services. It could save him a long walk, or a bullet in the belly. "Well, yes...I guess for all practical purposes..."

"Thought so. Saw your bag back in your jeep. We got a girl with a broke arm an' a busted head, up there in the shade by them rocks. You bein' a doctor's proof enough that Mellissa's got the power to Call, even when she's delirious.

"Anyway, you fix her up an' we'll do you a real favor. We'll take you with us when we go off in yer Jeep, 'stead of leavin' you stranded out here."

Josh shrugged. There was no answer possible. Protesting would obviously be useless. Besides, he really ought to do what he could for the girl, if she was hurt.

Red Beard walked up cautiously and removed Josh's revolver, then backed away again.

"So where will you be taking me?" Josh asked casually. "You can't be headed for the Arizona border. The feds are back in control, there. And beyond them is Indian Nation."

Long Hair motioned for him to start walking, up toward the Jeep. Red Beard answered him.

"We're goin' to the holy places west of here, in the canyons and the Land of Enlightenment."

Josh stopped, stunned. "The Weird Zones? You can't mean that! You must be crazy!"

Long Hair nudged him with the rifle.

"Move! You may be skeptical now, but you'll thank us when we meet God, and the sky turns into one big rainbow."

News From 2025:
A Glitch in Medicine Cabinet 3.5

Through its Hoechst-Monsanto subsidiary, Fuzzypal Inc announced today that a potentially serious bug will delay release of the next version of the conglomerate's lead product, *Medicine Cabinet®*.

"There is no cause for alarm," assured company spokesman Chow leLee. "Rumors of a virus in the template are overstated. We just want to tweak the security parameters a bit, before offering a free update to consumers."

The news sent Fuzzypal stock down a few points, but analysts don't expect serious losses for the wetware giant. Jacques Peabody of Analyque Zaire explained—"People want the features they were promised in version 3.5. When it comes to combining all the elements—from flesh-editing to headsheets to self-image processing—only *Medicine Cabinet* offers everything in one convenient package. Don't forget who invented chemsynth-in-a-box."

This comment brought jeers from FreeFloatingConsensusFive, a pseudonymical leader of the Open Organism Movement, seeking to replace Fuzzypal's proprietary system with universal free access to the registry of identified organic templates (RIOT).

"By strangling competition and colluding with government so-called *safety* agencies, *Medicine Cabinet* holds everyone back from where we could have been, by now. Haven't you noticed that every version has glitches that prevent people from synthesizing with true inventive freedom?

"That's why almost everybody who owns a home-chem unit sticks to the same ten thousand pathetic and boring organic compounds. The same pseudo-spices, plaque inhibitors, fatsplitters, muscle-stims, endorphins and sense-enhancers. Never before has human creativity been so thoroughly stifled!"

FreeFloatingConsensusFive was especially harsh in hisherits

condemnation of the Telemere Act, which mandates that most Medicine Cabinets come equipped with sensors to lock out healthy users under thirty years of age.

"There are over a million teens and tweens using illegally rewired units today, proving that the so-called Age-Socialization Curve is a myth. The worst thing you see on the street nowadays is the snake-skin fad, some watergills and other harmless retro-devo stuff. No poisoned aquifers or fancy plagues...at least none that a roffer can't detect with his sniffer and cancel with a quickie-antidote.

"No one worries about psychotropics in their BigMacs anymore."

When we asked the gov't public safety mavens about this, they just dittoed us their standard white paper—already five hours old—insisting that desktop chemishing is safe, when part of a conscientiously applied program of molecular hygiene and regular protective care. Rumors of a sniff-proof viral protein coat were dismissed as hysterical fantasy.

"*I predicted this,*" commented Bruce Sterling, a retired old fart, from his observation pedestal at the ROF enclave in Corpus Christi Under. The vener-*i*-able futurist seemed about to say more, but was interrupted by a Greg Bear partial, transmitted from a hibernation cave near Vancouver D.C.

"*No, you didn't,*" growled the partial. "*I did!*"

Thankfully, the rest of its remarks were quashed under injunction by a thoroughly embarrassed anonymous tribune, suspected to be yet another reminent ROF.

Meanwhile, Fuzzypal announced that it is proceeding with plans to acquire Gelatinous Cube in a hostile takeover. "Our dark minions are on the way," trumped Fuzzypal chief Check Portal, standing before a regiment of selfmobile stock certificates, each one double-recrypted and armed with hyperoxygenated proxies.

"We need Web technology in order to survive as a bloatcorp. So GC had better give it up or face a major ink bath."

We asked a seer-oracle at Analyque Zaire to psychologue this statement.

"I guess the day we all expected has come at last. Check Portal's mind has totally humptied. All the king's centaurs won't patch it this time.

"Anyway, the Web is just a passing fad," commented M'Peri N'Komo more soberly. "In the long run, nobody is going to want to remain fused to a continent-spanning network of sticky strands, no matter how many advantages it offers. There's just too much individual—or cranky monkey—in most of us to sit still for so long.

"If we wanted that sort of thing, we would still be squatting in dark rooms, watching TV and typing stupid chat-noises on the Old Internet," hesheit concluded. "Thank heaven-on-earth we managed to see through *those* traps in time!

"I'll bet you a year's supply of fresh flint nodules that this web-craze will turn out to be more of the same."

Seeking a New Fulcrum:
Parapsychology and the Need
to Believe in a New Transcendence

Lately we've been hearing more from a corner of the New Age that was strangely quiet for a while. *Parapsychology.* This perennial favorite keeps returning to grab the public's imagination, so maybe it's time to try for a little perspective.

Let me admit from the start that I have a murky and conflicted relationship with the quaint concept of "psi."

On the one hand, trained as a physical scientist, I find little to admire about a field that has almost nothing to show after two hundred years of strenuous and diligent effort. Every year, the claims that are made by proponents shrink as our horizons of measurement advance. A field that once purported to find treasures, cure illnesses, convey infinite energy and speak with the dead now craves marginal evidence for a few statistical anomalies in some randomized card tricks. That's pretty hard to respect.

On the other hand, I now make my living as a creator of futuristic worlds in literature, film and other popular media where "what-if?" can be all the justification you need! And despite my reputation as a "hard" science fiction author—known for technically well-grounded extrapolation—I nevertheless have been known to write stories in which characters use telepathy, clairvoyance, telekinesis and the like. (I certainly treat psi with more respect than the silly notion of UFOs! For more on *that* weird mania, see: http://www.davidbrin.com/)

Is it contradictory for me to portray our descendants using methods that I find implausible here-and-now? Why do I find it irresistible, as a novelist, to ponder future eras when people may communicate with each other without words and manipulate objects without tools?

For the same reason that generations of true-believers invested so much time, money and passion, chasing faint, tantalizing clues and self-deceptions in a fruitless search for manipulative powers of the mind. Because such powers go to the heart of what humans deeply *want!*

Take my own background. Surrounded at an early age by delusionally illogical adults, I recall first hearing about telepathy and trying desperately to *use* it for months, in a futile attempt to comprehend or get through to the volatile, powerful and unpredictable beings around me. Oh, I don't relate this anecdote in order to draw sobs; many people had similar experiences, and that's the point. Most, perhaps all of us, have yearned at times for some shortcut to understanding our fellows. Trapped for an entire life in just one head, one subjective reality, what human being hasn't wondered—

*"What makes **him** tick?"*

"Does she like the things I like?"

*"Does he experience the color **red** the same way that I do?"*

"How can I persuade others to see the real me?

Testimony for this yearning can be found in the extraordinary complexity of human language, so vastly more sophisticated than anything needed for simple hunting or gathering. It must have been advantageous for our ancestors who gained a leg up in conversation, persuasion and reciprocal understanding. Much of human progress has involved developing newer and better means of communication.

Some invent telephones and internets. Others—especially in the long era before electricity—would take peyote and seek communion via a spirit world. Is that so surprising? Wouldn't you have done the same thing?

Take another basic human imperative...our incessant drive to alter or control the environment around us. Is it "telekinesis" when we cause physical objects to move and react, far away, with a touch on a keypad or a word spoken over the phone? Of course not. And yet, a Seventeenth Century cosmopolitan like Descartes might draw no other conclusion, if he witnessed a modern person activating the house-lights with a finger's touch.

If I recall correctly, John Henry Newman claimed that human concepts of causation derive directly or indirectly from the experience of intending to do something physical, then seeing and feeling our body do it. If so, it's easy to see how we might start hoping to see an intended effect just by *looking* at something...or someone. In fact, now that we spend hours with things like TV remotes and computer mouses, we have a visceral experience of causing effects in remote objects outside our body, without there being a viscerally obvious mechanical explanation.

Already there are devices that respond to crude aggregate brainwave patterns, in order to activate machines at the command of physically handicapped people. Is it a stretch to imagine more sophisticated versions that will focus on narrowly localized states within the frontal or temporal lobes, responding to specific volitional cues...in other words, *choices?* Might our descendants use such tools routinely, commanding advanced machines to perform intricate tasks simply by wishing it to happen?

If telekinesis and telepathy don't yet exist, they surely *will*, as technology enables us to get more of what we want, quicker and with less expenditure of our precious attention or effort. (Isn't that what technology is for?) Our great-grandchildren will send messages by thinking them. What's to stop them? They will cause objects to move and the environment to change around them, by the efficient means of wanting that it be so.

The first few generations will know about the machinery in the walls, that make these things happen. Will later generations take it all for granted? Or even forget the machinery is there?

Perhaps parapsychology is something other than its enthusiasts imagine. Not a trail leading back to ancient wisdom, but more of a *prediction*. More an expression of human desire than an exploration of existing or ancient talents.

Well, that's one perspective. And certainly I do not expect psi enthusiasts to accept it! Because there are other forces than mere wishful thinking at work here—factors motivating some to look away from the future and fixate on the past. Nostalgia. Romanticism. Resentment of scientific authority...while yearning to *become* the authority on something wonderful. Something to compete with the scientific world that some outsiders malign as soul-less.

At the lowest level, a hunger for publicity — or profit — can propel garish and often unscrupulous claims. It is a realm rife with charlatans, who make money by persuading others to hand over the contents of their wallets. (True psychics would make it off the stock market or by finding buried treasure, no?)

I'm not saying that all enthusiasts are like this. Many are sincere. A few even want to legitimize the field, to bring parapsychology in from the wilderness and make it part of the scientific process that has brought us so far in just a few hundred years.

Alas, the behavior of a more gaudy element drives many scientists to over-react by spurning the entire conceptual realm of direct mental control...even mental control over our own bodies! Professionals who openly admit the necessity of using placebos in drug experiments will, perhaps in the same breath, deny any possibility the a patient's emotional self-image might directly affect the course of disease! It's an excessively narrow-minded reaction that does them—and science—no credit.

Let me shift gears and talk briefly about the Continuity Expression.

It's a simple trick of geometry and physics that we learned about early as undergrads, at Caltech. You draw a box in space, perhaps containing some matter. To keep things interesting, let's say that the material is in motion, a fluid or gas. Maybe a river. Or light flowing from the sun. First carefully measure what's inside the box. Also, keep an accurate accounting of anything that crosses all six faces of the box, entering or leaving through the boundary.

Assuming that nothing is created or destroyed, the resulting expression must balance. If a net *outward* flow is seen, the total amount of stuff remaining inside should decrease by exactly the amount that departed. It's a simple, rather obvious concept that enables us to derive everything from gas dynamics to the transfer of photons in the solar interior. The Continuity Expression has been essential to developing an understanding of particle physics within the blazing targets of high-energy accelerators.

Now add in the notion of *information* in the formal sense, as both a thermodynamic and a mathematical property. Some physicists get all spooky about information, especially down at the level of the quantum. But on one thing they agree. It takes *energy* to convey information from one patch of space to another. And most of them feel that information must obey relativity—the speed-of-light limit. In fact, information is nearly always carried, across any appreciable distance, by some form of electromagnetic radiation.

Combine these two notions and you quickly see another reason why scientists have trouble with parapsychology. Telepathy and other psi phenomena appear to involve transfers of information from one person or place to another. One individual's brain state gets partially transposed to another brain, far away. And so on. Neurons fire that might not otherwise have fired, as the recipient thinks some new thoughts that weren't generated from within or by normal sensory input. Something *entered* the second brain to stimulate these changes.

But what entered? If we carefully eliminate all the mundane stimuli of radio, sound, light, smell...what's left? Mystics claim *unknown channels beyond the ken of science,* but the Continuity Expression lets you check for unknown channels, indirectly! By measuring even minute changes within a given volume that cannot be explained in normal ways. It's how x-rays and radioactivity were discovered.

You want open-mindedness? Physicists have looked for other, un-known channels. They've looked *hard*, with the incentive of a Nobel for anyone who finds one! The Continuity Expression lets them trawl for clues either within the box or crossing the boundaries.

If it's strong enough to affect neurons in a systematic way, don't you think they would have found it by now?

Oh, that won't set back the enthusiasm of a true believer. For example, many still hold faith in the old mind-matter dualism of Descartes. Neurons react *to* the mind, not vice versa. And the mind operates on a plane of its own.

Sound silly and old-fashioned? I agree, sort of. And yet the contrarian in me has an answer. If you stretch your imagination, there could be some support for the dualist view!

Picture some future time when thinking beings may occupy simu-lated software realms within some vast cybernetic space. Realms that emulate reality with fine attention to every detail. We don't yet know how far simulation can be extended, or whether there are inherent lim-its. Some very smart people believe there aren't, in which case there's no guarantee that *you,* reading this paragraph right now, aren't living in such a simulation. (Two SF stories in this volume study this theme.)

What is reality? It's an old sophomoric conundrum, one that only gets more irritatingly relevant as time goes on. I fear it may become *the* cliche of the next century. Get used to it.

In a software world, brain-body dualism might easily be true! So could "hidden channels," especially if some denizens of the simula-tion occasionally gain access to bits of lower-level language code.

Again, we can't disprove any of this...and if it ain't true now, it could plausibly become true, tomorrow.

Want another reason for the ongoing fascination with psi? For some people it may have to do with the disappointing state of our *fulcra*.

A fulcrum is a pivot that enables a lever to work. Archimedes said, "Give me a fulcrum, a lever that is long enough, and a place to stand...I will move the world."

Today, even while trying to solve pressing contemporary problems, some of us also pause and dream even bigger dreams than Archimedes had. To visit faraway stars. To terraform planets. To commune with whales or aliens. To acquire infinite supplies of energy, resources, and lifespan.

Back in the middle of the 20th Century—a time of wretched de-spair on many levels—some of these dreams actually seemed within

grasp. Proponents of atomic power claimed their *fulcrum* would eliminate poverty, reshape the City of Tomorrow and blast huge, Orion-
Class spacecraft—bearing whole colonies—to Mars. Even Einstein's
speed limit still had a provisional quality, sounding more like an advi-
sory notice than The Law.

Today, physics still seems exciting in abstract. Finding the Higgs
boson is neat, all right. Black holes in the center of the galaxy? Terrific.
I just love pictures from the Space Telescope and salivate over the idea
of orbiting interferometers.

But none of those things offer any obvious new fulcrum—no apparent way to vastly expand the range of cool things we can *do!* Most
of the assertive spirit of derring-do has already moved on to biology, a
field that seems rife with new ways to alter human reality, both for
well and ill. But 21st Century biology is so large-scale, so expensive
and massively *corporate,* that its new fulcra appear to come at the price
of sacrificing all individualism or romance.

Wouldn't it be nice to have a shortcut? A way around all the com-
mittees and buildings and laboratories and budgets and accountability structures of Big Scale Science? How about a *personal-scale fulcrum,*
that anybody with the right talents or connections might cobble
together...or even create out of sheer will power, using the almost-in-
finite power of desire?

Oh, yes. I understand the wish. The need. The reason why science doesn't always satisfy. Sometimes mere pictures from space just
don't seem enough. It would be thrilling to learn that some cheap and
easy route had been found, to evade the prim rules of Einstein and
Boltzmann and the daunting problem of cosmic scale.

Hey, where do I sign up?

Oh, I could go on and on. There are so many implications of telepathy alone, not to mention all the other purported psychic marvels...is
it any wonder that I toy with them, now and then, in works of fiction?
Even while I cast a skeptical eye toward them, in my role as a licensed
Doctor of Natural Philosophy?

In fact, I confess sharing some of my colleagues' hostility—at a mild
level—toward the whole notion of parapsychology. Not because I think
it's a Great Big Threat To Rational Thinking or that a few crackpot
dreamers will bring the house of science crashing down. (What panicky silliness!) But for another reason altogether.

When you get right down to it, I dislike psi because *I don't think
it's anything real grownups should be bothering with, right now.*

Even if the next wave of super-cautious parapsychology experiments do manage to replicate some statistical anomalies in a card trick, or reproduce vague drawings at-a-distance, or even find a treasure or two...I cannot respect a field that tries to resurrect the *elitism of magic.* The belief that some special sub-race of beings living among us have inherent powers that raise them high above the common herd—not just in the quantitative way that genius and hard work can lift you, but in the profoundly qualitative sort of way that a speaking man stands apart from a mute chimpanzee.

That is what the romantic impulse has always boiled down to, folks, ever since way back when Byron and Shelley rejected the egalitarianism of the Enlightenment. All the way to the mystics of the Nazi SS, extolling their vision of a master race. Altogether too much of the so-called New Age has a nauseatingly similar agenda—to flatter believers that they are special, loftier than others, because of some quality deep within that a very few possess.

Not something learned or earned or created through hard cooperative work, but a trait of specialness that smolders within, waiting for the right incantation to ignite it in full glory...or full fury.

Didn't we have enough of that during all the thousands of years that romanticism ruled the zeitgeist of every human culture? Doesn't that appalling history - in dismal, ignorant, hierarchical societies— tell us something important? History warns that romanticism, for all its obvious *artistic* appeal, can be utterly poisonous when it infects a society's political structure, or the halls where earnest people study the hard difference between *true* and *false.*

Science and the other fruits of Enlightenment offer a much better way.

Oh yes, the sheer egotistical roar of romance can be alluring! Each of us, trapped forever in a single subjective theater, wants to believe we're special, the hero of the story. Some get to find a sense of importance from doing useful work. Many are lucky enough to participate in the adventure of science, or some other endeavor that contributes to a new kind of mature, shared adventure. Millions achieve value simply by working hard, being good citizens, and raising a generation of people slightly better than themselves.

Others yearn for something to raise them up out of the herd. Out of mundanity, to a realm of genuine specialness. Intervention by a power from the outside...or a power from within. What's the difference? Either way, the fantasy offers hope. And hope spawns belief.

To sum up, parapsychology boils down to a whole bunch of metaphors. (Doesn't everything?)

To an angry or frustrated romantic, psi can seem a means of transcending dreary everyday life, leaving the mundane neighbors behind.

To those focused on the future, it suggests cool powers that our children may take for granted, mediated by loyal machines. Powers that will democratize and elevate everybody.

To those focused on the past, psi is yet another auspicious magic, returning to Ancient Wisdom, snubbing the prim, book-keeping tyranny of the Continuity Expression, and its coldly dispassionate ilk.

To a frightened little child, psi may seem to offer a way to communicate and understand.

To a science fiction author, psi can offer a way out of some awful chapter, when you've written the hero into a jam and there seems to be no other...

Well, never mind that last bit. In fact, forget I mentioned it!

Anyway, when you get right down to it, we do love our charlatans and their tricks, don't we? Maybe that's the biggest reason why some myths keep on breathing with a life of their own.

So just ignore that man behind the curtain, pulling all the levers....

...and pay heed, instead, to the Great and Powerful Oz.

And now an item written especially for NESFA Press and the Boskone convention…in honor of Boston…

A Professor at Harvard

Dear Lilly,

This transcription may be a bit rough. I'm dashing it off quickly for reasons that should soon be obvious.

Exciting news! Still, let me ask that you please don't speak of this, or let it leak till I've had a chance to put my findings in a more academic format.

Since May of 2001, I've been engaged to catalogue the Thomas Kuiper Collection, which Harvard acquired in that notorious bidding war a couple of years ago, on eBay. The acclaimed astronomer-philosopher had been amassing trunkloads of documents from the late Sixteenth and early Seventeenth Centuries—individually and in batches—with no apparent pattern, rhyme or reason. Accounts of the Dutch Revolution. Letters from Johannes Kepler. Sailing manifests of ports in southern England. Ledgers and correspondence from the Italian Inquisition. Early documents of Massachusetts Bay Colony and narratives about the establishment of Harvard College.

The last category was what most interested the trustees, so I got to work separating them from the apparent clutter. That is, it *seemed* clutter, an unrelated jumble…till intriguing patterns began to emerge.

Let me trace the story as it was revealed to me, in bits and pieces. It begins with the apprenticeship of a young English boy named Henry Stephens.

Henry was born to a family of petit-gentry farmers in Kent, during the year 1595. According to parish records, his birth merited noting as *mirabilis*—he was premature and should have died of the typhus that claimed his mother. But somehow the infant survived.

He arrived during a time of turmoil. Parliament had passed a law that anyone who questioned the Queen's religious supremacy, or persistently absented himself from Anglican services, should be imprisoned or banished from the country, never to return on pain of death. Henry's father was a leader among the "Puritan" dissenters in one of England's least tolerant counties. Hence, the family was soon hurrying off to exile, departing by ship for the Dutch city of Leiden.

Leiden, you'll recall, was already renowned for its brave resistance to the Spanish army of Philip II. As a reward, Prince William of Orange and the Dutch parliament gave the city a choice: freedom from taxes for a hundred years, or the right to establish a university. Leiden chose a university.

Here the Stephens family joined a growing expatriate community—English dissenters, French Huguenots, Jews and others thronging into the cities of Middelburg, Leiden, and Amsterdam. Under the Union of Utrecht, Holland was the first nation to explicitly respect individual political and religious liberty and to recognize the sovereignty of the people, rather than the monarch. (Both the American and French Revolutions specifically referred to this precedent.)

Henry was apparently a bright young fellow. Not only did he adjust quickly—growing up multilingual in English, Dutch and Latin—but he showed an early flair for practical arts like smithing and surveying.

The latter profession grew especially prominent as the Dutch transformed their landscape, sculpting it with dikes and levees, claiming vast acreage from the sea. Overcoming resistance from his traditionalist father, Henry managed to get himself apprenticed to the greatest surveyor of the time, Willebrord Snel van Leeuwen—or *Snellius*. In that position, Henry would have been involved in a geodetic mapping of Holland—the first great project using triangulation to establish firm lines of location and orientation—using methods still applied today.

While working for Snellius, Henry apparently audited some courses offered by Willebrord's father—Professor Rudolphus Snellius—at the University of Leiden. Rudolphus lectured on *"Planetarum Theorica et Euclidis Elementa"* and evidently was a follower of Copernicus. Meanwhile the son—also authorized to teach astronomy—specialized in the *Almagest* of Ptolemaeus!

The Kuiper Collection contains a lovely little notebook, written in a fine hand—though in rather vulgar Latin—wherein Henry Stephens describes the ongoing intellectual dispute between those two famous Dutch scholars, Snellius elder and younger. Witnessing this intellectual tussle first-hand must have been a treat for Henry, who would have known how few opportunities there were for open discourse in the world beyond Leiden.

But things were just getting interesting. For at the very same moment that a teenage apprentice was tracking amiable family quarrels over heliocentric versus geocentric astronomies, some nearby Dutchman was busy crafting the world's first telescope.

The actual inventor is unknown—secrecy was a bad habit practiced by many innovators of that time. Till now, the earliest mention was in September 1608, when a man "from the low countries" offered a telescope for sale at the annual Frankfurt fair. It had a convex and a concave lens, offering a magnification of seven. So I felt a rising sense of interest when I read Henry's excited account of the news, dated six months earlier (!), offering some clues that scholars may find worth pursuing.

Later, though. Not today. For you see, I left that trail just as soon as *another* grew apparent. One far more exciting.

Here's a hint: word of the new instrument, flying across Europe by personal letter, soon reached a certain person in northern Italy. Someone who, from description alone, was able to re-invent the telescope and put it to exceptionally good use.

Yes, I'm referring to the Sage of Pisa. Big *G* himself! And soon the whole continent was abuzz about his great discoveries—the moons of Jupiter, lunar mountains, the phases of Venus and so on. Naturally, all of this excited old Rudolphus, while poor grumpy Willebrord muttered that it seemed presumptuous to draw cosmological conclusions from such evidence. Both Snellius *patris* and *filio* agreed, however, that it would be a good idea to send a representative south, as quickly as possible, to learn first-hand about any improvements in telescope design that could aid the practical art of surveying.

So it was that in the year 1612, at age seventeen, young Henry Stephens of Kent headed off to Italy...

...and there the documented story stops for a few years. From peripheral evidence—bank records and such—it would appear that small amounts were sent to Pisa from Snel family accounts in the form of a "stipend." Nothing large or well-attributed, but a steady stream that lasted until about 1616, when "H. Stefuns" abruptly reappears in the employment ledger of Willebrord the surveyor.

What was Henry up to all that time? One might squint and imagine him counting pulse-beats in order to help time a pendulum's sway. Or using his keen surveyor's eye to track a ball's descent along an inclined plane. Did he help to sketch Saturn's rings? Might *his* hands have dropped two weights—heavy and light—over the rail of a leaning tower, while the master physicist stood watching below?

There is no way to tell. Not even from documents in the Kuiper Compilation.

There *is,* however, another item from this period that Kuiper missed, but that I found in a scan of Vatican archives. An early letter from the Italian scientist Evangelista Torricelli to someone he calls "Uncle Henri"—whom he apparently met as a child around 1614. Oblique references are enticing. Was this "Henri" the same man with whom Torricelli would have later adventures?

Alas, the letter has passed through so many collectors' hands over the years that its provenance is unclear. We must wait some time for Torricelli to enter our story in a provable or decisive way.

Meanwhile, back to Henry Stephens. After his return to Leiden in 1616, there is little of significance for several years. His name appears regularly in account ledgers. Also on survey maps, now signing on his own behalf as people begin to rely ever-more on the geodetic arts he helped develop. Willibrord Snellius was by now hauling in ƒ600 per annum, and Journeyman Henry apparently earned his share.

Oh, a name very similar to Henry's can be found on the membership rolls of the Leiden Society, a philosophical club with highly distinguished membership. The spelling is slightly different, but people were lackadaisical about such things in those days. Anyway, it's a good guess that Henry kept up his interest in science, paying keen attention to new developments.

Then, abruptly, his world changed again.

Conditions had grown worse for dissenters back in England. Henry's father, having returned home to press for concessions from James I, was rewarded with imprisonment. Finally, the King offered a deal, amnesty in exchange for a new and extreme form of exile—participation in a fresh attempt to settle an English colony in the New World.

Of course everyone knows about the Pilgrims, their reasons for fleeing England and setting forth on the *Mayflower,* imagining that they were bound for Virginia, though by chicanery and mischance they wound up instead along the New England coast above Cape Cod. All of that is standard catechism in American History One-A, offering a mythic basis for our Thanksgiving Holiday. And much of it is just plain wrong.

For one thing, the *Mayflower* did not first set forth from Plymouth, England. It only stopped there briefly to take on a few more colonists and supplies, having actually begun its voyage in Holland. The expatriate community was the true source of people and material.

And right there, listed among the ship's complement, having obediently joined his father and family, you will find a stalwart young man of twenty-five—Henry Stephens.

Again, details are sketchy. After a rigorous crossing oft portrayed in book and film, the Pilgrims arrived at Plymouth Rock on December 21, 1620.

Professor Kuiper hunted among colonial records and found occasional glimpses of our hero. Apparently he survived that terrible first winter and did more than his share to help the young colony endure. Relations with the local natives were crucial and Professor Kuiper scribbled a number of notes which I hope to follow up on later. One of them suggests that Henry went west for some time to live among the Mohegan and other tribes, exploring great distances, making drawings and collecting samples of flora and fauna.

If so, we may have finally discovered the name of the "American friend" who supplied William Harvey with his famous New World Collection, the core element upon which Edmond Halley later began sketching his Theory of Evolution!

Henry's first provable reappearance in the record comes in 1625, with his marriage to Prosper White-Moon Forest—a name that provokes interesting speculation. There is no way to verify that his wife was a Native American woman, though subsequent township entries show eight children, only one of whom appears to have died young— apparently a happy and productive family for the time. Certainly any bias or hostility toward Prosper must have been quelled by respect. Her name is noted prominently among those who succored the sick during the pestilence year of 1627.

Further evidence of local esteem came in 1629 when Henry was engaged by the new Massachusetts Bay Colony as official surveyor. This led to what was heretofore his principal claim for historical notice, as the architect who laid down the basic plan for Boston Town. A plan that included innovative arterial and peripheral lanes, looking far beyond the town's rude origins. As you may know, it became a model for future urban design that would be called the New England Style.

This rapid success might have led Henry directly to a position of great stature in the growing colony, had not events brought his tenure to an abrupt end in 1631. That was the year, you'll recall, when *Roger Williams* stirred up a hornet's nest in the Bay Colony, by advocating unlimited religious tolerance—even for Catholics, Jews and infidels.

Forced temporarily to flee Boston, Williams and his adherents established a flourishing new colony in Rhode Island—before returning to

Boston in triumph in 1634. And yes, the first township of this new colony, this center of tolerance, was surveyed and laid out by you-know-who.

It's here that things take a decidedly odd turn.

Odd? That doesn't half describe how I felt when I began to realize what happened next. Lilly, I have barely slept for the last week! Instead I popped pills and wore electrodes in order to concentrate as a skein of connections began taking shape.

For example, I had simply assumed that Professor Kuiper's hoard was so *eclectic* because of an obsessive interest in a certain period of time— nothing more. He seemed to have grabbed things randomly! So many documents, with so little connecting tissue between them.

Take the rare and valuable first edition that many consider the centerpiece of his collection—a rather beaten but still beautiful copy of *"Dialogho Sopra I Due Massimi Sistemi Del Mondo"* or "A Dialogue Concerning Two Systems Of The World."

(This document alone helped drive the eBay bidding war, which Harvard eventually won because the Collection also contained many papers of local interest.)

A copy of the *Dialogue!* I felt awed just touching it with gloved hands. Did any other book do more to propel the birth of modern science? The debate between the Copernican and Ptolemaic astronomical systems reached its zenith within this publication, sparking a frenzy of reaction—not all of it favorable! Responding to this implicit challenge, the Papal Palace and the Inquisition were so severe that most of Italy's finest researchers emigrated during the decade that followed, many of them settling in Leiden and Amsterdam.

That included young Evangelista Torricelli, who by 1631 was already well-known as a rising star of physical science. Settling in Holland, Torricelli commenced rubbing elbows with friends of his "Uncle Henri" and performing experiments that would lead to invention of the barometer.

In correspondence that year, Torricelli shows deep worry about his old master, back in Pisa. Often he would use code words and initials. Obscurity was a form of protective covering in those days and he did not want to get the old man in even worse trouble. It would do no good for "G" to be seen as a martyr or *cause célèbre* in Protestant lands up north. That might only antagonize the Inquisition even further.

Still, Torricelli's sense of despond grew evident as he wrote to friends all over Europe, passing on word of the crime being committed against his old master. Without naming names, Torricelli described the imprisonment of a great and brilliant man. Threats of torture, the coerced abjuration of his life's work...and then even worse torment as the gray-bearded *Professore* entered confinement under house arrest, forbidden ever to leave his home or stroll the lanes and hills, or even to correspond (except clandestinely) with other lively minds.

What does all of this have to do with that copy of *"Dialogho"* in the Kuiper Collection?

Like many books that are centuries old, this one has accumulated a morass of margin notes and annotations, scribbled by various owners over the years—some of them cogent glosses upon the elegant mathematical and physical arguments, and others written by perplexed or skeptical or hostile readers. But one large note especially caught my eye. Latin words on the flyleaf, penned in a flowing hand. Words that translate as:

> *To the designer of Providence.*
> *Come soon, deliverance of our father.*

All previous scholars who examined this particular copy of *"Dialogho"* have assumed that the inscription on the flyleaf was simply a benediction or dedication to the Almighty, though in rather unconventional form.

No one knew what to make of the signature, consisting of two large letters.

> *ET.*

Can you see where I'm heading with this?

Struck by a sudden suspicion, I arranged for Kuiper's edition of *"Dialogho"* to be examined by the Archaeology Department, where special interest soon focused on dried botanical materials embedded at the tight joining of numerous pages. All sorts of debris can settle into any book that endures four centuries. But lately, instead of just brushing it away, people have begun studying this material. Imagine my excitement when the report came in—pollen, seeds and stem residue from an array of plant types...*all* of them native to New England!

It occurred to me that the phrase *"designer of Providence"* might not—in this case—have solely a religious import!

Could it be a coded salutation to an *architectural surveyor?* One who established the street plan of the capital of Rhode Island?

Might "father" in this case refer not to the Almighty, but instead to somebody far more temporal and immediate—the way two apprentices refer to their beloved master?

What I *can* verify from the open record is this. Soon after helping Roger Williams return to Boston in triumph, Henry Stephens hastily took his leave of America and his family, departing on a vessel bound for Holland.

Why that particular moment? It should have been an exciting time for such a fellow. The foundations for a whole new civilization were being laid. Who can doubt that Henry took an important part in early discussions with Williams, Winthrop, Anne Hutchinson and others— deliberations over the best way to establish tolerance and lasting peace with native tribes? How to institute better systems of justice and education. Discussions that would soon bear surprising fruit.

And yet, just as the fruit was ripening, Stephens *left,* hurrying back to a Europe that he now considered decadent and corrupt. What provoked this sudden flight from his cherished New World?

It was July, 1634. Antwerp shipping records show him disembarking there on the 5th.

On the 20th a vague notation in the Town Hall archive tells of a meeting between several guildmasters and a group of "foreign doctors"—a term that could apply to any group of educated people from beyond the city walls. Only the timing seems provocative.

In early August, the Maritime Bank recorded a large withdrawal of 250 florins from the account of Willebrord Snellius, authorized in payment to "H. Stefuns" by letter of credit from Leiden.

Travel expenses? Plus some extra for clandestine bribes? Yes, the clues are slim even for speculating. And yet we also know that at this time the young exiled scholar, Evangelista Torricelli, vacated his home. Bidding farewell to his local patrons, he then mysteriously vanished from sight forever.

So, temporarily, did Henry Stephens. For almost a year there is no sign of either man. No letters. No known mention of anyone seeing them...

...not until the spring of 1635, when Henry stepped once more upon the wharf in Boston Town, into the waiting arms of Prosper and their children. Sons and daughters who presumably clamored around their Papa, shouting the age-old refrain—

"What did you bring me? What did you bring me?"

What he brought them was the future.

Oops, sorry about that, Lilly. You must be chafing for me to get to the point.

Or did you cheat?

Have you already done a quick mentat-scan of the archives, skipping past Henry's name on the *Gravenhage* ship manifest, looking to see who *else* disembarked along with him that bright April day?

No, it won't be that obvious. They were afraid, you see, and with good reason.

True, the Holy See quickly forgave the fugitive and declared him safe from retribution. But the secretive masters of the Inquisition were less eager to pardon a famous escapee. They had already proved relentless in pursuit of those who slip away. While pretending that he still languished in custody, they must have sent agents everywhere, searching...

So look instead for assumed names! Protective camouflage.

Try *Mr. Quicksilver,* which was the common word in English for mercury, a metal that is liquid at room temperature and a key ingredient in early barometers. Is the name familiar? It would be if you went to *this* university. And now it's plain—that had to be Torricelli! A flood of scholarly papers may come from this connection, alone. An old mystery solved.

But move on now to the real news. Have you scanned the passenger list carefully?

How about "Mr. Kinneret"?

Kinneret—one of the alternate names, in Hebrew, for the Sea of Galilee.

Yes, dear. That Kinneret.

I'm looking at his portrait right now, on the Wall of Founders. And despite obvious efforts at disguise—no beard, for example—it astonishes me that no one has commented till now on the resemblance between Harvard's earliest Professor of Natural Philosophy and the scholar who we are told died quietly under house arrest in Pisa, way back in 1642.

It makes you wonder. Would a Catholic savant from "papist" Italy have been welcome in Puritan Boston—or on the faculty of John Harvard's new college—without the quiet revolution of reason that Roger Williams set in motion?

Would that revolution have been so profound or successful, without strong support from the Surveyor's Guild and the Seven United Tribes?

Lacking the influence of Kinneret, might the American tradition of excellence in mathematics and science have been delayed for decades? Maybe centuries?

Sitting here in the Harvard University Library, staring out the window at rowers on the river, I can scarcely believe that less than four centuries have passed since the *Gravenhage* docked not far from here on that chilly spring morning of 1635. Three hundred and sixty-seven years ago, to be exact.

Is that all? Think about it, Lilly, just fifteen human generations, from those rustic beginnings to the dawn of a new millennium. How the world has changed.

Ill-disciplined, I left my transcriber set to record *Surface Thoughts,* and so these personal musings have all been logged for you to savor, if you choose high-fidelity download. But can even that convey the emotion I feel while marveling at the secret twists and turns of history?

If only some kind of time—or para-time—travel were possible, so history could become an observational...or even experimental...science! Instead we are left to use primitive methods, piecing together clues, sniffing and burrowing in dusty records, hoping the essential story has not been completely lost.

Yearning to shed a ray of light on whatever made us who we are.

How much difference can one person make, I wonder? Even one gifted with talent and goodness and skill—and the indomitable will to persevere?

Maybe some group *other* than the Iroquois would have invented the steamboat and the Continental Train, even if James Watt hadn't emigrated and "gone native." But how ever could the Pan American Covenant have succeeded without Ben Franklin sitting there in Havana, to jest and soothe all the bickering delegates into signing?

How important was Abraham Lincoln's Johannesburg Address in rousing the world to finish off slavery and apartheid? Might the flagging struggle have failed without him? Or is progress really a team effort, the way Kip Thorne credits his colleagues—*meta-Einstein* and *meta-Feynman*—claiming that he never could have created the Transfer Drive without their help?

Even this fine Widener Library where I sit—bequeathed to Harvard by one of the alumni who died when *Titanic* hit that asteroid in 1912—seems to support the notion that things will happen pretty much the same, whether or not a specific individual or group happens to be on the scene.

No one can answer these questions. My own recent discoveries—following a path blazed by Kuiper and others—don't change things very much. Except perhaps to offer a sense of satisfaction—much like the

gratification Henry Stephens must have felt the day he stepped down the wharf, embracing his family, shaking the hand of his friend Williams, and breathing the heady air of freedom in this new world...

...then turning to introduce his friends from across the sea. Friends who would do epochal things during the following twenty years, becoming legends while Henry himself faded into contented obscurity.

Can one person change the world?

Maybe not.

So instead let's ask: What would *Harvard* be like, if not for Quicksilver-Torricelli?

Or if not for Professor Galileo Galilei.

The Robots and Foundation Universe: Issues and Hints Left for Us by Isaac Asimov

"It is the business of the future
to be dangerous." —A. N. Whitehead

Ah, robots.

Ever since Karel Capek coined the word "robot" in his stage play "R.U.R.," its meaning has gone through steady transformation. The fleshy slave-workers of Capek's drama would today be called "androids" or be likened to the replicants of the movie *Bladerunner*. Robots became associated with metal and plastic...computer chips and cool, artificial intelligence without direct connection to protoplasm.

Like aliens, robots have served as foils for the two great drivers of sci-fi plotting—the Other Who Must Be Feared...and the Innocent Other Who Must Be Protected From Vile Humanity...especially our wretched and oppressive institutions. We all remember many examples of both kinds. From the viciously genocidal machines of *Terminator* and *The Matrix* to cute little robots who are pursued by nasty generals in *Short Circuit* and *D.A.R.Y.L.*

Some science fiction tales did try to move beyond these awful cliches. I am reminded of Robert Heinlein's *The Door Into Summer,* whose hero, a tinkerer-inventor, wants to build household robots that are actually useful in the home, without necessarily writing sonnets or planning extinction for all humankind. Indeed, this gradual introduction of utilitarian models better predicted events than any of the clanking humanoids that spun off the pages and screens of bad sci-fi over the decades.

No discussion of robots would be complete without turning our attention to the biggest and most impressive science-fictional universe in which robots hold a major presence—the "Robots and Foundation" universe that was created, over the course of a lifetime, by one of SF's Grand Masters...the good doctor Isaac Asimov.

I was originally asked to comment on this topic, in part because I had the honor of being chosen to "clean up"...to tie many of the loose ends that Isaac left dangling when he so unfortunately left us, some years ago. Along with my collaborators and pals, Gregory Benford and Greg Bear, I helped create the new *Second Foundation Trilogy,* with the blessing of Isaac's heirs, his wife Janet and daughter Robin. As author of the final book in that loose trilogy (the books all involve the same character, but can be read separately), I tried to bring together all of Isaac's themes in a final grand adventure, titled *Foundation's Triumph.*

And now, by request, I'll let you in on some of the background story...

Isaac Asimov first began pondering human destiny while working in his father's candy store, at a time when the world was in turmoil. Vast, inscrutable forces appeared to be working on humanity, making whole populations behave in unfathomably dangerous ways—often against their own self-interest. Countless millions believed that the answer lay in prescriptions—in formulas for human existence—called ideologies.

Young Isaac was too smart to fall for any of the ideologies then on sale. From Marxism to fascism to ultra-capitalism, they all preached that human beings were *simple* creatures, easily described and predict-able according to incantations scribbled on a few printed pages. As a scientist and a trained observer, he could tell that these scenarios were wishful thinking, having more in common with religion than real sci-ence. And yet, Isaac could easily understand why people yearned for a model—a paradigm—for human behavior. Surrounded by irrational-ity on all sides, Isaac dreamed that maybe, someday, someone might discover how to deal with the quirky complexity of people...if not in-dividuals, then perhaps the great mass of humanity.

He had no idea how to solve such a problem, and was too sensible to expect formulae from the fools preaching and ranting contradictory slogans on mid-Twentieth-Century radios. But what about the far fu-ture? How about when human beings filled the galaxy? Might so many individual foibles cancel out, letting *mathematics* describe human momentum, the way dynamic formulas of chemistry's gas laws sim-plify the behavior of vast numbers of molecules?

Take this notion and combine it with young Isaac's reading mat-ter; one summer he devoured Gibbon's *Decline and Fall of the Roman Empire.* Now stir in a little yearning for adventure and you can start to see a pattern developing. One that would eventually turn into one of the great classics of mid-Twentiethth-Century science fiction.

It all starts with Hari Seldon, a character that most critics closely identify with Asimov, the writer-scientist himself. Seldon only appears as an active character at the very beginning of the *Foundation Trilogy*. But his shadow stretches onward, across all of the many short stories and novels that span five hundred years of history and many thousands of starry parsecs.

Only in later novels will we learn of meddling by another trade-marked Asimov character, the mighty immortal robot, Daneel Olivaw. At first, here in Asimov's first great work—the Trilogy—the tale appears to be limited to human beings. Ten quadrillion human beings...and an idea. One of the biggest ideas.

The idea that we—or maybe just a few of us—might look ahead, spot the inevitable mistakes and jagged reefs, and somehow chart a course around the most dangerous shoals, leading eventually to a better shore.

That is quite a concept to explore! But Isaac Asimov's fertile mind did not stop there. Another matter roiling in his brain was the problem of Robots. Far too long maligned as Frankenstein monsters, in magazines with lurid covers, they seemed to him filled with far greater possibilities. Yes, the simpleminded approach was to make them objects of dread. But what if we could program them to grow with us? And maybe to grow *better* than us...while remaining loyal to the last?

The result—Asimov's universe of Robot Stories—became another instant classic of science fiction.

The Foundation Universe and the Robots—for many years, these two cycles of fiction stayed separate. Then Asimov did something controversial. He combined them. It seemed a strange decision at the time. But in the long run, that combination brought about a great conversation. A conversation between Asimov and his readers. And one that Isaac kept thrashing back and forth with himself.

Like a truly honest scientist, he re-evaluated. Each and every decade, Isaac found hidden implications in his universe. Things that were already tacit, between the lines. With meticulous honesty, he bared these implications and explored them...till the next decade started another round.

First he wrought the *Foundation*, treating a quadrillion humans as "gas molecules" whose destiny could be calculated through Hari Seldon's wondrous new science of psychohistory.

Later, Isaac realized that *perturbations* would interfere with statistical predictability, even in such a marvelous new science. So he introduced a secret cabal of psychic-mathematicians (the Second Foundation) who would be dedicated to guiding the Seldon Plan back in line, should the galaxy drift too far down a wrong path.

But a decade or so afterwards, Isaac realized the moral flaw of the Second Foundation...that it left humanity led forever by a secret, inherited aristocracy! This was offensive to Isaac's democratic sensibilities. He solved this by bringing both halves of his life-work together...by inserting robots into the Foundation Universe. Daneel Olivaw and his scrupulously honest followers would act behind the scenes, manipulating even the Second Foundation, all for our own best interests, of course. Picture dedicated *court eunuchs,* who cannot conspire to become lords, because they will have no offspring. They can be trusted...or can they?

A little while later, Isaac realized something...free will had been reversed! The mechanical servants had memory and volition, they were rare, precious and powerful, while humans—as numerous and powerless as insects—had amnesia about their past and no control over their future. Now that didn't sound like such a great future either!

He sought a way out of this...and came up with Gaia! This is the ultimate robotic plan for humanity, for us to transcend together into a single, all-powerful mental being (a concept we've seen positively portrayed by Arthur C. Clarke in *Childhood's End* and *2001*...and negatively in *Star Trek's* infamous Borg). The Gaia/Galaxia resolution that Isaac put forward in *Foundation's Edge* would eventually deify humanity, restoring our memory and authority over robots again, in a fashion that Daneel Olivaw would find acceptable, allowing him at last to put down his ancient burden and step aside for a long deserved rest.

Only then Isaac took things to the *next* level, and realized...

Well, he dropped plenty of hints, before he died. Isaac made it pretty clear...at least to Benford and Bear and me...where the next dilemma lay.

In continuing Isaac Asimov's epochal saga, Gregory Benford, Greg Bear and I faced a daunting challenge—to keep adding ideas and possibilities to the Foundation/Robots setting. Concepts that captivate the reader. Visions that are new, awesome and wonderful, illuminated in stories filled with interesting characters and vivid adventure. And yet, we had to remain true to Isaac's overall vision of a startling and intellectually stimulating future.

As I said earlier, Asimov added an entire course to our endless and ongoing dinner-table conversation about destiny. His shoes were hard to fill. Fortunately, Isaac did lay down a terrific supply of hints, especially in books that he completed before he died. Clues to mysteries and logical quandaries that he clearly meant to deal with someday.

But we also had to capture the delightful *flavor* of an Asimovian tale. Isaac was, above all, a lover of mystery stories, and this carried over into his science fiction. Furthermore, readers of his works have come to expect certain traditions.

The protagonist faces adversaries whose masked motives are peeled away through logic and insight, with successive reversals offering delicious surprise.

Tantalizing mysteries. Isaac left "hanging questions" in many books...using these as hooks for the next tale. New books should continue this tradition of asking more unanswered questions.

Ethical quandaries. Isaac wasn't afraid of presenting readers with morally ambivalent situations. The hero must choose among several paths, each with advantages and drawbacks. Villains have reasons for their actions.

Issues of cosmic relevance. Isaac dealt with *Destiny*.

Frequent referral to events in other books. While each can be satisfying on its own, Isaac's readers loved catching brief references to events that took place elsewhere in his universe. (In *Foundation's Triumph* I refer *Pebble in the Sky, The Stars, Like Dust, I, Robot* and *The Naked Sun!*)

These traditions combined into a classic futuristic universe, a stage where we could watch a play as vivid and timeless as anything by Hugo or Dumas.

And there is Hari Seldon, a monumental figure, able to see so much about human destiny, yet also feeling trapped by strange forces that he barely understands...until achieving a strange triumph at the very end. His struggles to bring humanity to a sanctuary of happiness are epochal.

Alas, Isaac did not have time to continue exploring the implications. Mortality catches up with us all. But the logic is right there—a path implied by several dozen delicious clues he laid down, over the years.

What matters is to stay enthralled, to remain ready to be provoked by new thoughts, to keep pushing back the curtain a little bit, learning and discussing more about our future. Whether the topic is robots...how to keep them loyal and interesting...or almost any other dramatic device of science fiction...

The adventure continues. Enjoy. And keep thinking.

An Ever-Reddening Glow

We were tooling along at four nines to *c,* relative to the Hercules cluster, when our Captain came on the intercom to tell us we were being tailed.

The announcement interrupted my afternoon lecture on Basic Implosive Geometrodynamics, as I explained principles behind the *Fulton's* star drive to youths who had been children when we boarded, eight subjective years ago.

"In ancient science fiction," I had just said, "you can read of many fanciful ways to cheat the limit of the speed of light. Some of these seemed theoretically possible, especially when we learned how to make microscopic singularities by borrowing and twisting spacetime. Unfortunately, wormholes have a nasty habit of crushing anything that enters them, down to the size of a Planck unit, and it would take a galaxy-sized mass to 'warp' space over interstellar distances. So we must propel ourselves along through normal space the old-fashioned way, by Newton's law of action and reaction...albeit in a manner our ancestors would never have dreamed."

I was about to go on, and describe the physics of metric-surfing, when the Captain's voice echoed through the ship.

"It appears we are being followed," he announced. *"Moreover, the vessel behind us is sending a signal, urging us to cut engines and let them come alongside."*

It was a microscopic ship that had been sent flashing to intercept us, massing less than a microgram, pushed by a beam of intense light from a nearby star. The same light (thoroughly red-shifted) was what we had seen reflected in our rear-viewing mirrors, causing us to stop our BHG motors and coast, awaiting rendezvous.

Picture that strange meeting, amid the vast, yawning emptiness between two spiral arms, with all visible stars crammed by the Doppler effect into a narrow, brilliant hoop, blue along its forward rim and deep red in back. The *Fulton* was like a whale next to a floating wisp of plankton as we matched velocities. Our colony ship, filled with humans and other Earthlings, drifted alongside a gauzy, furled umbrella of ultra-sheer fabric. An umbrella that spoke.

"Thank you for acceding to our request," it said, after our computers established a linguistic link. *"I represent the intergalactic Corps of Obligate Pragmatism."*

We had never heard of the institution, but the Captain replied with aplomb.

"You don't say? And what can we do for you?"

"You can accommodate us by engaging in a discussion concerning your star drive."

"Yes? And what about our star drive?"

"It operates by the series-implosion of micro-singularities, which you create by borrowing spacetime-metric, using principles of quantum uncertainty. Before this borrowed debit comes due, you allow the singularities to re-collapse behind you. This creates a spacetime ripple, a wake that propels you ahead without any need on your part to expend matter or energy."

I could not have summarized it better to my students.

"Yes?" The Captain asked succinctly. "So?"

"This drive enables you to travel swiftly, in relativistic terms, from star system to star system."

"It has proved rather useful. We use it quite extensively."

"Indeed, that is the problem," answered the wispy star probe. *"I have chased you across vast distances in order to ask you to stop."*

No wonder it had used such a strange method to catch up with us! The COP agent claimed that our BHG drive was immoral, unethical, and dangerous!

"There are alternatives," it stressed. *"You can travel as I do, pushed by intense beams cast from your point of origin. Naturally, in that case you would have to discard your corporeal bodies and go about as software entities. I contain about a million such passengers, and will happily make room for your ship's company, if you wish to take up the offer of a free ride."*

"No, thank you," the Captain demurred. "We like corporeality, and do not find your means of conveyance desirable or convenient."

"But it is ecologically and cosmologically sound! Your method, to the contrary, is polluting and harmful."

This caught our attention. Only folk who have sensitivity to environmental concerns are allowed to colonize, lest we ruin the new planets we take under our care. This is not simply a matter of morality, but of self-interest, since our grandchildren will inherit the worlds we leave behind.

Still, the star-probe's statement confused us. This time, I replied for the crew.

"Polluting? All we do is implode temporary micro black holes behind us and surf ahead on the resulting recoil of borrowed spacetime. What can be *polluting* about adding a little more space to empty space?"

"*Consider,*" the COP probe urged. "*Each time you do this, you add to the net distance separating your origin from your destination!*"

"By a very small fraction," I conceded. "But meanwhile, we experience a powerful pseudo-acceleration, driving us forward nearly to the speed of light."

"*That is very convenient for you, but what about the rest of us?*"

"The...rest... The rest of whom?"

"*The rest of the universe!*" the probe insisted, starting to sound petulant. "*While you speed ahead, you cause the distance from point A to point B to increase, making it marginally harder for the next voyager to make the same crossing.*"

I laughed. "Marginally is right! It would take millions of ships...*millions* of millions...to begin to appreciably affect interstellar distances, which are already increasing anyway, due to the cosmological expansion—"

The star-probe cut in.

"*And where do you think that expansion comes from?*"

I admit that I stared at that moment, speechless, until at last I found my voice with a hoarse croak.

"What..." I swallowed. "What do you mean by that?"

The COPs have a mission. They speed around the galaxies—not just this one, but most of those we see in the sky—urging others to practice restraint. Beseeching the short-sighted to think about the future. To refrain from spoiling things for future generations.

They have been at it for a very, very long time.

"You're not having much success, are you?" I asked, after partly recovering from the shock.

"*No, we are not,*" the probe answered, morosely. "*Every passing eon, the universe keeps getting larger. Stars get farther apart, making all the old means of travel less and less satisfying, and increasing the attraction of wasteful metric-surfing. It is so easy to do. Those who refrain are mostly older, wiser species. The young seldom listen.*"

I looked around the communications dome of our fine vessel, thronging with the curious, with our children, spouses and loved ones—the many species of humanity and its friends who make up the vibrant culture of organic beings surging forth across this corner of the galaxy. The COP was saying that we aren't alone in this vibrant enthusiasm to move, to explore, to travel swiftly and see what there was to see. To trade and share and colonize. To *go!*

In fact, it seemed we were quite typical.

"No," I replied, a little sympathetically this time. "I don't suppose they do."

The morality-probes keep trying to flag us down, using entreaties, arguments and threats to persuade us to stop. But the entreaties don't move us. The arguments don't persuade. And the threats are as empty as the gaps between galaxies.

After many more voyages, I have learned that these frail, gnat-like COPs are ubiquitous, persistent, and futile. Most ships simply ignore the flickering light in the mirror, dismissing it as just another phenomenon of relativistic space, like the Star-Bow, or the ripples of expanding metric that throb each time we surge ahead on the exuberant wake of collapsing singularities.

I admit that I do see things a little differently, now. The universal expansion that we had thought due to a "big bang" is, in fact, at least 50% exacerbated by vessels like ours, riding along on waves of pollution, filling space with more space, making things harder for generations to come.

It is hard for the mind to grasp—so *many* starships. So many that the universe is changing, every day, year, and eon that we continue to go charging around, caring only about ourselves and our immediate gratification. Once upon a time, when everything was much closer, it might have been possible to make do with other forms of transportation. In those days, beings *could* have refrained. If they had, we might not need the BHG drive today. If those earlier wastrels had shown some restraint.

On the other hand, I guess they'll say the same thing about *us* in times to come, when stars and galaxies are barely visible to each other, separated by the vast gulfs that *we* of this era short-sightedly create.

Alas, it is hard to practice self-control when you are young, and so full of a will to see and do things as fast as possible. Besides, everyone *else* is doing it. What difference will our measly contribution make to the mighty expansion of the universe? It's not as if we'd help matters much, if we alone stopped.

Anyway, the engines hum so sweetly. It feels good to cruise along at the redline, spearing the star-bow, pushing the speed limit all the way against the wall.

These days, we hardly glance in that mirror anymore...or pause to note the ever-reddening glow.

We Hobbits are a Merry Folk...
...an incautious and heretical 1st draft about
J. R. R. Tolkien

Naturally, I enjoyed the *Lord of the Rings* trilogy (LOTR) when I first read it as a kid, during its first big boom in the 1960s...even though I did it unconventionally, by starting with *The Two Towers* and backfilling as I went along.

Likewise, I may be a bit off-kilter in liking, best of all, the unofficial *companion volume* to LOTR...perhaps the funniest literary work ever penned in the English (or any other) language. I refer to the *Harvard Lampoon*'s 1968 parody, titled *"Bored of the Rings."* Even if you revere and admire Tolkien...even if you take LOTR much too seriously...you will still find yourself unable to restrain guffaws at the adventures of *Frito*, son of *Dildo*, and his sidekick *Spam*...along with *Gimlet*, son of *Groin, Eorache*, daughter of *Eordrum*, and *Arrowroot*, son of *Arrowshirt*, son of *Araplane*...

Oh, it's true that many of the jokes refer to 1960s TV commercials. (Here's one hint; there was a jingle that went "Things go better with Coca-Cola.") Still, when the Dwarfish language features phrases like "A Dristan Nazograph!" and when Tom Bombadil comes out as the zonked hippie, Tim Benzedrine, and when Goodgulf runs afoul of the *Ball-hog* dribbling underneath the Mines of Andrea Doria...well, there's something timeless and adorable about this work of zonker genius. Any author should be flattered to receive such inspired satire. It means you've arrived.

But let's get serious. Some of what I say below may seem unconventional, provocative, heretical...and even self-destructively foolhardy in the face of the pseudo-religious reverence that's accorded to *Lord of the Rings*. So let me start by saying that I consider Tolkien's trilogy to be one of the finest works of literary universe-building, with an inter-

205

nal logic and consistency that's excelled only by his penchant for crafting "lost" dialects. (Long before there was a Klingon Language Institute, expert aficionados—amateurs in the classic sense of the word—were busy translating Shakespeare and the Bible into High Elvish, Dwarf-ish and other Tolkien-generated tongues.) And yes, LOTR opened the door to a vast popular eruption of heroic fantasy, setting up many others who followed with exacting devotion to his masterful architecture.

Indeed, the popularity of this formula is deeply thought-provoking. Millions of people who live in a time of genuine miracles—in which the grandchildren of peasants may routinely fly through the sky, roam the Internet, and elect leaders who must call them sir or ma'am—slip into delighted wonder at the notion of a wizard hitchhiking a ride from an eagle. Many even find themselves yearning for a society of towering lords and loyal, kowtowing vassals! It demonstrates how resonant such themes must be, deep within us.

Indeed, it makes sense if you remember that, for 99.44% of human existence, flight was a legendary prerogative of demigods. And a man was meaningless out of context with his king. It's only been two hundred years or so—an eyeblink—that "scientific enlightenment" began waging its rebellion against the nearly-universal feudal pattern, a hierarchic system that ruled our ancestors in every land where people had both metallurgy and agriculture. Only in the Eighteenth Century did a new social and intellectual movement finally arise capable of seriously challenging the alliance of warrior lords, priests and secretive magicians.

The effects of this revolution have been momentous, utterly transforming our levels of education, health, liberation and confident diversity. The very *shape* of society changed, from pyramidal, with a narrow elite atop a vast and ignorant peasantry, toward a *diamond* configuration, wherein a comfortable middle class outnumbers the poor. For the very first time, let me emphasize. We can argue endlessly about the detailed accuracy and implications of this analogy, but not over the fact that a profound shift has occurred, driven by a genuine scientific-technical-educational revolution.

And yet, almost from its birth, the enlightenment movement was confronted by an ironic *counter*-revolution, rejecting the very notion of progress. The Romantic Movement (of which C. S. Lewis and J. R. R. Tolkien were proud and avowed members) erupted as a rebellion against the rebellion! Calling the scientific worldview "soul-less," they joined Keats and Shelley and most European-trained philosophers, plus a multitude of poets, in spurning the modern emphasis on pragmatic experimentation, production, universal literacy, cooperative enterprise and flattened social orders.

In contrast to these 'sterile' pursuits, Romantics extolled the traditional, the personal, the particular, the subjective and metaphorical. Consider how this fits with the very *plot* of *Lord of the Rings,* in which the good guys strive to win re-establishment of an older, graceful and "natural" hierarchy against the disturbing, quasi-industrial and vaguely technological ambience of Mordor, with its smokestack imagery and manufactured power-rings that can be used by anybody, not just an elite few. Those man-made wonders are deemed cursed, damning anyone who dares to use them, usurping the rightful powers of their betters. (The high elves.)

The anti-modern imperative has strong resonance, all right. Indeed, some of its criticisms have validity! Without romance, we'd be sorry creatures, indeed.

Still, scientific/progressive society has been known to listen to its critics, now and then. Name one feudal society whose leaders did that. Were any orcs or "dark men" offered coalition cabinet positions in King Aragorn's postwar cabinet, at the end of the Ring War? I think not.

Which brings us to another of the really cool things about fantasy—you can identify with a side that's 100% pure, distilled good and revel as they utterly annihilate foes who *deserve* to be exterminated because they are 100% evil! This may not be politically correct, but then political correctness is really a bastard offspring of egalitarian-scientific enlightenment. Romanticism never made any pretense at equality. It is hyper-discriminatory, by nature.

The urge to crush some demonized enemy resonates deeply within us, dating from ages far earlier than feudalism. Hence, the vicarious thrill we feel over the slaughter of orc foot soldiers at Helm's Deep. Then again as the Ents flatten even more goblin grunts at Saruman's citadel, taking no prisoners, without a thought for all the orphaned orclings and grieving widorcs. And again at Minas Tirith, and again at the Gondor docks and again...well, they're only orcs, after all. What fun.

This tendency is taken much further—to an extreme that shows the basic moral problem of romanticism—in a work that was coincidentally by the *other* fellow who filmed a version of *Lord of the Rings,* one Ralph Bakshi, whose animated feature called *Wizards* was, in my opinion, just about the most evil thing produced ever since Goebbels ran the Nazi propaganda mill. In *Wizards,* Bakshi contrasts two cultures living on a post-apocalyptic Earth. One consists of pretty, pastoral and traditional pixies or elves, dwelling in a bucolic Wagnerian paradise amid vast open countryside. The other group is a tribe of "mutants"—ugly, earthy, and vaguely technological—who have been savagely repressed by the elves, forced to dwell in a single lightless canyon-ghetto for thousands of years.

Bakshi goes out of his way to emphasize both how pathetically incompetent and cowardly the mutants have been, whenever they have tried to escape, and how immense are the expanses that the pixies might share, if they ever acquired a grain of charity in their hearts. No matter. The narrator explains that the suppression of this hapless minority group is a good thing, for no other reason than a purported difference in their essences, between "good" and "evil." The audience worries when the mutants finally get a leader who inspires them to get some courage. Persuaded by the narrator and the pretty protagonist, viewers actually cheer when the doughty pixie army surrounds the ghetto, launching a pre-emptive strike that annihilates every mutant, down to the last cub.

Now most lovers of Tolkien have always hated Ralph Bakshi. They consider his version of LOTR to be quite wretched. And yet, one can see the commonalities of *theme*. Bakshi may represent the dark side of this "force," but it's based on the same underlying premise.

Let's not ignore, but instead openly acknowledge the underlying racialism and belief in an inherent aristocracy that J. R. R. Tolkien wove into the books, without even much attempt at subtlety. He couldn't help it, coming from the imperialist and class-ridden culture that raised him.

Moreover, the characters whom the reader comes to know best—Frodo, Sam and even the king-in-waiting, Aragorn—are *themselves* not very snooty or racist! The snootiest and most relentlessly aristocratic characters stand off to the wings, like preachy, secretive and patronizing Elron, letting others do the fighting for them...bloody elfs. (I'd point out endless parallels with a fellow named Yoda, but that would diverge a bit *too* far!)

Um, was that passage just above iconoclastic and heretical enough for you?

Oh, but in fact J. R. R. Tolkien was *himself* far more critical of the situation portrayed in his universe than any but a few of his myriad readers have chosen to notice! There are moments scattered throughout LOTR when he seems ahead of his time—the 1930s—in warning that romanticism can take the road to genocide. He was disturbed to see the Nazi SS, for instance, embrace many of the same Nordic mythic stories and symbols that he used as source material. (And that I examine in my Wildstorm/DC hardcover graphic novel— *The Life Eaters.)*

In later books, Tolkien even cast an analytical eye upon the elvish hierarchs of his own universe, in much the same way that Isaac Asimov re-evaluated his Second Foundation and meddlesome robots. But those self-critiques never had the widespread readership or influence of the original LOTR.

In the end, neither Tolkien nor his close friend C. S. Lewis could ever cross the gap that a Cambridge don, just down the road, was writing about, at roughly the same time—the infamous "two cultures" gulf that C. P. Snow claimed to find unbridgeable, between the world of science and that of the arts. Try as he might, and even faced with the blatant romantic excesses of Nazism, Tolkien could not escape his own deep conviction that democratic enlightenment was the greater evil. That it would ruin all the beauty he found in aristocratic-mystical hierarchies of the past.

Which is a pity, in light of what happened later, in the final third of the 20th Century, when C. P. Snow's "gap" between two cultures was crossed time and again by unfettered spirits—by technologically-savvy artists and by scientists who love art.

Indeed, *science fiction* bridged the two cultures gap with a super-highway. But that's another story.

Finally, may I offer a little mind-stretching exercise? Let's start by remembering that *history is written by the victors.*

How do we know that Hitler was as bad as we are told? Because we live in a democracy that has given Holocaust deniers plenty of opportunities to make their case, and all they ever come up with is blatant drivel. That's how. We see and hear countless witnesses to the Nazi horrors, conveyed via a media that, for all its faults, is relatively free and competitive. As implausible as the story of deliberate mass genocide might have seemed, in fiction, the reality was undeniably true and worse than anything previously imagined.

Allied propagandists did not have to make up any of it.

Ah, but things were different in kingdoms of old, where one official party line was promulgated and alternative sources of information routinely squelched.[1] And that's in *every* kingdom, mind you. Go ahead; name one where it didn't happen. (Note how the Norman propagandists went to work on poor old King Harold, even while his body was still cooling after the Battle of Hastings.)

My point? Well, LOTR is obviously an account written after the

---

[1] It happens even in democracies, e.g., the Gulf of Tonkin "incident" and some of what we see in the headlines today!

Ring War ended, long ago. Right?

So how do we know that Sauron did have red-glowing eyes?

Isn't some of that over-the-top description just the sort of thing that royal families used to promote, casting exaggerated aspersions on their vanquished foes, in order to reinforce their own divine right to rule? Next time you re-read LOTR, count the number of examples…then unleash your imagination to take the story a bit farther. Have fun!

Ask yourself—"What might *'really'* have happened?"

Then ponder something that comes through even the party-line demonization of a crushed enemy. This clear-cut and undeniable fact. *Sauron's army was the one that included every species and race on Middle Earth,* including all the despised colors of humanity, and all the lower classes.

Hm. Did they all leave their homes and march to war thinking "Oh, goody, let's go serve an evil dark lord"? Or might they instead have thought *they* were the "good guys," with a justifiable grievance worth fighting for? Like maybe "rebelling against an ancient, rigid, pyramid-shaped hierarchy topped by invader-alien elfs and their Numenorean-royalist-colonialist human lackeys"?

Here's the mild sub-scenario. Those orcs and low-elves and dwarves and dark-skinned or proletarian men who fought for the Ringlord were *fooled* by Sauron's propaganda.

Fair enough! Even that slight variation adds flavor to an already-great tale, making you pity Sauron's dupes a little, even though you still cheer as they're slaughtered down to the last corporal and private.

Want a scenario that's even more daring? Picture, for a moment, *Sauron the Eternal Rebel-Champion,* relentlessly maligned by the victors of the Ring War who control all the bards and scribes (and movie-makers) and never let the people hear the truth. Sauron, champion of the common Middle-Earther! Vanquished but still revered by the innumerable poor and oppressed who sit in their squalid huts, wary of the royal secret police with their magical spy-eyes, yet continuing to whisper stories, secretly dreaming and hoping that someday *he* will return…bringing more rings.[2]

Naw…I'm not being serious. (Though *one* novel or satirical short along this theme would be cool!)

---

[2] Note how it's easier to imagine an alternative to red-glowing eyes if you've read about them in a book. But after viewing a movie, it's almost impossible! Your brain feels that it's witnessed real events, even though you know it's just a version chosen by the director. Interesting…

No, my real point is much more general.

It's this—don't just *receive* your adventures. Toy with them! Re-mold them in your mind!

It's how you get practice not just being a passive consumer, or critic, but a creative storyteller in your own right!

And remember this too—enlightenment, science, democracy and equal opportunity are still the true rebels, reigning for just a few gen-erations in just one or two corners of the Earth—a few bare moments amid all the elite chiefdoms and romantic magicians that dominated our ancestors for half a million years.

Don't you think a little pride in that rebellion might be in order? A radical revolution-in-progress. One that (among many other things) taught born-peasants like you to read so you can enjoy epic books. One that makes vivid movies that cater to your taste for adventure. One that offers you choices.

One that gave you a chance.

Self-critical almost to a fault, this culture may not be as romantic as those old kingdoms...but isn't it *better*?

You are heirs of the world's first true civilization, arising out of the first true revolution. A revolution of enlightenment. Take some pride in it.

Let's keep kings and wizards where they belong. Where they can do little harm.

Where they entertain us.

In fantasies.

The Other Side of the Hill

"Deserts grow.

"The sky glowers with deadly rays and the seas grow poisonous.

"Today I have come to tell you of our decision. You will get your way. Our people have no choice but to depart with the rest of you. To flee this unhappy, cursed world."

Head bowed, calloused hands clasped before him, Mas Wathengria spoke from the High Council's circle of deliberation, his voice heavy with age and defeat.

"North Glacier Clan submits to majority will," he concluded. "We will join the exodus."

The other members of the Council shared looks of astonishment, having grown accustomed to decades of righteous northern stubbornness. At last, Keliangeli, the Grand Das of Farfields Clan, thumped the stone floor with her staff, and exclaimed.

"We are united, then! All can join now, without bitterness or anguish over leaving kinfolk behind."

Wathengria answered with an acquiescent drooping of his ear-fringes. "No clan or colony will stay on Bharis, Das Keliangeli," he agreed. "My people will participate in the abandonment of our mother world, but only because it is too late to turn back."

The stooped, gray-fringed Das appeared not to hear him, so excited was she. "With the resources of North Glacier no longer wasted, we can push the schedule forward two years, and leave before another famine comes!"

Mas Wathengria nodded gravely. It would be rude, having submitted, to voice recriminations. Anyway, he was too tired. Keliangeli called it "waste" to set aside some of the last arable land on Bharis, sparing it the kind of intense overuse that had ruined most of a once-beautiful planet. Starvation and pestilence had twisted judgment and

213

reason. The Das and her followers were desperate enough to try anything, even use up what was left of this world in order to flee toward a distant star. North Glacier, with its fresh water and abundant ores, had long held out. But the siren song of a robot, circling a faraway globe, now beckoned with lush green hints of fecundity. Wathengria had lately begun to sense his leadership slipping away. As shipbuilding became a planetwide mania, heedless of new damage brought on by the reckless pace, even his own clan's blessed isolation offered no protection.

"My ecologists tell me that once the ships are built, and the exodus prepared, little more than seven hundredths of the land on Bharis will remain suitable to support life in any decency. You, all of you, have thrown our lives like dice into the wind. They tumble even now, up in the sky." He pointed to the Fleet, which glittered like gems in early evening, crossing the heavens much swifter than the stars. "North Glacier cannot but join the cast."

"We are overjoyed to have you with us, Mas Wathengria," the Bas of Sheltered Oasis cried out, oblivious to Wathengria's irony. "Oh, yes!" Das Keliangeli added. "On our new home, you will help teach us how to keep and preserve it against the sorts of mischief our ancestors unleashed on Bharis. You will be our conscience."

Wathengria suppressed a hot response. True, their ancient forebears had done the worst harm, with their wars, noxious pollution and mismanagement. But today's folk were multiplying the damage, even as they sought to flee. "My specialists will accompany you to the new world. Perhaps you will learn from them, although I doubt it. As for myself, I plan to stay and take the Lesser Death, in stasis within the hall of my progenitors. One of our race should remain to explain this wasteland, should the ancient gods of myth ever return to look in dismay upon poor, ruined Bharis."

The Mas coursed his eyes around the circle. On a few faces, he noted signs of shame. But within moments of turning and departing the hall, he heard their voices rise again behind him, the moment forgotten amid new, excited plans. *I notice no one even protested my personal decision to stay,* he thought. *Probably, they're all relieved to hear the last of my carping. My caustic criticism.*

From his transport, Mas Wathengria looked down on the valley of Lansenil. The Council Chambers stood next to one of the few remaining sites of untarnished beauty on Bharis. If they had chosen a more desolate and representative place, Mas Wathengria might have been more optimistic for his race.

Forested slopes gave way to the paler shades of crops and pocket gardens, and then the harbor spires of Sea Haven, one of three remaining cities. Haven was not yet a desert of wind-blown dust. Still, Mas Wathengria tried not to look closely as his machine passed over cracked marble monuments, stained by ancient pollution and more recent, inexorable decay. Squinting past the fuming shipworks, he peered instead with his mind's inner eye toward the better days of his youth. Longingly, he filled his mind with remembered beauty to take with him to an icy tomb.

One compensation. The animals and plants that remain will have peace at last. We "thinking creatures" will no longer be a menace.

Too late, alas. Much, much too late.

Sounds of celebration continued even after the airlock sealed, cutting off the noise of continuing revelry aboard the mother ship. The crew on Ras Gafengria's exploration craft were on duty and free of intoxicants, but that did not make them sober. They went grinning to their tasks, babbling excitedly, drunk on the tincture of hope.

It was tempting to give in to the contagious happiness. Who wouldn't feel joy at the prospect of landing on a beautiful world after half an aeon of cold sleep! Orbital surveys had already confirmed what the robot probes earlier promised. More than twice as much of this planet's surface area supported life as tired old Bharis. Green regions ran like thick veins across every continent. As for the oceans—no one living had ever seen so much good water. The cartographer kept muttering happily, over and over—seas covered nearly a third of the globe!

Ras Gafengria wanted to share the others' covetous triumph. She could appreciate the wonder of this place. After all, here was an entire ecosystem to study...and perhaps take better care of, if she and others like her had their way.

But the message, she thought. *It's hard to take pleasure in any of this, after seeing my father's message.*

The pilots banked the boat into an aerodynamic braking dive to save fuel. Soon they were passing high over an ocean. Instruments detected planktonic life, something they could not have done an equal distance above old Bharis. Amazing. Yet, Gafengria's thoughts kept pulling back to the image in the viewing tank of the mother ship...an image of Mas Wathengria, the old man's face almost unchanged from when she had seen it last, impassively watching his people march into the ships. Leaving him behind. Alone.

The Council had not wanted to distract from the joy of a million and a half newly awakened exiles. So the leaders only invited a few to come see the strange message that had caught up with their fleet while passengers and crew slept. Patient computers had stored the transmission until arrival, when the officers and councilors wakened to view it.

The first thing Gafengria had noticed was the date—five hundred and forty turns after Departure! So, the old man's stasis unit had held, even without anyone around to perform routine maintenance.

She had expected words, but what happened next was far more startling. Her father's wrinkled sardonic visage shrank as he stepped back from the camera, and...into the holo tank next to him appeared the image of an alien creature!

The figure was tall, bipedal and slender, with dark cranial filaments that lay motionless atop its scalp. The narrow, fleshy face was inset with two small but penetrating eyes, above and on both sides of a fleshy, protruding nose.

Wathengria remained silent for a long interval, as if knowing the effect this scene would have on those later to view it. Only when the shock had abated slightly did his speech begin.

"My dear, departed people," the Mas had said. *"I hope your new world is everything you prayed for. If, indeed, you've learned a lesson, perhaps you will take better care of it than you did our poor beloved Bharis. You'll notice, though, I haven't held my breath!"*

The message went on. *"By the time you see this, another several hundred years will have passed. Nevertheless, I'm giving in to a little hastiness, rushing to transmit so you can be introduced to Bharis's new tenants.*

"They're really very nice people. The Mhenn, as they're called, seem to adore our tired old world! They've settled into Sea Haven now, and they want you to know..."

The chief pilot interrupted Gafengria's recollection. "We're approaching the coast now, noble Ras," he said. A collective sigh filled the cabin as the shoreline neared. Scattered vegetation grew upon the dun slopes, left and right as far as the eye could see, even from this great height. None of the people had ever encountered such a sight.

"Over there!" One of the pilots pointed to the eastern horizon. "One of the anomaly clusters! Shall we fly closer?"

Gafengria assented and they adjusted course toward an elevated clump of brown and tan shapes, shinier than the surrounding dunes. From space, the regular, geometric features had caused some to speculate that they might be cities. The prospect of inhabitants with prior claims to this planet disturbed the Council...though such a rich world surely had room enough for two races.

The youngest pilot gasped. "They *are* habitations!"

The chief pilot magnified the screen. "Perhaps, once. But they look long abandoned."

The ship cautiously slowed, skirting some distance from the

rounded stone shapes. The extent of the constructions soon left no doubt this had been a great city, indeed. Giant, spidery bridges and archways still connected many of the concave structures, whose blank, oval windows stared empty, like the eye sockets in a skull. The alienness of the architecture was almost as eerie as was the desolate loneliness of total abandonment.

The younger pilot pointed again, this time to a broad, flattened area not far away. "Firing pits," he pronounced. "A launching field."

"Don't jump to conclusions. We can't be..." The senior pilot abruptly stopped and stared. The cartographer gasped. As they topped a gentle rise, an immense cube of shining metal came into view, glittering under the slanting sunshine. Gafengria covered her eyes, wishing the giant thing would go away. She had a premonition about it, which caused her fringes to shrink down to their roots. It did not feel good.

"The Council calls," their comm operator said. "Command wants us to approach the artifact. Shipboard image enhancement indicates *writing* along the sides, inscribed in binary code!"

In hushed awe, the pilots brought the boat nearer. Ras Gafengria sank back in her seat, while the comm operator tuned to the frequency of the linguists, onboard the mother ship. Those experts babbled urgently about ciphers and contexts and translation possibilities. About analogies and similarities...

"It's all terribly ironic," Gathengria recalled her father pronouncing across the light years. *"These Mhenn are also refugees! They, too, fled a world that could barely support them. They didn't use robot probes to search for a new planet. Their method appears to have been more direct, though I can't say I really understand it well enough to explain it.*

"Anyway, here they are. They awakened me, and I told them where you'd all gone. They're very much like us, you know." His smile had been bitter. *"They may look strange, but it's uncanny how much like us they truly are."*

Holograms from the cubic artifact filled the tank in front of Ras Gafengria. It was a full body portrait of an alien being, a roundish shape coated with tentacles. To her surprise and relief, those who had left this monolith weren't at all similar in appearance to the "Mhenn" shown in her father's message.

Thank the gods, Ras sighed. *That* irony would have been too much to bear—that one species should deplete its home world in order to fly to a refuge that had been depleted by another race in *its* own desperate effort to flee to the first...

As a matter of fact, that tragedy was logically impossible. For one thing, the Mhenn had come from a direction opposite to the one the people had fled towards. And anyway, her father had said the Mhenn were *pleased* with their new world. In fact, the poor creatures had seemed pathetically ecstatic, calling their new home a "paradise." How devastated their own planet must have been, then, to think so highly of tired old Bharis!

Ras noticed that the others on the boat had stopped talking. "What—?" she began. The cartographer turned and whispered. "The translation, noble Ras! They've translated the inscription!"

Blinking, she saw that the alien figure in the holo tank was moving! Over the hum of the hovering engines, a tinny voice accompanied the movements, soft and lilting. In text below the figure flowed the mother ship's translation, in the language of Bharis.

"...So we were forced to decide...to remain and face continued famine, or to take a desperate gamble, squandering our last resources to fling our race of heroes across the stars...The (undefined term) choice was obvious to all but a few (undefined term)... By the time the necessary (undefined term) transmitters were completed, our world was humbled...ruined...less than a quarter of her land arable...dead in so many..."

"Less than a *quarter?*" The voice of the assistant ecologist cracked. "They call that ruined? The message can't be correctly translated!"

But Ras Gafengria sighed, seeing it all in utter clarity. So. They had been spared the irony that was superficially most cruel, only so they might have nightmares over a far more subtle joke the Universe had played on them. Or that *they* had all played on the Universe.

She closed her eyes and wished the onetime denizens of this world good luck in their quest. *May they find their bountiful new home. Though to satisfy them, it need be so rich as to stagger my imagination. They don't deserve success, of course, but neither did we...nor the Mhenn, presumably.*

In her mind she envisioned a chain of intelligent but short-sighted races, each getting more mercy than it merited, joyful to inherit the leavings of the one ahead of it in line. Each conditioned to see its new, leftover wasteland as a heaven.

She thought of Wathengria's wry words, and wished he had not taught her so well the burdensome gift of honesty.

"*The Mhenn had a terrible time,*" the Mas had said. "*But they kept faith, and knew they would find a world as nice as Bharis, someday. Amongst them, there is a saying almost as old as their race. When times were hard, they repeated it to one another for encouragement. For the courage to move on. Loosely translated, it goes something like this—*

" 'Over the mountain, the plant life will be a more pleasant shade of green.'

"Now I must end this message, and begin trying to teach the new tenants of Bharis how to take care of her. Perhaps this time I will have better luck.

"May fate bless you, my wayward children. As little as you deserve it, may you also find the grass greener, and the waters sweeter...on the other side of the hill."

Author's note: This story was one of my very first published. It may not be high art, but nothing at all has changed to make the central point obsolete. We still face the fundamental truth—a people who deserve the stars will be people who first learned to be wise at home.

Acknowledgments

From the author

My appreciation to many who read or critiqued earlier versions of these stories and essays. The list includes Cheryl Brigham, Tappan King, Ralph Vicinanza, Lou Aronica, Mark Grygier, Stefan Jones, Steve Jackson, Joe Miller, Ruben Krasnopolsky, Vernor Vinge, Robert Qualkinbush, Dan Brin, Pat Mannion, Amy Sterling Casil, Jim Moore, Robert Hurt, Robin Hanson, Steinn Sigurdsonn, William Calvin, Trevor Sands, Nick Arnett, Stanley Schmidt, George Scithers, Greg Bear, Gregory Benford, Wil McCarthy, Joseph Carroll, and David Hartwell...along with members of the Caltech, UCLA, UCSD, and University of Chicago Science Fiction Clubs. And to all of you out there who let me do this for a living. Gee, thanks. Right or wrong, I'll try to be interesting.

— David Brin, Ph.D.

From the editor

My great thanks to several people, without whose aid this project would not have happened:

Ann Broomhead, Pam Fremon, Sharon Sbarsky, and Tim Szczesuil for their help with initial proofreading.

George Flynn, a damned fine professional whose copy editing skills and willingness to work on projects like this one make all of us look better.

Alice N.S. Lewis, whose graphic eye makes me green with envy.

Mark Olson, for his patience and kindness in making sure the details didn't get missed.

This book was typeset in Adobe Garamond (with titles set in ITC Kabel Medium) using Adobe Pagemaker, and printed by Sheridan Books of Ann Arbor, Michigan, on acid-free paper.

— Deb Geisler
December 2002

THE NEW ENGLAND
SCIENCE FICTION ASSOCIATION (NESFA)
AND NESFA PRESS

Recent books from NESFA Press:

- *Tomorrow Happens*, David Brin $25
- *A New Dawn: The Complete Don A. Stuart Stories* $26
- *Cybele, with Bluebonnets*, Charles Harness $21
- *The Best SF: 1964* $25
- *Dimensions of Sheckley: Short Novels of Robert Sheckley* $29
- *From These Ashes: Complete Short SF of Frederick Brown* $29
- *Martians and Madness: SF Novels of Frederick Brown* $29
- *Adventures in the Dream Trade*, Neil Gaiman (**tpb**) $16
- *Strange Days* by Gardner Dozois $30
- *The Warrior's Apprentice*, Lois McMaster Bujold $25
- *Entities*, Eric Frank Russell $29
- *Major Ingredients* by Eric Frank Russell $29
- **The Complete SF of William Tenn**
    - *Immodest Proposals* (Vol. 1) $29
    - *Here Comes Civilization* (Vol. 2) $29

Details and many more books available online at: www.nesfa.org/press

Books may be ordered by writing to:
NESFA Press
PO Box 809
Framingham, MA 01701

We accept checks, Visa, or MasterCard. Please add $3 postage and handling per order.

The New England Science Fiction Association:

NESFA is an all-volunteer, non-profit organization of science fiction and fantasy fans. Besides publishing, our activities include running Boskone (New England's oldest SF convention) in February each year, producing a semi-monthly newsletter, holding discussion groups relating to the field, and hosting a variety of social events. If you are interested in learning more about us, we'd like to hear from you. Write to our address above!